The Life of a
Banana
PP Wong

Legend Press Ltd, The Old Fire Station,
140 Tabernacle Street, London, EC2A 4SD
info@legend-paperbooks.co.uk | www.legendpress.co.uk

Contents © PP Wong 2014
The right of the above author to be identified as the author of this work has
been asserted in accordance with the Copyright, Designs and Patents Act
1988. British Library Cataloguing in Publication Data available.

Print ISBN 978-1-9100532-1-8
Ebook ISBN 978-1-9100532-2-5
Collection ISBN 978-1-78507-979-5
Set in Times. Printed in the United Kingdom by Clays Ltd.
Cover design by Gudrun Jobst www.yotedesign.com
Collection Design by Gudrun Jobst www.yotedesign.com

PP Wong was born in Paddington, London, and spent her childhood in Surrey, Wembley and Sheen. She also lived for a number of years in Bedok, Singapore.

After completing a degree in Anthropology and Law at the London School of Economics, PP Wong worked as an actress for six years. She acted in lead roles at the Soho Theatre in *Moonwalking in Chinatown* and BBC Radio 4's play *Avenues of Eternal Peace*. Her very first role was "Screaming Vietnamese Girl" in a James Bond movie.

She is now a writer and also the editor of www.bananawriters.com. With thousands of readers from more than thirty countries, the website is a voice for East Asian and South East Asian writers.

PP Wong currently divides her time between London and Singapore.

The Life of a Banana is PP Wong's first novel.

Visit PP at
ppwongauthor.com
or on Twitter
@ppwong_

For my love Mark X---ng

Funniest
Bestest
Sharpest
Mostest

&

Mamie the greatest storyteller of all

Love
Ha ha
Sacrifices
Stamping ants

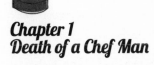

Chapter 1
Death of a Chef Man

"Just be glad that cat is in a better place. If this were Guangdong, she'd be in a peasant's belly by now."

"That's s-o-o-o racist."

"I can't be racist to my own race. Mama said it ain't possible."

"I don't remember Mama ever saying that."

"Well, Mama did."

I'm not sure if my brother Lai Ker is right, but Mama isn't here any more. She's in heaven with Papa and my ancient cat Meow Meow. Grandma forced me to give Meow Meow to the RSPCA - she's twenty years old and I know what happens to old pets. Grandma told me she had to go 'cos she was "dirty", "smelly" and "carrying millions and millions of germs". She also said I couldn't keep my Bart Simpson clock with the dent on his forehead. Lai Ker is allowed to bring his Xbox, but only after we clean it with baby wipes. But he can't bring any of the big-leafed plants he grows in his room and sells to his mates 'cos Grandma's two gardeners are already really busy.

We didn't always live with Grandma. For twelve years, I lived in a cosy trio - Mama, Lai Ker and me. We were the Kwans of 187C Kilburn Road - the British Chinese family who played loud pop music and spoke with cockney-Chinese accents. Lai Ker was more cockney; Mama was more Chinese and I was something in between. We only saw Grandma, Auntie Mei and strange Uncle Ho once a year 'cos Mama said Grandma was a super busy lady and didn't have time for us. Every time we saw Grandma she wouldn't talk to Mama unless it was to complain.

"Why you not put more soy sauce in fish? It taste like armpit."

"Your kitchen so dirty, rats must be having disco here every day."

"Your flat too small - only fit in midgets."

Mama would just ignore Grandma, and carry on as if Grandma wasn't there. I asked Mama why she never fought back and she said that when people fight it means they care.

Mama always tried to teach me what was right or wrong. She told me lots of things like how I must never leave any rice on my plate, if I did I would get giant spots on my cheeks for every grain of rice left. Also, I should always leave the plastic on TVs, mobile phones and sofas 'cos they last longer that way. But I'm never gonna know what Mama thinks about anything any more 'cos Mama is not here. Mama is gone forever and there's nothing I can do about it.

Mama died on my twelfth birthday.

It was raining lots. But it wasn't the normal half-hearted London rain that can't make up its mind if it's heavy or not. London rain usually bugs you enough so that you need an umbrella but it's not heavy enough to run through and have fun with, and you definitely can't play "dodge the thunder and lighting". The kind of rain that happened on my birthday was the sort of rain that made us feel like our roof might collapse. It was fun and loud and kind of scary.

Sitting round an old oil heater, I opened my presents wrapped in cool paper that had Rudolf the red nose reindeer printed all over it. I got a computer game from Mama and some Toblerone, with a bite taken from Lai Ker. I was super excited when Mama suddenly brought out a small chocolate cake. We only got the expensive, yummy, chocolately stuff on our birthdays. Mama looked at the time and tutted about how quickly the day had passed. Grandma, Auntie Mei and strange Uncle Ho would arrive soon. She started to panic loads 'cos we didn't have any candles. Mama always wanted things to be super perfect when they arrived. When Mama panicked, she would run up and down tutting and flapping her arms like those mad Chinese Opera singers. Lai Ker called her "Melodramama".

Mama quickly grabbed her old, floral umbrella and rushed into the rain.

The time was 4:23pm.

I remember the time 'cos she kept repeating Grandma was going to be here in seven minutes and she was never late.

"Aiyah! It's 4:23pm. Grandma will be here soon. It's 4:23pm already! I need to get the candles."

Mama ran into the thunderstorm to get the dreaded candles. On the way to the newsagent, she passed Xiong Mao Chinese restaurant. Mama often sneaked into the back kitchens of this restaurant to scrounge free food from her friend, chef Andy Cheung. Lai Ker gave Maths tuition for Andy Cheung's ten-year-old son and the free food was the chef's way of repaying the favour. Chinese people call this *Guanxi*, which basically means "You scratch my back and I'll scratch yours."

Mama would do her usual tug of war ritual with Andy Cheung. It would start off with Mama being all embarrassed when Andy Cheung gave her MASSIVE portions. Since it was my birthday I'm sure they would have been more massive than usual. He was nice like that. Mama as usual would ask for smaller portions; Andy Cheung would push the cartons of food back to her and she would push them back again saying the portions were too big.

Push food forward, push food back, push food forward,

push food back.

The ritual would last for about three minutes until Andy Cheung would finally open Mama's bag, force the food in and nudge her out of the door. She always did that ritual with Andy Cheung. I don't know how long the ritual lasted that day but it wasn't the reason why Mama died. Lai Ker said it was, but I know the truth, Mama did not die 'cos of the stupid tug of war ritual.

Mama died 'cos it was my birthday.

If it weren't my birthday, Mama wouldn't have gone out to get the candles. She wouldn't have passed Andy Cheung's restaurant and dropped in to get a birthday treat for me. Then she wouldn't have had to do the stupid tug of war ritual with Andy Cheung next to the cheap oven that the owners of the restaurant refused to repair. Then she would have been far away from Andy Cheung's kitchen when the oven exploded. Then her photo wouldn't have been on the front page of the local newspaper. Then I wouldn't have spent my twelfth birthday in a morgue.

Mama died 'cos it was my birthday. She died 'cos of me.

Chapter 2
Four Wus and a Funeral

Mama died on a Friday and the funeral was on the Monday. Lai Ker said Monday funerals were twenty percent cheaper than Saturday funerals. Grandma chose a beautiful white church with huge stained glass windows. It looked more pricey than any of the other religious buildings on offer. The church was decorated with yellow roses - Mama's favourite. Auntie Mei got her friend who did celebrity weddings to arrange the flowers. I thought the flowers with giant diamante ribbons made the church look too happy. Lai Ker said the "major bling" was giving him a headache. Before the service, I found five empty bottles of Tiger Beer in his room hidden by a pile of messy takeaway cartons.

It was a closed casket service. Auntie Mei said Mama's charred body would be too upsetting for the countless friends who had come to say goodbye. I know what she meant. The image of Mama's blackened body had been forced right to the back of my mind, but it liked to appear when I closed my eyes to sleep. Mama's once sparkly eyes were gaping holes and her tanned flesh was tarred black.

She wasn't Mama any more; she was just a black, horrible shell.

The 200-seated church was stuffed full of old school friends, neighbours and even my childhood postman.

Grandma placed a half-page advert in *The Times* to invite anyone who had ever known Mama. It was weird seeing the fish and chip shop owner and our bin man at the funeral.

Grandma sat through the service with a really frozen look on her face. She did not weep, she did not cry, she did not let one teardrop fall. I saw her glance at her wristwatch twice. Once, during Mama's good friend Mrs Alsanea's poem, and also when Mama's primary school friend, Maggie Chin, told the story of when Mama let her stay on the sofa during her divorce. When I saw Grandma looking at her watch I hated her lots.

Auntie Mei bit her lip a couple of times and gripped her handbag tightly through the whole service. She did not cry either. But after the service I caught her crying loads and loads in the car park behind the bins. All I could see were her red nailed hands going up and down as they covered her face. Auntie Mei always tried to be nice to Lai Ker and me but found it hard when it came to chatting to us. Lai Ker said it was 'cos she was one of those people that doesn't know what to do with kids 'cos she only ever talked to grown ups.

When it was time for everyone to say goodbye to Mama, tons of people were crying. I saw the Pakistani lady from our local newsagent wipe a couple of tears. It felt really strange that the woman I bought Mars bars from was crying over Mama.

It didn't feel real at all.

Grandma and Auntie Mei went up to say goodbye together. They were both pale and looked like ghosts walking in slow motion. Grandma didn't look at the coffin or even touch it. She looked in a daze and just walked past it. Auntie Mei followed before returning to get Uncle Ho. He refused to go up to the coffin. She tried to make him but it was like his ginormous bum was stuck with Velcro to the chair. She pulled on his arm and he'd go up a little bit then down again, up a little bit more, then down again.

"I'm fine, you go ahead."

"Ho, are you sure?"

"I'm fine, you go ahead."

"You have to say goodbye to your sister. Come on?"

"I'm fine, you go ahead."

"This is the last time you are going to see her. Please come with me to say goodbye."

"I'm fine, you go ahead."

Later, when Mama's coffin was put into the ground, Uncle Ho shut his eyes tightly and put his hand to his forehead. I saw tears rolling down his unshaven cheeks. His face was screwed up tight like someone had given him a bitter pill to swallow along with his other meds. He stayed like this for a good ten minutes. Uncle Ho was the only person in the crowds of people who did not walk up to the coffin and say goodbye. I wish I could have done the same but I wanted to be brave for Mama. I told Lai Ker to go up first and he propped himself up against me to stand. He complained of feeling sick and rubbed his temples loads. I watched him walk to the coffin in a zigzagged way. He almost knocked over the pastor on his way to the coffin and did not stop to say sorry. The coffin was patted speedily and he leaned on a flower arrangement that came crashing to the floor. There was a big gasp from the crowd of people. Grandma marched him back to his seat and he leaned his head on my shoulder. I could smell the alcohol on his breath. I wanted to tell him off for making a fool of himself at Mama's funeral and to start behaving. I wanted to tell him I needed him to be strong. I wanted to tell him he was all I had left. But my sorrow had gobbled up all my words.

I made myself walk up to the coffin.

My insides twisted so painfully and my legs became so wobbly I thought I might collapse. I tried to concentrate on each step and counted from one to ten over and over again.

One

Two

Three

Four
Five
Six
Seven
Eight
Nine
Ten

My heart was hurting so much and everything in the room became dead quiet. Mama used to say, "I love you forever and a week," that way I knew she loved me every day of the week not just one day. I remember thinking, "She's not here, not for today or tomorrow or the day after that. Mama is gone."

When I put my hand on her coffin, everything was blurry and I could feel the tears falling on my lips. I patted her coffin one last time and whispered my final goodbye.

"Bye Bye Mama. I love you forever and a week."

Chapter 3
My Family and Other Animosities

Mama's only been gone for six days but it feels like forever. I'm standing in Grandma's posh hallway with Chinese antiques and exotic stuffed animal heads. I can feel my eyes starting to tear up and I bite my lip hard. I want to be strong, 'cos that is what Mama would have wanted. She said it was important to be strong 'cos that way people can't trample over us. But I don't feel strong, I feel like a walking jelly person, all wobbly and shaky inside. A stuffed baby deer is staring back at me; it looks sad like Bambi when his mother died. There's a sick smell of roses in the air and Lai Ker is trying his best not to touch anything in case he breaks it.

Grandma gestures at us to join her at the bottom of the huge, spiral staircase. I try to listen to her, but I can't stop staring at the golden, carved roses snaking through the bannisters. Each rose is so beautiful like they belong to the garden of the Queen. Grandma walks to the middle of the staircase and looks a lot taller than five foot.

"Xing Li you go red room. Lai Xing you go blue room. We start lunch thirty minutes. Never be late. If late you like gravestone 'Late Lai Xing', 'Late Xing Li' so never be late. That is that."

Grandma turns her back to us and I see her tiny feet carrying her s-l-o-w-l-y up the stairs. I guess that's the end

15

of her welcoming speech. We make sure she is definitely gone before Lai Ker and I touch EVERYTHING. A giant bronze horse with massive teeth, a grandfather clock made of seashells and tons of floral vases that are probably from the Ming dynasty. Lai Ker flops down flat onto the pale pink rose carpet with Chinese writing on it. It looks super clean but the design is probably a thousand years old.

"Xing, THAT lady needs to get out of Emperor Ming's arse and into the twenty-first century."

"Yeah, a trip to Ikea will sort her out."

I give a quick last check up the stairs and then lie down next to him. We wave our arms and legs up and down as if we are making snow angels. The carpet feels like hundreds of rabbits all knitted together. Lai Ker jumps up and starts bobbing his rock hard, gelled, spiky head in and out of a dozen antique vases. He's been joking with me more than usual since Mama died. I start smiling a bit. He looks like the pop out beavers we used to hammer with a mallet in our local arcade. Mama still has the high score in Kilburn Fun House. Lai Ker is sixteen and almost grown up, but the pimples on his tanned forehead remind him he isn't a man - not just yet.

"Shall I piss Grandma off and headbutt one of these vases?"

"Dare you."

"Nah, don't wanna mess my hair. Gotta keep it perfect for the ladies."

"Bet if you did, you'd smash it into pieces. Your hair's so hard you could bounce a tennis ball off it."

Actually once when Lai Ker was sleeping, I tried bouncing a rubber ball off his head and it was definitely bouncier than the floor. I got a punch in return. Lai Ker makes a big show of patting his porcupine head while looking in a giant mirror that is literally ten times my height. I'm crap at Maths, so I can't calculate what five foot four-and-a-half inches times ten would be, but the mirror is basically big. My armpit length black hair is messy as usual and my small flat nose that turns up at the tip is flatter than usual and there are huge, puffy bags under my tadpole shaped eyes. Before I can put my fingers through my hair, Lai Ker starts to nudge me towards the kitchen with his razor sharp elbows.

"Let's not keep the old bird waiting."

I nudge him back, but my elbows aren't as pointy. I wish I had really pointy elbows - it helps when you want more room during rush hour on the tube or for getting to the front of the sales in Primark.

Grandma's kitchen is completely white and German - a silver and white mish-mash of Miele, Bosch and Siemens appliances. She says German brands are the best 'cos they are the most sterile. Her chef has prepared a feast on a grand, circular table with a white tablecloth. Lai Ker and I drool in unison.

1) Deep-fried crab claws!
2) Scallops with prawns and honeyed snow peas!
3) Roasted five-spice chicken!
4) Braised e-fu noodles with garlic lobster!
YUM!

The smell of ginger, garlic and exotic spices is so strong I can feel the flavours whooshing up my nose and into my mouth. I have to poke Lai Ker to remind him to wipe the drool with his sleeve. Lai Ker's gone straight for the lobster and gobbles the food up like a hamster filling his cheeks with nuts. I stab a few gigantic scallops and prawns - my chopstick looks like a messy barbecue skewer. I'm chomping on my perfect garlicky scallop, when I notice Auntie Mei and Grandma have not touched a thing. Grandma gives me a dirty look.

"You think you so clever eat so fast? When grow very fat and go Weight Watchers who blame but you? In Wu house we eat proper, we respect. UNDERSTAND?"

Grandma makes a big show of having the first choice of food; she spots the largest scallop from across the table and stabs it with her chopsticks. At seventy-two her eyesight is super sharp. Her tiny, beady eyes scan her surroundings like an alligator about to eat an unsuspecting chicken. She has twig-like arms and her olive skin is spotty, like she spent too long in the sun as a child.

I feel something bumping me out of the way and realise it's Uncle Ho's tummy. It gives me a shock! He slips in and out of the kitchen in a hurry like he's nicking the food or something. He is wearing a stained grey tracksuit, has an unkempt beard and his curly mop of black hair is plastered down with coconut oil. He reminds me of a fat, wet poodle. Uncle Ho stuffs his plate with more food than Grandma and Auntie put together before running to his room and slamming the door.

We eat in complete silence with clicking chopsticks and ticking clocks.

TICK-TOCK TICK-TOCK TICK-TOCK

Click, click, click, click

Chomp, chomp, chomp

TICK-TOCK TICK-TOCK TICK-TOCK

Click, click, click, click

BURP

That was Lai Ker.

Grandma gives him an icy stare. I try to catch Lai Ker's eye, but his mouth is too full of food. Greedy pig. All the sounds are way louder in Grandma's house and I can't take it.

TICK-TOCK TICK-TOCK TICK-TOCK

FINALLY, Auntie Mei speaks - she says her words perfectly, like a posh Shakespearean actress. Auntie Mei is really beautiful and tall and classy like a Chinese Audrey Hepburn, but a bit curvier.

"Ma, I'm delighted to tell you that tomorrow I have a BIG audition."

Silence

"Ma, tomorrow I have a BIG audition."

Silence

"Ma, it is for a film produced by the makers of *Dallas* - a science fiction film with cowboys. I'm meeting a HUGE casting director who is flying in from LA."

Grandma looks at me for the first time during dinner and rolls her eyes.

"Apart from Brad Pitt cameo, *Dallas* not so great. When she get million-pound contract then can get excited eh? No point excited over stupid nothing."

Auntie Mei sadly shakes her head and makes a tall, white hill on her bowl with the rice. The room becomes dead silent again and I can hear the pak choi crunching between my teeth. Grandma makes us wait and wait and wait. Then she does a big AHEM and tells us some "vely important things" in her strong Chinese accent. She says Lai Ker and me are Wus - no longer Kwans. We have to work hard now and go to Cambridge or Oxford University. Then we must become a banker, lawyer or doctor; only one of the three though 'cos they are the best jobs and earn the most money. Lai Ker has already bagged being a doctor, so I guess that means I'll be a banker 'cos they have lots of dosh. Though I'm not very good at adding things. As if reading my mind, Grandma says I've got to be smarter at Maths and she's got me a special tutor called Mrs Wing. She's arriving tomorrow morning and is going to give me "special pre-school" training in Maths before I start my new private school called West Hill. I have to listen to everything Mrs Wing says or there will be trouble. Lai Ker isn't getting a tutor, only me. Also, Grandma tells me I'm not allowed to take the tube until I'm sixteen. I can only take it if I have Lai Ker or an older relative with me 'cos there are a lot of pee-do-files on the tube and it's hard to escape if you are stuck in a tunnel. BUT I can walk to school by myself 'cos it is only fifteen minutes away. If I meet a pee-do-file or mugger I can spray him with my pepper spray and run. Grandma hands me a pepper spray. It's all shiny and much heavier than hairspray.

Grandma clears her throat and continues her speech with

a massive AHEM. Then she tells me that if it's snowing I can use the chauffeur, but only if Grandma or Auntie Mei aren't using him. We can only play computer games if we get good grades and we must not do anything that will bring shame to the Wu name. This includes breaking the law, getting expelled or being in the school choir. Grandma then takes out a large feather duster and lays it right in the middle of the table. Mama used to tell me stories about Grandma's dreaded feather duster. She said when Grandma got mad, she would whack the soft part of her legs behind her knees so it would hurt extra bad. Grandma stares at us for a few seconds without blinking - I want to wave my hand in front of her eyes to make her blink.

"Now you both listen here for IMPORTANT thing. You act good. I act gooder. You act bad. I act badder. UNDERSTAND?"

Grandma picks up the feather duster and whacks it HARD onto the table. It almost breaks and I can see even Lai Ker is scared.

"UNDERSTAND?"

We both nod together. I reach for Lai Ker's hand under the table and he gives it a tight squeeze. I miss my old flat with the ragged green carpets and rusty radiators.

Chapter 4
The Big Snore

It feels weird being in my new room.

It's decorated in different shades of red; tomato red velvet curtains; strawberry red carpets; stop sign red sofa; marker pen red walls; blood red bed spread. Lai Ker's room is all blue, Grandma's is brown and Auntie Mei's is pink. I didn't know you could buy pink TVs, but Auntie Mei has a cinema-sized pink TV with diamante buttons - it's a flat screen as well. Lai Ker and me sneaked into her room when she was having a shower. It's like triple the size of our old flat. In fact, her wardrobe is the size of our living room and kitchen. I haven't managed to sneak into Uncle Ho's room yet 'cos he literally triple bolted his door. Lai Ker couldn't pick the locks and we stopped trying when we heard Auntie Mei leaving her shower. I only got to see Grandma's room for five seconds before Lai Ker heard an AHEM near the bottom of the stairs. Grandma's room is a little bigger than Auntie Mei's and is chock-full of Chinese antiques including a real sugarcane rocking chair and this giant fireplace that's so big you could park a car in it.

CREEEEAKKKKKKK

It sounds as if someone is walking down the stairs but everyone is asleep. REAL CREEPY!

I wrap a quilt tightly round my body and tiptoe into the

corridor. It feels like someone spray painted the air with ice. My heart thumps loudly as I zoom past five stuffed animal heads in the corridor. A lion, a polar bear, a beaver, a reindeer and a crocodile. Anyone that keeps stuffed animal heads in their home is definitely in the loopy category. Seventy percent of mass murderers collect weird things like dead butterflies and animals. I once saw a serious docu on TV talking about it.

Creeping into Lai Ker's room, I make out his snoring body in the moonlight. Lai Ker likes to talk in his sleep and snores loudly. He isn't the best bed buddy but at least I'm not going to be alone. We have to stick together now, two peas in a pod or as he says, "Two pisses in a pot". Lai Ker can sleep through thunderstorms, loud hoovers and fireworks. When he was eight, he slept through the repo man taking away our TV.

I lock Lai Ker's door and lie on his bed top to toe just like when we were little. It's super crammed but I feel safe. There is no way I'm returning to my room tonight and if I have to sleep with Lai Ker's smelly feet in my face, then so be it.

I wake up to Lai Ker dripping cold water into my right ear hole.

"Wakey Wakey lil sis. Rise and shiny."

"STOP IT!"

Grabbing the towel, I chase him round the room, whacking him as hard as I could.

Knock, knock, knock.

Judging from the tiny knocks it has to be Auntie Mei.

"Xing Li, Mrs Wing is arriving in fifteen minutes. You had better be ready and stop messing around. Breakfast is waiting for you on the kitchen table."

"Okay. I'm coming."

Lai Ker grins and wiggles his thick eyebrows at me.

"Enjoy your special lessons thicko."

I run to my room to get changed. With the darkness of the night gone, the stuffed animal heads don't look as bad. In fact, the mounted black and white beaver with its puffed out face reminds me a little of Meow Meow. I remember where

22

she is and swallow hard.

Mrs Wing charges £85 per hour. She's from Cambridge and has some important certificate from Harvard Business School. Maths tuition is something she does for fun in her retirement. She's the only secondary school Maths tutor with a company registration number and a regular advert in *The Times*.

> **Mrs Wing gives your child wings.**
> **Child guaranteed an A. If not, your money back.**
> Terms and conditions apply.

Grandma says she only just managed to get me on Mrs Wing's list of students 'cos they play mahjong together. Mahjong is a Chinese game that loads of old people play. I don't know the rules but I know you have to shuffle hundreds of small tiles with pictures and Chinese words on them. I think you need to be clever to make sure you get all the good tiles so you can beat the rest. The only person who can beat Mrs Wing at mahjong is Grandma. When Grandma plays mahjong, she shuffles the tiles so quickly it gives her opponents headaches.

The lesson with Mrs Wing is about as fun as watching Grandma clip her yellow nails. She goes on and on for HOURS about fractions and percentages. She doesn't smile - not once. Instead she frowns lots and scribbles tons of notes about me in her gigantic book with the red leather cover.

When I share my awful "special" Maths lesson with Lai Ker, he is simpo-thetic for about a second before going back to play Super Hairy Ninja 4 on the computer.

"Look lil sis. If you want to be a proper Chinese you HAVE to be good at Maths. If you want to be a fake Chinese, then go bleach your hair blonde and call yourself Mary."

I believe most of the things Lai Ker tells me 'cos he's really smart and gets As in everything yet is pretty cool too. Of course I'd never tell him that to his face, but I do wonder if he is right all the time. Like he's always going on and on about what makes me a "true" Chinese person and what makes me not a "true" Chinese person. He says "true" Chinese people work fast so they can secretly play more while all the other people are slaving away.

"Lil sis, time is important. Life is about playing more and working less. People always think Chinese people are working hard but actually they're smart and they've finished the work by lunch break so they can play games on their computer."

He also told me that "true" Chinese people always keep their Chinese names.

"Xing, you don't see those rich white blokes living in Asia changing their names from Charlie to Chang or Mike to Ming do you? Gotta be proud of your culture innit."

Lai Ker also has this thing called *Chinks Have Mouths* or *CHM* for short. He says if I'm not smart enough or cool enough or loud enough I won't be a "Chinese person with a mouth", and will be "ignored by society". Lai Ker and his dodgy friend Jimmy Tang taught me the meaning of *CHM*. Standing up to white boys, cracking jokes mid-lesson and putting fingers up at racist sales assistants in posh shops are all examples of *CHM*. They said if I want to be a "true" Chinese person with a mouth, I have to be like them. I hope I can find my mouth soon, but I don't know exactly what my mouth is yet.

I think Lai Ker is the best at *CHM* 'cos at St George's he was always in detention 'cos of fights with the big white boys. That quickly stopped them from calling him "yellow wanker". Jimmy Tang was not far behind in having the best *CHM* but now he's moved to Hong Kong with his parents. Jimmy Tang's grandparents left Hong Kong to go to London for a better life, but his parents left London for Hong Kong to start an even better life. He said it was to do with glass in the ceiling at Jimmy Tang's dad's work place. Guess they have better decor in Hong Kong or something. I wouldn't know though as I've never been to Asia. The furthest I've been is Bath and that was 'cos Mama won us tickets by entering a competition in *The Sun*. She said it was destiny 'cos she found the newspaper on the bus she took to her job at the nursing home. Lai Ker says *The Sun* needs to be more multicultural as we never have topless Chinese models on page 3.

"Xing, another example why we need to have *CHM*."

I thought the reason was 'cos Chinese girls have small boobs, not 'cos there aren't enough Chinese people with *CHM*.

Chapter 5
The School for Scuttlebutts

I arrive at West Hill Independent Secondary School with butterflies in my stomach and rain dripping down my nose. Grandma said I was "the lucky luckiest girl in London" to get a place at such a good school.

"I pull hundred strings get you there. So you better work hard."

"Is Lai Ker coming with me?"

"No, he study Hampstead Independent School. Much better without bimbos distract him."

"But he's never really had a girlfriend."

"Ah you see, right. That why he do so well in school."

West Hill is not like my old school St George's. For one, the school looks like a castle without a moat and there are tennis courts and a massive rugby pitch with a guy who is paid to mow it. Also, the corridors are very long and made of marble and airy instead of smelly. Kids carry tennis rackets and everyone has the latest touch screen phone. Oh, and they can afford swimming pool water that turns dark blue when you pee in it. Kids at West Hill all have last names like Fenn-Wright and Palmer-James while at St George's we had Chatterjees, Chiwetels and Angobungs. I'm well nervous being at West Hill. Lai Ker isn't here so no-one has got my back. Also, Mama isn't here any more, which is crap. On my first day at St George's, Mama put my favourite strawberry milk and Wotsits in my lunch box. Then she walked with me into the school and talked to the teachers to make sure they'd look out for me. I wouldn't want her to do that now 'cos I'm not a baby any more. But just knowing that I could chat to her after school would be enough to get rid of the sick feeling in my stomach.

Have a good day at school. I love you forever and a week.
No!

I mustn't think about Mama 'cos just a tiny memory, any tiny memory of her hurts my heart. When grown ups talked about having their hearts broken I never understood. But now I know that when your heart is broken for real it really hurts. Every time I think of Mama it feels like there is a little person wearing spiky shoes trampling up and down my heart. It kills!

I walk into classroom 3B.

Smart Victorian-type wooden desks with inkwells are positioned in neat rows. They face an old chalkboard that has smiley faces, flowers and the word "Welcome" drawn on it. In the right hand corner of the room sit a large group of teenage girls with straightened hair and perfect tans. They stare at me from top to toe. A tall model-like blonde girl with green eyes gestures at me and whispers something to the group. Muffled giggles follow and I feel my heart starting to beat quicker. Near the gigantic arched window is perched a group of skinny boys. The ringleader is softly strumming on his guitar, singing to himself. He reminds me of a younger version of Cliff Richard. Mama was a big fan of Sir Cliff and used a poster of the film *Summer Holiday* to cover the mould on our kitchen wall.

The boys look up very briefly from their mobile phones when I pass and then go back to writing text messages. I sit at an empty desk near the front. My neighbour is a small, mixed-raced boy with blue glasses listening to his iPod. With his freckled, caramel skin I think he's cute in a bookworm way. He sits with closed eyes, tapping his foot on the floor to the rhythm of the music. His shoulder-length dreadlocked hair is moving from side to side as if he is in a trance.

"Good morning class."

"Good morning, Mrs Wilkins."

"Class, before we begin, I would like to announce we have a newcomer all the way from China."

(I was born in Hackney)

"Her name is… "

Mrs Wilkins pauses and squints her eyes as if she were reading another language. She looks at me as if she has a giant question mark over her head, and then shrugs her shoulders.

"X?"

"Ing?"

"Axe-ing Lee?"

The class burst into laughter and repeat my mangled name over and over again like Etonites chanting at a rugby match. I feel my face going all red, but at least I'm not going bright, bright red 'cos Chinese skin doesn't really go very red unless we drink alcohol. The only person who isn't laughing is the dreadlocked boy.

"AXE-ING, AXE-ING, AXE-ING."

Mrs Wilkins arches her thin pencilled eyebrow and looks slightly amused.

"Settle down class, we have to be welcoming to all."

I hear the blonde model girl hiss "Axe-ing, maybe her chink parents were farmers with axes," causing her female followers to stop their giggles with their manicured hands. The dreadlocked boy stiffens slightly when he hears the word "chink". I clench my fists and dig my nails into my palms until they hurt. My whole body is starting to shake. I feel tiny like a mangled ant that has just been squished by a five-year-old. Mama or Lai Ker usually fought my battles for me. Mama could do a mean right hook when provoked. I wipe my wet hand against my grey woollen skirt and swallow hard.

"Mrs Wilkins."

She peers and squints at me over her black sixties-shaped

glasses.

"You-got-my-name-wrong. My-name-is-Xing-Li. It-is-pronounced-Xing-with-an-S-sound.

There is a short silence before a chubby, gingered-haired boy starts jeering "Sing-song, Sing-song". In a matter of seconds the whole class has joined in again.

"Sing-Song, Sing-Song, Sing-Song."

Hot tears fill my eyes and I bite my lip until I can taste blood in my mouth.

Shirley
Hannah
Isabelle
Teddingham.

That is the name of the model-like blonde who has decided I am not welcome at West Hill. Her friends call her "Shils" for short and she is the queen of West Hill. She told everyone that I'm some refugee on an assisted place and the school only let me in 'cos they felt sorry for me. Assisted place kids usually don't have posh accents and 'cos I don't sound like Prince Charles, no-one believes that Grandma is rich. When I was in the lunch queue, Shils tripped me up and told me off for being a "clumsy chinky bitch". Then one of her mates stepped on my hand when I tried to pick up my sandwiches.

The West Hill bitches are taller, more athletic and greater in numbers than me. In the time it would take to give Shils a bloody nose, her catty crew would have pinned me to the floor. I can't channel Lai Ker's *CHM*. I've spent the first day keeping quiet while making the toilet by the library my cool hang out place.

When the school bell rings, I run out of class so quickly I don't know where I'm going and end up getting lost. The school is so big with so many doors and exit signs and corridors labelled with loads of numbers and letters. I pass the mixed-raced dreadlocked boy who did not laugh at my name. He's walking along corridor D4-003 as if he were strolling along a beach in Hawaii. Messy hair, perfect posture and sky blue glasses carefully placed upon his nose. I should ask him really, but he's listening to his iPod and doesn't look like he wants to be disturbed. Oh yes! This is Chemistry lab 2D; I was here this morning when Shils "accidently" spilt some iodine onto my shirt sleeve. I know where I am now - kind of.

After school, I'm too embarrassed to tell Lai Ker about Shils. He won't understand 'cos he's already found his "mouth". His first day of school started similar but ended totally different. The rugby star of Hampstead tested the water when he asked Lai Ker, "Do you sell illegal DVDs?"

Lai Ker calmly replied, "Yeah, I've got some in the back of my trunk along with my nunchucks and black belt in kung fu."

After showing some made up kung fu moves such as "Monkey peels the banana" and "Giraffe eats a mouse", he was left alone by the Hampstead toffs. They even asked him to join them for rugby tryouts. Lai Ker sounds really happy with his new school. He says none of the guys are as cool as Jimmy Tang and they're all kinda thick, but he'll whip them into shape. He's gonna take up rugby and try and become Britain's first Chinese rugby player. But I'm not to tell Grandma. When he asks me how my first day went I say it was f-i-n-e.

Dinner with Grandma is eaten in silence with the giant clock ticking away. I'm getting a bit used to the sounds now. Auntie Mei isn't joining us for dinner 'cos she's out filming a commercial. She's playing the role of a Thai girl selling a new brand of jasmine rice. Grandma was not pleased about this. She shouted A LOT at Auntie Mei yesterday. She was annoyed Auntie Mei is lying about being Thai and if she gets found out it will be shameful. Auntie Mei said white directors can't tell the difference and talked about when she went to an audition pretending to be Cambodian. They asked her to speak in her "native" tongue - she made up gibberish and got the job. Luckily the advert was only shown in the

UK. She told us yesterday she's played Filipino maids, Thai prostitutes and Chinese refugees. It must be super glamorous being an actress.

Grandma doesn't ask us how our first day at school went. She told us this morning, "As long you get good report card and no detention no need make big deal. Actions louder than words. You get it?"

If Mama were here she would want to know everything and then I bet she'd make up a joke about the posh kids and their million quid pool with the water that changes colour when you pee. She'd probably tell me what to do about Shils as well. But Mama isn't here so I don't know what to do. I miss her so much. When I think of her my eyes get all teary and I pinch myself so I won't start crying properly. I know once I let my tears fall down they will never be able to stop. My tears will fall and fall like rain. Then my room will become an ocean and that's not good because I'm crap at swimming. I'll probably end up drowning in my salty tears.

After dinner, I try to prepare my own lunch for tomorrow - spam and baked bean sandwiches, just the way Mama used to make them. When times were tight, Mama produced combos of recipes that would cause TV chefs to swear. We did not have a sofa or a toilet that flushed smoothly, but Mama said if she couldn't feed us, she had failed her duty as a Chinese mother. With her bank balance in minus, Mama had to seriously get creative with meals. Sitting around a red metal table we lived on baked beans mixed with rice, peas and generous lashings of soy sauce. A treat would be tinned spam wrapped in won ton pockets served with boiled spaghetti - the cheap kind that tasted like corn flavoured cardboard. Lai Ker's favourite dish was sweet and sour offal with cheese. Those were GREAT meal times, but Grandma was having none of it. She said since we are now Wus we have to eat like Wus.

"No more baked beans, no more ham or spam or pak choi covered with tomato ketchup. You Wu now, you eat proper Chinese food."

"But Mama's food was proper."

"Your mother feed you rubbish. That's why you not so brainy."

I didn't know there was a connection between eating baked beans and times tables. Lai Ker ate a lot of beans and he got the highest grade in his Maths GCSEs, even though he was watching *Terminator 2* the night before. Every day I have to add a new rule to the rules of the Wu household. Apart from this new rule about only eating "Wu" food, I've discovered the following rules.

1) Grandma is the queen. She has the final say on EVERYTHING

2) No speaking at meal times unless spoken to

3) No going on the tube by myself

4) No whistling

I discovered the whistling rule when I whistled the theme song for *Superman* and Grandma threw one of Auntie Mei's stilettos at my leg.

"Whistle bad luck, shut lips now."

Lai Ker insisted it wasn't so much the whistling, but more my choice of music.

"Bet if you'd whistled the *Star Wars* theme instead of *Superman*, Grandma wouldn't have had a problem. She quite fancies Han Solo. Ages ago she saw me watching *Star Wars* and she said *Hallison Ford not as ugly as guy playing Rude Skywalk*."

"Okay if you're so clever, I'd like YOU to try whistling in front of Grandma."

"I would but gotta not strain the muscles on my lips - need them for when the babes line up for kisses."

"Of course, mustn't strain your precious lips just in case a supermodel comes knocking on your door."

"Precisely, you're a lot smarter than you look. Maybe one day you'll be as smart as me."

"You wish!"

Lai Ker says that it's important for Chinese people to be smart 'cos smart people get the best jobs. Also, smart people get to secretly run the country 'cos they have the most money. He doesn't mean the MPs but more the people that own the MPs. Maybe if I keep my head down and work my arse off, I'll get good grades and Grandma will be nicer to me. When Shils and her friends marry rich bankers and become pretty divorcees without careers, I will be this super smart rich Chinese businesswoman ruling the world. Then I will have the loudest mouth of all, even louder than Lai Ker.

Chapter 6
The Hair and the Tortoise

"Sing-Song, does your grandma cook you dog?"

"Sing-Song, why do you eat lunch alone? Is it because you have no friends?"

"Sing-Song your bags are massive. Were you making chop suey in your parents' chinky takeaway last night?"

It's only been a week at West Hill but my lunch breaks have got into a special routine. Lunch break ugliness by Shils and her crew in the corridor followed by me rushing to the toilet by the library. Then I put the toilet lid down and start playing my DS while scoffing my lunch. If I can get through the break without getting wet toilet paper thrown over the top of the cubicle or someone tripping me up - then my lunch break is fine. I know as long as I keep my head down and stay in the toilet I will be okay.

Not happy, not depressed, but okay.

I start to daydream about what it would be like to grow up in a country where I am not seen as different. Somewhere where I am popular and don't have to explain my name or that I'm Chinese. It would be a really cool place where Asians and Jamaicans are just seen as doctors, school girls and business women. Not "the Chinese doctor", "the Asian school girl" or "the black businesswomen of the year". It would be a country where I was not seen as "ethnic" or "exotic" but just "me".

That would be great!

The class has been given an assignment of looking after giant African spur-thighed tortoises in pairs. They are almost the size of the giant tortoises that Darwin bloke found. Mrs Wilkins has spent the last forty years breeding them in her garden shed. She's fed the enormous beasts with lettuce mixed with rocket and wants to share her unusual pets with us. I'm really excited - looking after tortoises is a lot more fun than tackling history essays on the Romans and Geography projects about plankton. I've been paired with the peculiar dreadlocked boy with blue glasses. His name is almost as weird as mine, it is Jayeth Ming Anderson, but he calls himself Jay for short. I always see him sitting by himself listening to music.

We're sitting next to each other and it feels well awkward. The uncomfortable wooden chairs don't help; they give you a hiney cramp after thirty minutes. Jay is tapping his leg against his chair while I desperately try to sit as straight as I can. Mama said if you sit straight it means you are more confident. I find it hard to make eye contact with Jay and I find my cheeks getting hot. His foot starts tapping really quick. Then he speaks to me with an East London accent. It's been a while since I've heard someone my age speaking like me rather than with a la-dee-da accent.

"You looked after a tortoise before?"

"No."

"Me neither."

I gave my best attempt at chit-chat too.

"You looked after a pet before?"

"Nah, my dad's allergic."

"That sucks."

"Yup."

Jay's leg continues to tap on the chair; there is some kind of rhythm to his tapping.

"Why do you tap so much?"

"'cos I like it."

"What do you mean?"

"Like when I'm nervous it helps when I'm tapping to the fourth movement of Beethoven's fifth symphony."

I didn't know Beethoven had more than one symphony. I think he's joking but he looks dead serious. He gulps some water from his black water bottle with tiny white pianos printed on it. Then he takes out an ironed handkerchief from his right pocket and wipes his mouth before speaking again.

"West Hill not great, innit?"

"Yeah, I hate it… hate 'em."

"I hate the school but don't hate 'em."

"Why?"

"'cos that would mean I care what they think. I don't care. Best use my energy for better things."

"How?"

"How what?"

"How do you not care?"

"I just don't. I don't care what they say 'cos most of them are thick anyway. Like Shils and her crew have repeated like one or two years."

No wonder Shils and her side kicks all look way more grown up than me. Jay draws a quick sketch of a giant tortoise with massive glasses. It's actually pretty good. Without looking up, he asks me where I'm from.

"Well, my parents were both Chinese. But I was born in London."

"I know, what I meant was which part of London are you from?"

Jay is one of the only people ever to ask me which part of London I am from. About ninety-nine percent of the time when people ask me "where I'm from", they mean which country, even though London is the only home I know. It gets me confused. When I say, "I was born in Hackney and grew up in Kilburn," they look at me strangely. Some smile and say, "Yes but where are you REALLY from?"

"I was born in Hackney, grew up in Kilburn, now live in Kensington. You?"

"Born in Newham, grew up in Newham, still live in Newham. But my parents are from Jamaica and China. Dad's Jamaican, Mum's Chinese."

"That's really cool."

"What's really cool?"

"I guess your background."

"I guess… but I'm just me."

I have never met a Chinese-black person before, especially one with kick-ass dreads for his hair. Chinese-white kids are two a penny. Meeting a Chinese-black kid is SO rare it's like winning the lottery or finding a four-leaf clover.

Jay has stopped tapping now and I'm glad 'cos his tapping is starting to give me a headache. I'm trying to think what I can ask him without sounding uncool.

"So Jay, what kind of music do you like?"

"Classical." (I like pop.)

"How about computer games? Which one is your favourite?"

"I don't touch computer games. They'll fry your brain."

Jay opens the box with the giant tortoise. He's got a beautiful, yellowish shell with dark brown edges and is chomping on some lettuce with an enormous, scaly head. He looks super grumpy and doesn't care if we know it. I like him already! Jay smiles and pushes his sky blue glasses up. I notice he has some freckles on his nose. He must have got them from his Jamaican side 'cos Chinese people don't get freckles.

"Look Xing Li, THAT tortoise must be Chinese, look how much he eats."

"Yeah, definitely, he looks like my older brother when he's eating dinner."

"So your brother must be greedy with a fat head."

"Exactly."

We both start laughing, but not too loud 'cos Mrs Wilkins

is walking up and down the classroom. She's got a massive nose and looks like a skinny ant-eater who hasn't been fed for days. I stroke the tortoise's shell; it feels a lot smoother than it looks.

"Have you got any brothers or sisters?"

"Nah, there were some problems when my mum gave birth to me so it's just me and my parents. But it's okay. They're cool - most of the time anyway."

Jay touches the tortoise's head gently like he is patting a tiny dog. Suddenly, he takes his glasses off in excitement.

"Xing Li, you know what would be really cool?

"What?"

"We could experiment with this tortoise."

"Like what? I don't want to hurt him."

"Of course not, he's cool. I meant we could experiment and see what he likes to eat."

"Yeah that would be fun! See what he likes."

"But we've gotta be careful, if not Mrs Wilkins will kill us."

"Yeah she's weird, like there's something not right about a sixty-year-old woman keeping fifteen giant tortoises in her back garden."

"My mum would say she is a *Din Por.*"

"A what?"

"You know, a *din por* - crazy woman in Chinese."

"Hey, you can speak Chinese. My Chinese is crap."

"Yeah, my mum only spoke to me in Cantonese when I was little."

"Wish my mum did that. Her Chinese weren't so great, so she made me go to Chinese school."

"What, like on Saturdays?"

"No, on Sunday mornings. My brother and me used to hate it 'cos the lady in charge was such a con."

"What do you mean?"

"Like her idea of teaching us Chinese was to make us watch Jackie Chan films with subtitles and learn Chinese ribbon dancing. We didn't learn much Chinese at all. Oh, and she liked to show off her fake designer gear that she got from Hong Kong. Like she'd strut up and down the room carrying her 'Kartier' watch and 'Channels' handbag."

"That's weird."

"Yeah, I know."

The bell goes and we haven't started writing our eight-week plan for looking after the tortoise. Mrs Wilkins wants us to measure how much the tortoise eats, drinks and even poos. Jay says I can have the tortoise first, but I've gotta keep him updated if he dies. He gives me his mobile number. It's the first mobile number I've got from a boy. It's the first mobile number I've got from a classmate in West Hill. It's a good day today!

Chapter 7
CHM

The tortoise weighs a ton and I have to get Jay to help me carry him home. We have to stop every ten minutes to stretch our arms. The tortoise sleeps all the way home. With his eyes closed, he looks like a hundred-year-old man. Jay has to go when we reach the top of my road 'cos he has to rush home for a music lesson. I drag the box home a metre at a time. I can't wait to introduce the tortoise to the family. The tortoise opens his eyes and stares at the sky like he wants to grow wings and fly out of the box. I laugh! Imagine if the tortoise grew wings! Mama would be so excited if she were here. Once, we gave Meow Meow some wings made out of cardboard. She started purring lots and then tripped over the wings, we just laughed and laughed and laughed.

Grandma doesn't like the tortoise.

She says it's "ugly", "old" and "disgusting". I want to say, "a bit like you then" but I remember her feather duster and bite my tongue. I tell her it's for a school project that makes up a BIG amount of my grade. When she hears the word "grade", she narrows her eyes and says I can keep him in the shed. Poor tortoise will be cold in winter. I hope he doesn't hibernate on me. Grandma says the shed has a heater so he won't die and I should stop moaning.

"Tortoise lucky I don't eat for dinner."

She's not joking about this one; we had turtle soup last night. I thought it was fish at first until I saw the shell. Actually it was really tasty. Like it had these special herbs that really make your tummy warm without being too spicy. Which is like so nice in winter. I wonder who makes up what food is okay and what food is weird. Like I heard there are countries that keep cows and chickens as pets. They must think we're weird when we eat hamburgers and stuff like that. I asked Jay and he said that in Leviticus in the Bible they have a whole list of foods people could or couldn't eat. But then later in the New Testament it says we can eat anything we want. So, I guess that includes tortoises too.

It's really dark in the shed but a lot cleaner than I thought. There's no cobwebs or anything, just some old pots and stuff. It smells of wood - that's one of the nicest smells ever. I've got a big box and put lots of leaves and grass and shredded newspapers inside. The tortoise seems to like it and looks really comfy. I told Jay I didn't want to give the tortoise a name 'cos that will make the tortoise ours for real. Then it will be way too sad when we say goodbye. He agrees, he said he got well depressed when he had to give his dog Lemon away 'cos his dad couldn't stop sneezing. Every time he sees a lemon he gets sad 'cos he remembers his dog.

I can't wait for our silent dinner to be over 'cos I want to see what happens if I feed the tortoise some prawns. When Grandma isn't looking, I hide the prawns in my napkin. I also add some Chinese cabbage too. Lai Ker winks and helps me to get some green beans even though he says keeping pets is a waste of time.

"Lil sis, pets are selfish creatures that just take and take. I'd rather spend my money on a good beef steak instead."

"But you can't pat a good beef steak can you?"

"No."

"Also, you can't cuddle a good beef steak or feed it from your hand."

"No, but a good beef steak is tasty and that's all that matters."

It is REALLY cold outside; the air's so icy I have to take small breaths. I don't like it when it gets dark so early. It's much nicer when it is summer. Auntie Mei told me Singapore is really, really hot and when she's cold she wishes she could zoom to the beach in Singapore.

Mama and Auntie Mei were born in Singapore and came to the UK when Mama was five and Auntie Mei was one. Uncle Ho was born in London and is almost six years younger than Mama. Singapore is a tiny island near Malaysia and that's where my ancestors are from. It's weird thinking that Mama grew up on this sunny island far away. Maybe hot weather is in my blood 'cos I *hate* cold weather.

I open the shed. It's nice and warm in the shed.

Wait a second!

That's Uncle Ho sitting in the corner. He's kneeling down and watching the tortoise. Like really, really staring as if the tortoise is going to attack him or something. I can hear Uncle Ho breathing really hard. He sometimes sounds like he is hiding a tiny whistle in his nose, but that's normal for him.

"Uncle Ho?"

He turns around quickly like I've come up to him and said, "Boo". He doesn't say anything, just stares at me as if he is looking through me. I suddenly start speaking really quickly.

"Uncle-Ho-I-guess-you-beat-me-to-feeding-the-tortoise. He-doesn't-have-a-name-yet.We-just-call-him-tortoise. I-brought-some-prawns-you-can-feed-him-if-you-want."

I show him the prawns and he looks well suspicious. Then he walks quietly out of the shed.

Grandma says Uncle Ho has the "strange" disease. We are not to tell anyone about his disease ever. If people ask about him, we have to say he works as a writer and that is why he's weird and keeps to himself. Whenever Uncle Ho came to visit, he would sit in the corner watching the telly. Mama told me he liked to be left alone 'cos he's more shy than most people. The only person Uncle Ho really talks to is Grandma. She does everything for him and even helps him to bathe.

I squat down and the tortoise looks up at me; his nostrils twitch a bit. I dangle the prawns near his nose and he stretches his long head out. His nostrils twitch like crazy. *UM*. He gobbles the prawn up in one go. I give him the second prawn and he swallows it up whole. Jay will be super excited when I tell him. Mrs Wilkins told us tortoises are vegetarian - she is so wrong.

Lai Ker is not interested in my tortoise talk at all. He says he's very busy working out a business deal with Jimmy Tang and doesn't have spare time to "play with my food". Lai Ker's always thinking about business. When he was eight, he stole his classmates' rubbers and sold them back for 50p. Lai Ker said it was their toll for him sourcing the rubbers. Also, at my age, Lai Ker did other students' homework for a price. I have fond memories of helping him design leaflets with the "Homework Price List" on them. Maths homework was £2.50; English was £8.75 while large-scale Geography projects were twenty-five quid. "Packages" were delivered through primary school kids who were paid 50p per delivery. Unfortunately, Lai Ker's business went bankrupt when arch enemy Hamid Khan photocopied Lai Ker's work and sold it for half the price. Lai Ker punched Hamid and he ran squealing to the headmaster. The only reason Lai Ker was not expelled was 'cos he had won the super famous Young Olympiad prize in Mathematics three years in a row and the school needed him to attract other smart kids. Lai Ker always brags, "I do the crime, but I ain't never do the time. *CHM*."

"So what kind of business deal do you have with Jimmy Tang?"

"Ah, it's top secret my lil sis. Let's just say I've found the best market for a top product."

"What kind of product? Who's the market?"

"Patience, patience. I can't tell you all my business secrets.

Richard Branson didn't become a billionaire by sharing his secrets."

"Jimmy Tang's not exactly a Chinese Richard Branson, is he?"

"Well, he's getting there. He's already importing and exporting to ten different countries."

"You mean he opened an online store on eBay."

"Look, mock all you want. But Jimmy Tang and I are gonna be billionaires. I've found a great hole in the market at my school. When promoted the right way, I could sell shit to those posh, white kids. *CHM*, innit."

"What has this got to do with *Chinks Have Mouths*?"

"Well, if I make lots of money, I will be able to say what I want when I want. Look, you have to have a plan too. Rack your brains so you can be heard too. Maybe you can help me do some business with the posh kids in your school?"

"Maybe…"

But that would mean speaking to them. The only time my classmates speak to me is when they are making fun of Jay or me. Yesterday, Shils said loudly to her friends that assisted place kids are so thick we need special tutors to teach us how to write and use cutlery properly. Everyone heard and everyone laughed.

Lai Ker keeps telling me I need to have *CHM*. But I don't even know where to start. I'm really confused sometimes about who I am or what I want to be. I wish Mama were here, she would know what to do. She always told me to be proud of being Chinese 'cos one fifth of the world is Chinese and everything is made in China. Like all the toys we got from Oxfam were made in China. But how can I be proud of being Chinese 'cos if I weren't Chinese, Shils would leave me alone. She wouldn't make fun of my Chinese name, she wouldn't cuss my black hair and she wouldn't ask me if my grandma cooked me dog for my tea. If I weren't Chinese, I wouldn't have so much pressure to be good at

Maths and I would have bigger boobs. I wouldn't have to worry about people not saying my name correctly. I would look like everyone on the telly and wouldn't have to always explain London is my home, not China. But then if I were English, I would have stuff like fish fingers for dinner instead of yummy Chinese food. I would become a lobster in the sun, spend hours talking about the weather and get wrinkles quicker. Like Auntie Mei looks about twenty-eight when she's actually forty-three. Also, my house would be really muddy 'cos English people wear shoes in their home. Most importantly, if I weren't Chinese I wouldn't be Chinese like Mama. I don't know - it's confusing.

Chapter 8
Survival of the Fritters

"Ewwwww, that is SO disgusting."

"Yeah, what kind of food do these weirdos eat?"

"Looks like some kind of fried vomit."

"That is like so disgusting."

Jay and I have front row seats for Shils' short play of meanness. She speaks in a way that makes every remark personal. Yet her voice is loud enough to cause all our classmates to stop and stare. They always laugh. It's not the kind of laughter that you have when you watch something funny on telly and want to share the joke. It's more like the kind of cackling laughter that those witches in cartoons have when they are cooking someone in their cauldron.

Our lunchtime mocking usually happens on Mondays and Wednesdays. On Tuesdays, Shils has drama club and Thursdays are her netball practices. As for Fridays, anything could happen. Some Fridays she hassles us so much we don't get to eat lunch, other Fridays she doesn't give a toss about us. When she leaves us alone, it's bliss. Jay and me can eat lunch and we're free just like all our other classmates. But we never know if she will leave us alone or not. I get a horrible feeling of nausea and butterflies in my stomach on Thursday nights. Not knowing what is going to happen is worse than anything.

As a treat, Jay's mum often makes him the most delicious banana fritters I have ever tasted. Mama once tried to make fritters before, but we had run out of sugar and bananas so she made us savoury fried cucumber instead. When dipped in tomato sauce, Mama's fritters were actually quite tasty. But they were not the drooling delight Jay's mum's fritters are - fluffy melt in your mouth batter with a gooey, sweet inside that lingers on your tongue all afternoon.

YUM!

The secret is soaking the bananas in brown sugar over night, and then adding a small teaspoon of Jamaican rum to the mixture. She calls them the "Jay Fritters" 'cos the recipe is "half Chinese and half Jamaican". Jay always gives me half his share. He measures each fritter with his ruler and slices it down the middle. Sometimes the ruler cuts the fritter in a lopsided manner and one portion is a couple of millimetres out. Jay always insists I take the bigger half. I wonder what he would say if I told him about the ketchup and pak choi sandwiches Mama used to make. The sandwich was a recipe Mama made up when she needed to buy us new school bags and we were short of cash. She used to write down every item of food, school books, sweets and toilet rolls in her tatty diaries she bought from the bargain bucket at Mr Kapoor's newsagents. Until I started school, I thought it was normal for diaries to be a year behind.

I remember always hating the twenty-first day of the month 'cos it was what Mama called "Mean Reds day". On that day all the red bills would arrive. Mama would sit at the kitchen table sighing and shaking her head.

"What's wrong Mama?"

"Don't worry, grown up problems. Why don't you go play with Lai Ker?"

Mama refused to get help from what she called "English government money". Lai Ker told me her job paid less than what Mama would have got if she signed up to all the benefits: Jobseekers Allowance, Single Parent Allowance, and Housing Benefits. When Mama recycled Lai Ker's old clothes for me to wear or I had to wear the shoes that I had grown out of six months ago, I would be annoyed at Mama for not taking the "Benefits". Some of my previous classmates in St George's got great stuff from their parents' "Benefits". They got to buy things such as Nike trainers and touch screen phones. Each time Mama introduced us to her new recipes of barely edible food we'd wrinkle our noses in disgust and then gobble up the food hungrily. I sometimes saw Mama bite her lip to stop the tears.

I'd do anything to have some of that food now.

Jay never asks me about Mama and I like it that way. Today we're going bargain hunting after school at Oak Lane Market. I can sneak to the market for about thirty minutes, then rush home to do my homework. The flea market was started in the sixties by a bunch of hippies who wanted to sell their "special" brownies and recycle their old clothes. It's an amazing place where you can get anything and everything - from pickled quail's eggs to patchwork trousers. I've already spotted a stuffed lion's head for £140; it would not look out of place in Grandma's house. Jay is looking at second hand CDs and I'm trying on five quid shoes. There are some really cool silver platforms with leopard bows. Jay loves peering at the prices of things over the top of his glasses. He looks like an old man when he does that. If the item is what he calls "Cheap as Mr Chan's chips", Jay takes his glasses off in excitement. As part of his assisted place grant with West Hill, Jay gets weekly lunch money. His parents want him to learn "responsibility" so he can use the money on anything he wants. Sometimes Jay will eat jam sandwiches for a week so he can buy a classical album by a composer I've never heard of.

"Jay, guess what?"

"What?

"I fed the tortoise prawns and he REALLY liked them."

"Seriously? Man that tortoise must be a boy then."

"Why do you say that?"

"Well, guys like meat."

"Yeah, but so do girls. I like meat too."

"Yeah but I think boy tortoises are car-knee-vols. Read that on the internet somewhere."

"Guess it must be true then."

Jay and me talk about everything that matters like whether Mr Singh or Mr Chan sells the oiliest sausage and chips or if Miss McCall (the wide-shouldered gym teacher with the tiniest Adam's apple) used to be a man or if Mr Lewis is the secret father of our classmate Mark Lewis. They have the same ginger hair and blue eyes and right dimple on their cheek. As for the Shils issue, Jay says we should "blank her" and that's that. I'm trying to get him to have lunches in the disabled toilet to avoid the heckling on Monday and Wednesday. Jay shakes his head and taps his foot to the rhythm of Chai-Koi-Ski's 1812 Overture. I recognise that one now.

"Xing, it's well germy to eat in the toilet, where would we sit?

"It's really roomy in there. Guess we could put a newspaper or library book on the floor and sit on that or something. I don't know."

"No way, we're eating in the lunch room just like everyone."

"Yeah but at least if we're in the toilets Shils won't be able to say all that crap about our lunch in front of everyone. Before I met you, I used to eat in the girls' loo, it's not TOO bad."

"She can say what she wants."

"I know but I hate it. Wish I could just not worry about it."

"Well you shouldn't. I know who I am and so should you."

"But how do you know who you are?"

Jay frowns and takes his glasses off.

"I guess 'cos of my parents, things like Shils don't bother me. Like they had to put up with a lot more crap than we do."

"What do you mean?"

"Like when they got married... like you know, my mum is Chinese and my dad is Jamaican."

"So?"

"Well, 'cos of that they don't see their families any more."

"What like never?"

"Never. When my Jamaican granddad met my mum he told her that she could be his girlfriend but never his wife."

"Seriously?"

"Yeah. They wanted my dad to take over their furniture business with this girl in Jamaica. So they didn't want him to marry my mum. But my mum's parents were worse, they didn't even want to meet my dad. They said, "If you marry a black man, we will never see you again.""

"That's real sad."

"Yeah I guess, my mum looks real sad about it sometimes. But my parents have got a new family in their church, so they're okay."

"I guess they've got you too."

"Yeah I guess, when I don't get on their nerves."

"Don't worry, I get on my grandma's nerves all the time."

"Well, I don't want to piss them off all the time. Like my dad also puts up with loads 'cos he's a classical musician."

"What's wrong with that? You have to be super smart to play classical stuff."

"Yeah but it's a real problem 'cos there're only like three black classical musicians in the UK."

"But he's good at playing, right?"

"He's amazing. Like when he plays it makes people cry. But it don't stop people being real bad to him."

"What do you mean?"

"Well, like when he first started work. Like he wasn't even a kid any more, yet they were like making fun of him."

"Like how?"

"Like making jokes about him not having enough black rhythm when he got some notes wrong and asking him to "channel his Bob Marley". Like they did it in a sarcastic la-dee-da way so you had to laugh as if it was a joke but it hurts inside."

"Yeah I know what you mean."

"Yeah. Anyway, let's not talk about this any more. It's the past. My dad says forgive and forget. He knows who he is, God knows who he is and that's all that matters."

"Yeah, I would love to hear him play some time."

"Yeah, that would be cool. He is like a hundred times better at music than me."

I know who I am and so should you.

Maybe one day when I become grown up and confident I will be able to say it too. Like I know I'm Chinese but then my only home is London and I can only speak English not Chinese. So I'm weird like that. I guess until I grow up and know who I am, I just have to focus on surviving Mondays and Wednesdays and Fridays at West Hill without losing my lunch in the process.

Chapter 9
This Little Grandma Went to Market

When I get home, Grandma is standing at the door tapping her watch. She looks well annoyed.

"YOU thirty minutes late."

I look at my watch, it's 4:45pm, I come back at this time every day. Do I dare ask if her watch is wrong? She is almost shouting.

"Xing Li I say meet 4:15pm, remember? We have get school sports uniform. Now too late to take car as car went for service at car shop 5:30pm. TERRIBLE time. TERRIBLE GIRL. I wait AGES."

Oh no! I completely forgot Grandma told me last night I need to get my PE kit today. At West Hill I've been wearing an old T-shirt and shorts while waiting for my sports uniform to be ready and Grandma said it would be ready for sure TODAY. In PE, Shils said my favourite white T-shirt with Hello Kitty on it makes me look like a "loser five-year-old". The class kept doing the L sign with their hands every time the teacher wasn't looking. So, I do need to get my new PE kit ASAP.

West Hill has a special PE kit that you can only get in a posh department store called Harold & Sons. It has a white cotton T-shirt with the school crest, a horrible yellow hockey skirt, a red tracksuit with zips and navy blue knickers. The navy blue knickers are the most important 'cos if you don't wear them, you get a demerit point. My netball teacher Miss Sparks makes the girls line up in the changing room. They have to lift their skirts one by one. If we're not wearing navy knickers she notes it down. At first I thought Miss Sparks was a pervert, but it didn't make sense 'cos she is going out with a really good looking bloke. Saw him picking her up once on his Harley. Then I found out that checking navy knickers is normal at posh schools. Also, you can get demerit points for wearing muddy shoes, not clearing your tray at lunch and for being late for class as well as a hundred other things that I can't remember. If you get three demerit points, you get a detention. If you get twenty demerit points, you get suspended for a week. Lai Ker's school is Catholic so you get penance points: five penance points is detention and thirty is suspension. Lai Ker wants to get thirty, so he can have time off school to work on his business plan with Jimmy Tang. He still hasn't told me what business it is. But he says it's going well and he's earning lots of cash.

Grandma is super annoyed now 'cos we are late and we have to take the tube. She nudges me along with her elbows. They are more pointy than Lai Ker's.

"Hurry up, hurry up, HURRY UP."

I almost slip on some dead leaves on the way to the station. Grandma grabs my arm with her iron grip before I fall down. She is well strong.

"Careful, you get accident then die for nothing."

At the station, Grandma looks confused at the ticket machine. She presses a button and it says "ERROR".

"Xing Li, Grandma test you, SEE if you clever. SEE how quick you buy tickets."

Grandma gives me a fifty-pound note. It's red; I've never seen one before. I buy return tickets to town and Grandma looks pleased.

"Okay you past first test. But still not as clever as Lai

53

Ker. Second test now. SEE how quick you find platform and collect train. You got five minutes."

Grandma taps her watch and I rapidly find our platform in three minutes and twenty-two seconds. We get into the train and before I can sit down, Grandma pulls me back. Oh yeah, have to offer Grandma the seat first. I gesture for her to sit down, waving my hand in what posh people call a "flurry". She ignores me and is busy taking wet wipes out of her bag. Before I can say a word, she is wiping the seats with her wet wipes. People are starting to stare. Grandma uses three wet wipes for each seat. Then Grandma takes a tissue out and unfolds it S-L-O-W-L-Y. She puts it on her seat. My mouth is a little open and she gives me a dirty look.

"Why look so shock? What more shock is you sit down on warm seat and get rectal cancer."

During our long journey to Harold & Sons, Grandma keeps silent. She only speaks when a blind person comes in with a Labrador.

"LOOK so dirty bring dirty dog on train."

"But Grandma he's blind."

"That's why he can't see how dirty dog is."

A young English woman in a business suit shakes her head and quietly tuts.

"Why you tut tut? YOUR BUSINESS BE RUDE TO OLD WOMAN?"

The woman turns red and looks down. The rest of the carriage pretends to read their newspapers. I'm SUPER embarrassed. Now the whole carriage is going to think Chinese people are twats! Mama said we always have to be careful of how we behave in public 'cos how we behave can affect how people see the entire race of Chinese people. Like if we are rude, people will think all Chinese people are rude and if we are thick, people will think all Chinese people are thick. Also, if we are smart, people will think all Chinese people are smart. It's the same for blacks too. She said that's how the world works for ethnics. I remember when we went

54

out for dinner for Lai Ker's sixteenth birthday; we went to a very posh restaurant called Gourmet Hot Dog. The hot dogs were HUGE and came with French cheese called E-damn. The waiter was super rude but Mama said we had to leave the twelve percent tip, if not, people would think Chinese people were cheap. It's so complicated, like so much pressure to be good all the time.

Harold & Sons is REALLY huge and beautiful and expensive. The handbags cost more than anything I have ever seen. Grandma hurries me up the escalators. Wow! They've made it like you are inside an Egyptian tomb with real gold everywhere. Grandma stands to the left of me on the escalator and blocks everyone. Mama said they used to go grocery shopping in Harold & Sons like it was their local market. This was until Grandma discovered online shopping.

OH MY GOODNESS!

There is a pervert behind me and he is touching my arse.

WHAT SHALL I DO? WHAT SHALL I DO?

I feel my cheeks getting hot. Suddenly Grandma turns around on the escalator and grabs the pervert's wrist. I can see her nails digging into his wrist as she waves his hand in the air.

"EVERYBODY ATTENTION. THIS PERVERT MAN HERE PUT HIS HAND ON MY BUM. THIS IS THE HAND HERE."

Grandma keeps waving the man's hand really quickly.

"THIS PERVERT MAN HERE PUT HIS HAND ON *OLD LADY* BUM. THIS IS THE HAND HERE." Everyone looks shocked, but I'm not embarrassed 'cos this time I don't think Grandma is acting like a twat. Even if she is and that makes people think Chinese people are twats, they must think the man is MORE of a twat. The old man pervert goes all red. He struggles to get out of Grandma's grip, but she makes sure his hand is waving in the air until we reach the top of the escalator.

The sales assistant lady in Harold & Sons is measuring me for my PE kit. She smells of sweet perfume that reminds me of this purple disinfectant Mama used to clean the toilet. It came in a huge plastic bottle and was called Luscious Lilac for Loos.

"Twenty-three inched waist, no bra. That will be XS for the top and the navy knickers. Thirty-two inched hips, probably an S for the skirt and tracksuit bottoms. A little less snug than an XS, but that way your granddaughter can grow into it."

"No, we take M for top, M for tracksuit, M for skirt, S for blue knickers."

"Madam I'm terribly sorry, but that will be far too large for your skinny granddaughter."

"No problem, she grow into them. YOU also say she grow into them. No point waste money then have buy new clothes when she become big and fat."

"But Madam, she will be swimming in them."

"NO, no, she got swimsuit already."

"I mean Madam, they will be too big for her, size wise."

"Big better than small."

The lady looks at her friend at the till and rolls her eyes. They both have what Lai Ker calls "poo under their noses", you know that snooty look people have when they lift their noses ever so slightly higher than you. The sales assistant gestures wildly like she is doing charades with the uniform.

"Madam, do you un-der-stand what I am saying? The u-ni-form for your granddaughter will be TOO big."

"DO YOU UN-DER-STAND ENG-LISH? I WANT PAY NOW."

Grandma snatches the PE kit in one swift movement and drags me to the till. As the lady packs my new clothes into a ginormous green bag, she stares at the huge diamond and jade bracelet on Grandma wrist.

"Thank you Madam. Have a nice day."

It is a mad dash getting home. Grandma is rushing and

pushing and poking people with her umbrella when they get too near to her on the tube. She tells me to hurry up and keeps looking at her watch every two seconds.

"Hurry up Xing Li. I much older than you. You so slow because eat many cakes."

I can hardly keep up with her even though she is so tiny. She weaves in and out of the crowds like a bee ready to sting if someone gets in her way.

We finally arrive home; I'm breathless. Auntie Mei is sitting outside with her super warm fur coat that looks like a hundred chinchillas are stuck to it. Her usually perfect hair looks like someone rubbed a massive balloon all over it and her mascara is running.

"Ma, where have you been?!"

"We buy uniform. Xing Li make late."

"Ho has been asking and asking for you."

Auntie Mei is trembling so hard I can see the chinchillas moving up and down as if they are becoming alive again. Her face looks like she has used chalk instead of foundation.

"He's in one of his moods. He knew it was time for his shower and when I said you weren't in, he accused me of hiding you. The maids are all gone already, your brother is at rugby, and I didn't know what to do."

Auntie Mei tears up and slowly pushes the right sleeve of her coat up. There's blood soaking through a bandage. Grandma pushes past Auntie Mei and unlocks the front door in two seconds. There is broken glass and two of the vases have been smashed to the floor. I see the blood on the soft carpet where Lai Ker and I lay.

It feels eerie quiet.

Grandma runs up the stairs, two steps at a time. I follow her. I don't want to but I don't want her to be alone. I'm scared. I wish Lai Ker were here, I wish Mama were here. Uncle Ho is sitting on a chair outside the bathroom, all calm as if he is waiting for a bus. He's completely naked; he's got lots of moles and his fat tummy almost covers his bits but not everything. My knees are starting to shake, I can barely walk and the floor feels more slippery than usual. I'm not going to look at him - I'm going to look at my shoes. Grandma goes straight up to him and strokes his hair like he's a baby.

"Sorry Ho, I late to bath you. Xing Li take too long, she bad girl as late all time."

Uncle Ho slowly gets up and I stare so hard at my shoes I feel tears in my eyes. They go into the bathroom and lock the door. I can hear my heart.

Thump, thump, thump.

Then I hear the sound of the shower being switched on and loud splashes of water. I don't know why but I want to wait to see if Uncle Ho sings in the shower, but he doesn't. I can only hear the water - big splashes like a whale in a swimming pool.

Auntie Mei is sweeping up the glass near the door. I've never seen her do any housework before. She gives me a small smile and keeps on sweeping and sweeping in her chinchilla fur coat. I go and get a dustpan and brush to help her.

"Auntie Mei, what's wrong with Uncle Ho?"

Auntie Mei stops sweeping and bites her lip.

"He isn't very well, but you do not have to worry about it because Grandma is looking after him."

She keeps sweeping, I try to catch her eye but she acts as if every piece of glass is kryptonite that needs to be gotten rid of ASAP.

"Has he always been like this?"

"No."

Auntie Mei stops for a bit and then sighs.

"He was perfectly fine until he was seventeen."

"What happened?"

"He just became strange."

"Strange?"

"I apologise, I do not think I should be talking about this.

Grandma does not like me to talk about it and I know she does not want us to tell anyone. Can you promise me you won't tell anyone about tonight?"

"How about Lai Ker?"

"He's acceptable because he's family. However, definitely not anyone outside the family."

"Okay."

Uncle Ho has the "strange" illness Chinese families don't like talking about. I don't know why, maybe it's 'cos they are scared people will think they are strange too. When I was six years old, Uncle Ho broke my Barbie doll 'cos I wouldn't let him touch it. He pulled her head off and threw her across the room. No-one told him off, Mama said that I should forgive him 'cos he isn't well. I asked her if he has seen the doctor and she told me that Uncle Ho sees a doctor twice a week and he is getting better. Uncle Ho's doctor is called Dr Lincoln like Abraham Lincoln and he is a private doctor 'cos Grandma doesn't trust the NHS. He gives Uncle Ho pills that he takes every morning, a blue one and a white one. Uncle Ho has been going to Dr Lincoln for many years, I thought he would be better by now, but maybe his illness is something that takes a long, long time to cure.

Auntie Mei goes and gets a black bin liner and fills it with glass. Then she starts sweeping again even though I can't see any more glass bits. She says even though I can't see the glass bits, the tiny ones are still there - they're the dangerous ones to look out for. Next, Auntie Mei gets a yellow hoover to clean the floor and the carpet. She pauses for a bit by the blood stain on the carpet and then keeps hoovering away. Then she gets some baby wipes and rubs the floor, she shows me a baby wipe that has a tiny, tiny piece of glass on it.

"You see Xing Li, you have to be careful with glass, it's terribly tricky when it shatters."

I go and get carpet cleaner for the blood stain in the carpet and Auntie Mei looks pleased. I spray the cleaner and it expands like crazy, to a mountain of foam. The blood stains start to disappear like magic and leave a huge, damp patch. By the time Lai Ker comes home, most of the blood is gone.

"Hey lil sis, did Grandma promote you to be maid number 5?"

"No."

"Shame, I've got some smelly rugby gear that needs cleaning. You need to lick the mud off the shoes."

"Only after you lick the mud off my hockey stick before I whack you with it."

"Good comeback! I'm well nackered; posh white boys are a lot bigger. But Chinese people are quicker, I can just run through their legs and knee 'em in the balls."

"True."

"Anyway, I'm gonna have a shower. Is Uncle Ho out of the shower yet?"

"I don't know but you've got to be careful. He... "

Auntie Mei clears her throat loudly and interrupts me.

"Uncle Ho is having a horrific day. He's in a terrible mood. It would be best to wait for him to sleep before you have a shower."

"What do you mean t-e-r-r-i-b-l-e mood? Like he's got PMT or something?"

Auntie Mei keeps quiet and I can see her foot tapping on the floor.

"He's just feeling out of sorts. Please just be patient and have a shower later. You can have something to eat first. I'll go and see what we have leftover."

Auntie Mei grabs the bin bag and hoover. She is very red and her foundation is dripping off her nose but she is still wearing her chinchilla coat. Lai Ker sits down heavily next to the wet patch on the rug and starts twisting the rug ends.

"What's up with Uncle Ho?"

"He got really, really angry tonight 'cos Grandma was late for his shower."

"What time did she come home?"

"At 7:12pm and he usually takes his shower at 7pm."

"He's nuts."

"I know."

We sit in silence and stare at the damp patch in the carpet. The patch has trickled down the carpet and is the shape of a squashed baby octopus.

"Xing, you know Mama told me about him when I was very little."

"I thought Mama didn't like talking about him."

"She doesn't… she didn't but when I was little, she told me lots of stories about a strange boy and I put two and two together. She stopped telling me these stories when I got older but I'm not thick, I know what metal-fours are, learnt it in English class."

"What did she tell you?"

"She said the boy was really special like he lived in his own imaginary world and he had super powers."

"What else?"

"Let me see. Oh yeah, she said his family loved him and all that but he saw the world differently and that's what made him special. Like if someone was being nice to him, he wouldn't see it that way. Sometimes his imaginary friends would tell him to use his super powers to do bad things even though he didn't want to and that's when he would get scary."

"Mama never told me these stories."

"Maybe that's 'cos you're a girl and she didn't want to scare you. She knew I liked scary stories about vampires and monsters with super powers."

"What kind of bad things did the strange boy do?"

"Well Mama said when people made him annoyed, he would use his super powers to smash things like tables and windows and toys. But then his super powers became too strong; they took over him. He had to see a scientist who gave him magic pills to stop him. 'cos of his magic pills he became quiet and stopped smashing things."

"Did Mama say the boy was evil?"

"No definitely not evil, just messed up. She said the boy

had the best heart in the world but he just couldn't control his super power."

I suddenly remembered the stories Mama told me. They weren't about a strange boy with super powers. They were about a boy who had the kindest heart, the best heart. He liked to look after people and if anyone needed help he was there. If anyone cried, he cried for them too. Whenever his sister was in trouble, he'd fly to her side.

"Xing, Uncle Ho is nuts but he's okay. He has good days and bad days. You just have to ignore the bad ones. That's what Mama would have wanted."

"Even if I feel scared?"

"You don't have to be scared, he's family. You don't have to be best friends with him. But Mama loved him so we've gotta try too."

I think of the blood on the carpet and take a deep breath. If Mama loved Uncle Ho, I have to love him too. Even if every time I see him a cold chill trickles through my skin and gives me goose bumps.

Chapter 10
World War Wu

How boring is this history lesson? Mr Wool is going on and on about World War Two and how his grandparents had to wear gas masks and eat tinned spam and powdered eggs and fight the Germans. He likes to say, "Our ancestors did this and our ancestors did that." I feel a bit weird when he says "our ancestors" 'cos the truth is during the war my Singaporean ancestors didn't eat spam or powdered eggs or fight the Germans. They ate mouldy rice and maggots and the Japanese skinned my great grand-uncle to death.

Mr Wool is showing us pictures of "Our ancestors" in the war and talks about how brave they were and how it makes us proud to be British.

"We owe everything to our grandfathers and great grandfathers, because of their bravery we are able to be free."

Jay puts his hand up which is strange 'cos he only puts his hand up during Music class.

"Yes Jayeth?"

"Mr Wool, I don't see no black people in the pictures, where were they during the war?"

For some reason Mr Wool is going bright red.

"They were there too... don't worry young man, black people were also part of the war too. Erm... I'll see if I can find one in the picture. Ah, young man, see that little black boy carrying the Captain's gun? That could have been a relative of yours."

Mr Wool looks at me now.

"The Orientals were also part of the war. But mostly World War One."

Shils whispers to her friend.

"Yeah the chinks were part of the war too, cleaning people's homes and making the rail roads."

Mr Wool speaks to the rest of the class as if he is telling them some wonderful historical fact. He points at me with his fat fingers. He's got a fat face, fat hands, fat belly. Even his giant round teeth look fat.

"THIS young lady's ancestors may have been fighting alongside the British in the First World War. This is very exciting because we gave the Orientals a special name, as they were kind enough to help us. We called them Gerk-hers, spelt G-H-U-R-K-H-A-S. They were very helpful indeed."

I write the word down - GHURKHA. Must remember the funny Ghurk part of the word sounds like jerk. Mr Wool smiles and then changes the subject to trenches and goes on and on about the types of trenches "our ancestors dug". He speaks in a very s-l-o-w voice like he wants us to fall asleep.

"The t-r-en-ches had barbed wi-res and they had to dig th-em in the ra-in… "

Jay taps his leg against his chair while glancing at the clock. He does that in all our extra boring lessons. During a really boring Physics lesson, I counted Jay looking at the clock 233 times.

FINALLY after one hour of history story time, we go to our Music class in a really cool part of the school called The Music Laboratory. It's like a giant greenhouse with tall ceilings and all kinds of expensive instruments like electric keyboards, trumpets, drums, and violins - you name it. At my old school we only had a battered piano and a triangle. Music class is when Jay really comes alive. Bait-hove-am, Bart, Handle, Chopping and Wagger. He knows all the famous

64

classical men. Jay's dreadlocks swing from side to side as he waves his hand to answer Mr Bradbury's questions.

"Class, how old was Beethoven when he composed his first piece?"

"Four or five but the evidence isn't concluded."

"Which century was Wagner born?"

"Wilhelm Richard Wagner was born in 1813."

"Does anyone know what Handel's most famous composition is?"

"The Oratorio Messiah with the famous Hallelujah chorus."

Mr Bradbury studied at the posh Royal Academy of Music and I heard it's the best school. Jay talks a lot with Mr Bradbury about Wagger and Bart. He stays after class and I hear his voice echo down the corridor of West Hill. Jay says his dad knows double the amount of music stuff that he does. He used to study ten times more than his white classmates at music school and came first in his year. While they got drunk, he was swotting up on music stuff. Jay said his dad did this 'cos if he didn't know enough about music, the people in his orchestra would think not just that he was thick but that all black people are thick. That's why it was super important he got good grades.

Us girls are having our first swimming lesson in West Hill's Olympic-sized swimming pool. I want to see if the water really turns dark blue, but know even if I pee a little bit Shils will see and tell the rest of the class. Shils created a horrible new nickname for me, it's "Ano-bitch". The "Ano" part of the word is short for anorexic. I hate my nickname more than Sing-Song 'cos I've never liked my short, skinny body. It's so bony and yucky. Lai Ker always calls me "Chimp Arms" while making the noises of a chimpanzee. I shut him up by calling him "Chicken legs" while making loud clucking sounds. With Shils though, I only remember good comebacks after she has gone. When she's around my mind goes blank.

Shils shouts loudly at me from across the pool so all the girls can hear.

"Sing-song are you okay? You look TOO skinny; I hope you are eating okay. I never see you eating. If you want I can give you some of my lunch."

"I'm fine."

"Don't worry Sing-Song, we are here for you and your eating problems. That is what friends are for."

"I'm fine."

My whole body is starting to shake and I hold onto the edge of the pool. Shils swims up to me and whispers into my ear.

"What's wrong ANO-BITCH? You shaking from the cold? Not enough meat on your bones?"

She gives me a pinch, the sort of pinch that gives you a bruise. Then she whispers into my ear.

"You're all skin and bones. You're disgusting."

Miss Sharp goes to get the floats and within seconds Shils has pushed my head under the water. I can hear her laughing as I splash around. I feel someone else holding my legs down and another pushing on my shoulders. I struggle and struggle and my eyes get blurry. The chlorine is swirling up my nose and think I'm going to be sick.

I need some air, I need some air!

I kick and kick but someone grabs my ankles, I can feel their sharp nails gripping into my bone. They're laughing. The water is getting into my nose and I feel my head spinning. Just as I think I'm going to pass out, Shils lets go of me. I breathe in HARD and find myself coughing instead. My eyes are on fire, they feel so sore, my throat is swollen, my ankles hurt. I want to cry badly but I don't.

"Watch your back ano-bitch."

Shils and her gang swim quickly to the other end of the pool. The smell of the pool is making me feel sick. Everything sounds all echoey and strange like I'm in a cave. I get out of the pool and my legs feel weak and wobbly and goose pimply.

"Miss Sharp, I'm sorry, I feel sick."

Miss Sharp looks concerned and puts her hand on my forehead.

"Do you have a fever?"

"No I just feel really sick."

"Okay, well get changed and go and see the nurse then."

I wobble out of the pool, the room is moving up and down, in and out. I go to the changing room and I'm shivering so hard I can hear my teeth rattling. I keep hearing Shils' voice in my head.

Ano-bitch. Ano-bitch. Ano-bitch.

I can't get Shils' voice out of my head. It just keeps echoing round and round and round.

Ano-bitch. Ano-bitch. Ano-bitch.

I close my eyes and they sting - one half chlorine, one half tears. I kneel on the floor and I'm sick all over my expensive, new swimming costume that Grandma got from Harold & Sons.

I curl up on the freezing floor and start crying.

Chapter 11
The Worm Diet

My stomach still doesn't feel quite right but I feel a lot better.
The nurse gave me some Panadols and I slept for the rest of
the day. It was bliss being in the sick bay by myself. I could
look out of the window and watch the gardener planting tulip
bulbs. Mama used to like gardening, she'd put all kinds of
herbs on our windowsill. But then she had to stop 'cos the
chilli plant fell off and almost hit our landlord Mr Mills in the
head. I wish with all my heart that I could swap places with
the gardener. It must be nice being messy in the garden all
day, with no-one to bother you. You could dig and water the
plants. You could sing and not worry about anybody hearing
you. You could pluck the flowers and eat the apples. Plants
leave you alone, they don't hurt you - not the way people do.

I'm barely through the door and Lai Ker is dragging me
up the stairs. I don't even have time to take my shoes off.
Grandma's always telling off the postman when he wears
shoes into the house.

"Quick Xing, before THEY get home!"

"Where is everyone?"

"Grandma brought Uncle Ho to the doctor for an extra
top up of drugs and Auntie Mei is filming some crappy low
budget film."

Lai Ker tells me to close my eyes. I'm not sure, the last time Lai Ker asked me to close my eyes he put a dead frog on my head.

"I'm not gonna close my eyes."

"Look you have to, if not you'll miss the MAJOR surprise. I promise it won't be anything dodge."

"Okay but if you put another frog on my head I'll wallop Grandma's feather duster on your arse."

"Okay, okay just close your eyes."

I close my eyes and he covers them with his right hand while nudging me forward with his left elbow.

"Ow, easy on the elbow."

"Keep walking, keep walking."

I keep walking along the corridor and then suddenly the air smells like old sweat. Lai Ker takes his hands off my eyes and I breathe in quickly which isn't a good idea with BO air.

We're standing in Uncle Ho's room.

I don't know how Lai Ker managed to break into Uncle Ho's room but he has. The room is the largest room in the house. It's MASSIVE, like our old flat times five. The walls are painted white, like really shiny white and the carpet is completely white or at least it used to be as there are lots of old stains and smudges. There isn't a lamp or a table or a side table or books or even a TV - only a giant bed with white sheets. Uncle Ho must be bored without a TV. Though he does come downstairs to watch the 6 o'clock news every day. I try to avoid the living room from around 5:30pm onwards just in case he comes down early but he never does. In the corner near the giant window is a calendar. Every day that has passed has a giant red cross on it. Lai Ker is looking at the smudges on the floor, he points at a large red one next to the bed.

"You think that's blood?"

I know he's trying to scare me and I'm not going to fall for it.

"Nope it's ketchup, are you blind or what?"

Lai Ker grins and sits on the bed.

"This massive bed is well comfy, must've cost a bomb. Bet the old bird made sure he got the best. Always the best for Uncle Ho."

"Yeah. Have you seen his electric toothbrush in the bathroom? It probably 'cost more than an iPhone."

"Yeah and those grey tracksuit bottoms he wears. They're designer you know? Jimmy Tang nicked some from Selfridges."

"Really?"

"Yeah, they cost a bomb."

"By the way, how's Jimmy Tang?"

"He's alright, he's living it up in Hong Kong. Got a girlfriend and everything. Says over there his grandparents treat him like a hot shot 'cos he's from overseas."

"Wonder if people will treat us like hot shots if we return to Singapore."

"Maybe, but our accent will sound well funny to them. They'll probably skank us."

It's weird thinking about Singapore and what people are like there. Mama said it's really sunny with lots of palm trees and Chinese, Malay and Indian people, but mostly Chinese like us. How weird to think that there are more people that look like me over there than here.

"You still doing your business with Jimmy Tang? "

"Yeah, those Hampstead boys were lapping up the merchandise like anything."

"Were? You still haven't told me what you're selling."

"The less you know the better it'll be for you IF Grandma ever finds out. We've got into a bit of a problem you see. Someone screwed me over and told the headmaster, Mr Haywood."

"Does that mean you're in trouble again?"

"Nah you know the drill. I have to meet the old guy tomorrow. But don't you dare tell Grandma, she'd give me the feather duster special if she found out."

"Okay, my lips are sealed. Do you know what you're gonna say to him?"

"Not yet, but I'm gonna prepare a script later this evening. The usual, I write the script, you help me with the presentation."

Lai Ker has been to the headmaster's office hundreds of times. He could publish a book with all the scripts he's written. They involve sob stories that would make a tough headmaster cry or laugh depending on the situation. When he was fourteen, Lai Ker was caught "borrowing" St George's new projector - he wept buckets. Between his multiple rounds of "sorry", "very very sorry", and "very, very, very sorry", he told Mr Gurmani-Ward the projector was for a screening of a movie for poor kids from our local estates. As a child, Mr Gurmani-Ward's refugee parents could not afford a television. Lai Ker got a half-hearted telling-off plus a week of detention. What Mr Gurmani-Ward never found out was that Lai Ker's cinema for the poor showed X-rated films. He charged the horny teenage boys £10 for a ticket; popcorn was £3.49 plus VAT.

SLAM

The front door! Grandma and Uncle Ho are home. Lai Ker and I rush out of Uncle Ho's room and he almost drops the keys on the floor.

Click, click, cl… the third lock is stuck.

Lai Ker keeps jiggling it back and forth. Three locks! I run downstairs first and almost slip on the bottom step. Uncle Ho pushes past me and walks up the stairs; his belly almost topples me over. Grandma is taking off her shoes, she doesn't look up.

"Xing Li what I say about running? You fall down break arm, then go hospital, then miss school, then fail exams, then end up on street selling pirate DVD, then EastEnders spot you, then you act for them, then you get sacked and never ever work again."

"Sorry Grandma, I was just excited to, to… welcome

you home."

Grandma looks up at me and narrows her eyes.

"You being sarcastic like English girls in school?"

"No, no, I promise. I just wanted to welcome you home 'cos you told me… you told me that I should RESPECT my elders."

Grandma gives me a tiny smile that lasts for half a second.

"Okay respect done, now go do homework."

I smile and consider doing a little curtsey but she might accuse me of doing a "sarcastic" curtsey. So, I walk s-l-o-w-l-y up the stairs making sure each one creaks less. Lai Ker is already in his room looking completely calm. He's working on his headmaster's office script.

"Psst lil sis, you got any eye make-up?"

"Nope."

"I thought your age was the age that girls start to wear bras and tart up?"

I look down at my size AAA flat chest.

"Not me. I don't have any make-up. Auntie Mei has lots."

"Does she have any black eye shadow?"

"Yeah she's got lots. She said it makes her eyes bigger. Anyway why do you want eye shadow for - you becoming a tranny? Shall I get you red high heels as well?"

"Tsk tsk tsk. So young, so naïve. It's all about the illusion. Look, I've gotta get the bags under my eyes well big. That way Mr Haywood will think I'm racked with guilt over my business deals."

"Oh I see, like losing sleep 'cos you're so guilty."

"Precise-le-mont. It was that or try and lose a stone before tomorrow, so I look like I'm starving myself out of guilt like those monks who fast and whip themselves."

"Well, you could try and lose weight Auntie Mei-style. You'll never guess what I overheard her telling her actor friend on the phone."

"What? And you better not say Weight Watchers or the Doo-can diet. 'cos this conversation is already taking precious time from my script."

"Well, Auntie Mei told the other actor about this new diet."

"What like starvation?"

"NO! Basically they give you an egg of a worm and you swallow it. The egg hatches in your stomach and then the tapeworm lives there and eats all your food so you lose a HUGE amount of weight."

"You're a bloody liar."

"I'm NOT. I swear she wasn't joking. She said she nearly ended up in hospital 'cos of it."

Lai Ker shakes his head and shoos me out of the room.

"Look, I've got a lot to do. Get the eye make-up from Auntie Mei and then we can talk."

I wasn't lying. Auntie Mei doesn't make up stuff like that. She's really serious about diets 'cos she needs to have her bones showing when she is doing all her serious roles as Chinese prostitutes and starving refugees. I wonder if Jackie Chan had to do the tapeworm diet too?

Chapter 12
Second Prances

Lai Ker's snoring is travelling down the corridors; it's cutting like a chainsaw through the still creepiness of the Wu household. I put my head against the wall and hear Lai Ker sleepily scratching his nose so hard until his nostrils make a sticky sound. I wish I could sleep like Lai Ker. Even though he's meeting Mr Haywood tomorrow, he's snoring louder than ever. Mama said he sleeps the way Papa did - all snory and deeply. That's one of the only things Mama said about Papa 'cos she told me talking about him is too painful. I only know a bit about Papa 'cos every time I asked Mama about him she would tear up and I hated seeing Mama cry. Lai Ker said she cried because she loved Papa very much. On our windowsill in the kitchen there was a picture of him at the casino. He was dressed in a black suit with a red tie and looked quite handsome and muscular with a tanned face, black hair with a side parting, a long Roman nose and ears that stuck out a bit. Lai Ker looks a bit like him except Lai Ker has normal-sized ears and spiky hair.

This is what I know about Papa:
1) He was a nice man.
2) He was very serious and worked hard.
3) He worked as a crew-pier in a casino.

4) He hated having his photo taken.
5) He died of cancer of his man bits.

That's ALL I know and it sucks big time 'cos I should have asked Mama more about Papa. But I thought I had lots of time 'cos Mama was never ill - like never ever sick. When Lai Ker and me had chickenpox, mumps, flu, colds she would run around giving us Lemsip and hot water bottles. It was like she had an invisible force field that stopped her from being sick. I thought I had at least fifty years with Mama before she got old and senile.

If I had a time machine and could go back in time, there are so many questions I would ask Mama. I would ask her why she sneezed when we ate mints and why she always wore two pairs of socks instead of one. I would ask her why we only saw Grandma once a year and if she missed living in Singapore. I would ask her what she really thought about *Chinks Have Mouths*. Like did she think Lai Ker's right about how Chinese people really need to fight to be heard or are we okay? I'd also ask her if she was ever confused about who she was or if inside she was fine. Then I would ask her lots of questions about Papa. There would be loads of questions 'cos when Mama died, thousands of Papa's secret memories were taken with her too.

Memories that I can never, ever get back.

Happy ones, sad ones, funny ones and weird ones all disappeared into a dark, swirling, black hole. Like what was Papa's favourite food? Did he like to joke? What was his favourite film? Did he like sports? Was he like me? Unless I build a time machine I can never get any of the memories back. Never. They're gone forever. Instead, I have new memories that fill my brain. They don't go away even if I want them to. When I close my eyes at night I see darkness and water and chlorine and laughter and Shils whispering chink in my ear.

The Office

Mr Earnest Haywood sat in his antique leather chair and shook the fluffy, white hair on his head. If there were such a thing as a lookalike competition for Robert Redford's father, Mr Haywood would win first prize. Hampstead Independent School was an institution that prided itself on moral integrity. The Catholic headmaster had spent forty years instilling sound, moral values into his fine, young men. For him, the role of headmaster was not a vocation, it was a calling. Most of the boys at Hampstead School respected Mr Haywood - he was harsh but fair. The serious seventy-two-year-old believed adolescent boys needed a firm hand and wished he were still in the days of corporal punishment. In the past, he had always given boys a chance for prayer and repentance before their lashings of the cane. He staunchly believed in second chances.

Mr Haywood looked across his giant oak table and saw a young Chinese lad - Lai Xing Wu. There was not a drop of sweat on the young man's head and he was breathing at an even rate. For some reason the boy's short, spiky hair and ruddy cheeks reminded Mr Haywood of a baby hedgehog he had rescued as a child. Always the optimist, Lai Xing gave Mr Haywood a cheeky grin. After paying homage to headmasters' offices more than one hundred times, Lai Xing knew exactly what to expect. If he apologised profusely he would be fine. His mother's crying Chinese soap operas had taught Lai Xing the art of showing remorse; he was an expert in the field of crocodile tears.

Mr Haywood leaned forward in his chair and put on the gravest face he could find. He wanted Lai Xing to know the seriousness of his actions. Behind his desk hung a gold plaque with the words:

Not only so, but we also rejoice in our sufferings, because we know that suffering produces perseverance; perseverance, character; and character, hope.

Romans 5:3-5

"Lai Xing, it has come to my attention that you have been involved in some extremely shady endeavours. Do you have anything to say for yourself?"

Lai Xing began Act 1 of the script he had written the night before.

"I'm very sorry. Please forgive me kindest kindred Sir. Hampstead is the best school I have ever gone to. To think that I had any part in corrupting the finest young boys that you have taught so well has caused me many sleepless nights."

That morning while Lai Xing wrote the finishing touches to his script, his sister stole some grey eye shadow from his Auntie and helped smudge it under his eyes. Lai Xing looked like he hadn't slept all year. He continued with his dramatic rendition of Act 2 of the script.

"Mr Haywood, I come from a poverty stricken background and I know what it means to be part of the finest school. This is something that I did not take for granted. You see my foolish personality renders me to have a soft heart when it comes to bringing happiness, joy and laughter to others… "

Lai Xing proceeded to tell the heroic story of when he had rescued a drowning classmate. He had jumped fully clothed into the muddy river and had dragged the terrified student to safety. He omitted telling Mr Haywood that this was after he pushed the student in. Mr Haywood listened to Lai Xing as he vigorously acted out the swimming movements and the frightened screams of the drowning boy. He admired Lai Xing's enthusiasm and his endearing eloquence reminded Mr Haywood of when he was a boy. A young Earnest Haywood had won many dramatic prizes - he was especially proud of his four-hour monologue of Ulysses, set to music.

A week ago, Mr Haywood had discovered one of his students was committing an illegal act and was horrified. Images of drug taking and stolen school equipment came to his mind. He did not know the culprit or the solid facts, but he knew he would have to punish the sinner. The new French teacher, Mr Mark Boardman, had brought a quivering fourteen-year-old into the headmaster's office. When questioned, the young man admitted to buying something illegal from another student.

Throughout his fifty years at Hampstead, Mr Haywood had only dealt with two incidents of drugs. The first incident was when the effeminate Hockey Captain was caught smoking cannabis after his team lost 22-4. The second incident was with an American exchange student who was addicted to smelling Pritt Sticks. This was the first time Mr Haywood had dealt with a student actually selling illegal substances. He immediately wanted to find out the identity of the young drug dealer.

The cheek of the boy!

Mr Haywood demanded the student tell him who the supplier was and surrender the drugs he had purchased. Trembling from the tips of his curly hair to the ends of his toenails, the student opened up the palm of his right hand. Mr Haywood prayed the substance produced would be marijuana or ecstasy. A hard drug like cocaine could be the end of his unblemished career. He could see the tabloid headlines now.

Catholic Headmaster's Cocaine Bust.

Mr Haywood breathed out a wheezy sigh of relief. The boy was not carrying white powder in any form or shape. The headmaster did a double take and squinted. His eyesight was not what it used to be. In the sweaty palm of the student was a small, black, plastic square. It looked like a computer chip of some sort, but was too big to be a memory chip.

"Young man, what is the meaning of this?"

"It is a TF4 card sir."

"And what may I ask is a TF4 card?"

Mr Haywood liked to consider himself as a forward thinking, modern man. However, new technology made him uncomfortable. His granddaughter had taken one solid week to teach him how to send a text message. Mr Haywood had a PhD in English Literature from Cambridge University, but his granddaughter lost her patience when he couldn't grasp the concept of predictive text. Kind Mr Boardman sensed his bewilderment and continued to explain.

"Mr Haywood, TF4 cards are illegal. They allow the boys to download software from the internet, and use them on their handheld consoles or their mobile phones. Apparently once you have one of these you never have to pay for any computer game, song or software ever again."

Mr Haywood stared at the little piece of plastic that looked moist from the student's sweaty hand. He shook his head and Mr Boardman continued.

"… One of the students, Lai Xing Wu, has been selling them for quite a hefty sum."

Lai Xing had discovered TF4 cards from his good friend Jimmy Tang. Jimmy Tang was already selling the cards in twenty countries and he had taught Lai Xing the ins and outs of the IT industry. When Lai Xing arrived at Hampstead, his new upper-class friends had never heard of a TF4 card. He saw a business opportunity and decided to grab it with both hands.

Lai Xing continued to sit calmly in Mr Haywood's office. He was midway through the final act of his script and Mr Haywood was lapping up the Oscar-winning performance.

"I saw how much delirium these cards were bringing the boys. Their look of exclamation made it worthwhile. I didn't want to charge them, just their thankfulness was enough, but when they threw money at me I had to oblige. Mr Haywood, I am naïve about the decor of your fine establishment. Since my father died and then later my mother, I have been very lonely and, in a way, lost. I thought I would gain friends by my well-intentioned actions and deeply regret everything I have done. I am happy to accept any punishment you glimmer appropriate for my foolhardy actions. All I ask is your forgiveness."

He dramatically paused and mustered up some tears.

"Mr Haywood, all I ask is your forgiveness from the kindness of your heart."

Mr Haywood felt a deep compassion rising in his spirit. It

was the sort of compassion reserved for thieves that stole for their starving families and illegal workers who sent money to their aged parents. There was a hunger in Lai Ker that Mr Haywood identified with. His words were a bit flowery at times, but this boy knew what hardship was. Mr Haywood was orphaned at a young age too. Through the pain of losing one's parents there were times when decisions made were not black and white but grey.

"Lai Xing I quite understand the predicament you are facing. Being an orphan myself I know what it is like to not have the correct guidance. In a world like ours it is sometimes hard to know which path to take. When to say no and when to say yes."

"Yes, I completely agree Sir... Headmaster... Mr Haywood."

"However, you must not underestimate the serious error of judgment in your actions. Breaking the law is no laughing matter. Just one phone call to the police and you could find yourself in very unforgiving circumstances."

Lai Xing kept quiet, he wondered if this was the correct time to muster a few more tears. He struggled to understand which direction the aged headmaster was taking. Mr Haywood would make a brilliant poker player.

"Lai Xing I have made a decision. Your actions cannot go unpunished."

Lai Xing found his heart starting to beat at an accelerated rate. This was not a bodily function he was used to.

"Your actions cannot go unpunished. However, given your background and lack of strong male role models, I would like to propose that you meet here in my office every week for the remainder of the year."

"What like detention for a year?"

"Yes. That is my final decision."

For the first time, Lai Xing did not brag to his younger sister about getting off lightly. Perhaps the visits to Mr Haywood's office would have more of an impact on the young man's life than he would ever admit.

Chapter 13
I, Bruce Lee

"So my bro's going to detention for like a year, Grandma is hassling me about my B+ in Maths and I have no idea what we're doing for Christmas. What's new with you?"

"Well my dad finally finished writing his musical, we're going to Jamaica for Christmas and, oh yeah, the tortoise has like yellow poo."

"Seriously! Is it 'cos you fed him too many potatoes?"

"Maybe, but could have been the sweetcorn or bananas. Have no idea."

"Is he gonna to die on us then? THAT would be AWFUL."

"Nah he only had the poo for like one day. It's fine now."

We're eating lunch, tuna salad for Jay and yummy bak chang rice squares for me. The chef spent all day yesterday making them 'cos he has to squish together a ton of ingredients and tie them up in flat bamboo leaves. Glutinous rice soaked for six hours, pork, winter melon, dried prawns, dried mushrooms, garlic and his secret lamb mince. It's de-li-cious, like the best thing in the world. I got an extra one for Jay too and he doesn't have any scissors so he's using his red plastic protractor to cut the super tight knots on the string. Shils comes over.

Oh yeah. Forgot it was Wednesday.

My hands start to shake a bit but I don't want Jay to see so

I sit on them. Shils makes some remarks about me eating dog food 'cos my family ran out of proper dog. Jay and I tried to ignore her. She whispers in my ear.

"Woof woof."

Jay says any reaction will let Shils win; in the game of "Bullies and Bullied" the only weapon we have is zipping up our lips.

"Why are you ignoring me Sing-Song? Is it 'cos your English is so bad you don't understand a word I'm saying? Should I say *sayonara* instead?"

Jay takes out his headphones and jams them into my ear. By filling my head with classical music, I don't have to listen to Shils' evil taunts. The musical notes from the animal song by a famous composer called St Sands blast in my ears. Shils pokes my bak chang with her skinny fingers. It's nice having a loud orchestra drown out the world. Jay listens to this kind of music all the time. Violins, clarinets, flutes, cellos, clanging things. The first time Jay played St Sands to me was when Shils grabbed my history essay and tore it into confetti. The second time was when I refused to eat my lunch after Shils put some dead leaves in it. The third time was when Shils started a rumour that my mother used to sleep with white men for money. I wanted to punch her when she started that one. I went up to her but she was surrounded by like fifteen guys and girls, so I went to the toilet and sat there for thirty minutes until Jay found me and gave me his last banana fritter.

We do not look at Shils, we do not say a word. I try my best to concentrate on the small black stain on the table. Shils walks off but then she comes back. The Cliff lookalike and his posse arrive. They look embarrassed, but any thirteen-year-old boy would find it difficult to say no to someone who looks like she is one of the models in Lai Ker's Victoria's Secret magazine. Jay and I call Shils "Evil Barbie" behind her back. The boys give Shils a knowing look and she lifts her boobs up and pouts. Then the boys fling our lunches to the floor.

My bak chang is EVERYWHERE.

Meat and prawns and rice and mushrooms EVERY-WHERE.

"Waahhhhh. I Brucee Lee, I vely hungry, I swipe your lunchee."

They laugh and egg each other on as they do round house kicks near our heads. Each kick gets closer and closer until we can feel a whirlwind of smelly trainers swishing in front of our noses.

"Wahahhhhh. I vely goodie at Kung Fu. Wahahhhhh."

I can see Jay's dreadlocks starting to swing slightly as the kicks rotate half a centimetre from his glasses.

"Wahahhhhh, I give you lound house kick. Vely scarly Wahahhhhh."

Jay starts to tap his leg on the floor so hard I think his chair's gonna gather steam and shoot into space. He grabs my arm and we run to the library. We don't look back, we just run and run and run as fast as we can. Ignoring Shils is one thing, but getting kicked in the face is not something we want to stick around for.

We sit hidden amongst old Science textbooks; a dusty corner no-one goes unless they want somewhere quiet to sleep. Jay's tapping his foot on the ground - his trembling legs cause his rhythm to be a bit out of time. My heart is beating super fast and I can feel my skin all tingly and hot and shaky.

"They think just 'cos we're Chinese we think their Bruce Lee antics are funny."

This is the first time Jay has called himself a Chinese person. By calling himself Chinese it makes me feel we're in this together. Jay frowns and taps the chair with both his legs not just one.

"What is it with white people and Bruce Lee? My mum's last name is Lee and when she first arrived in the UK the customs officer asked her if she was related to Bruce Lee."

"Yeah people are well obsessed. Worst of all when people are drunk and see anyone looking remotely Chinese they just shout "Wahahhhhh", and expect you to respond."

"Yeah it don't matter if you are Japanese, Korean, Thai or even Filipino. They shout it at you whether you know kung fu or not. I mean Bruce Lee was the first Chinese guy in Hollywood and all that, which was kinda cool, but I seriously wish he hadn't started the "Wahahhhhh" phenomenon."

"Yeah, well annoying."

Grandma, Mama, Lai Ker, Auntie Mei and me, we've all had "Wahahhhhh" shouted at us at some point. The first time I had it was when I was eight. I was walking home with Mama when this guy in our estate jumped out from behind a wall and shouted "Wahahhhhh" at the top of his voice. Mama was so shocked she dropped her shopping on the floor. The guy then did the kung fu crane pose from that old film *The Karate Kid*. When Mama ignored him, he started laughing and said, "What's the problem China girl? Where's your sense of humour?" Mama replied, "I do have a sense of humour, I just don't laugh at stupid jokes." All of a sudden, the guy became furious. His face completely changed like he wanted to punch her or something. "Well if you chinks don't have a sense of humour, you can piss off to where you came from." Mama grabbed my arm and pulled me all the way home. She was gripping me so hard I could feel her nails digging in. When I told her she was hurting me, she hugged me and kept saying she was sorry over and over again. She hugged me as if she never wanted to let me go.

Jay and me sit on the floor of the library. The carpet is peachy and floral and looks like it is from Victorian times. It feels safer when we are low down and no-one can see us. Jay's foot tapping is less mad. He leans in and whispers to me. The tips of his dreadlocks almost touch my cheeks.

"Xing, do you wanna hear something random about Bruce Lee."

"What?"

Jay smiles like he is about to tell me the greatest secret in the world.

"Bruce Lee had… German blood!"

"No way? That's well random - thought he was as Chinese as could be."

"Nope, his mum was the mixed-raced mistress of his father. She had German blood. Bet Shils and her crew don't know that."

"Yeah, bet they didn't know a thing."

Jay is like a walking Wiki of strange, unknown facts and that's why he's different from everyone I have ever met. But I guess in West Hill different means that you aren't cool. On his first day at West Hill, one of the boys put chewing gum in one of Jay's dreadlocks and said it was an accident.

"Xing, did you know Bruce Lee won the 1958 Crown Colony Cha-Cha Championship?"

"Yeah? Bet he had moves Evil Barbie can only dream of."

"Man, bet she thinks the Cha-Cha is a type of dog."

"Yeah like Chihuahua."

"Hey, did you know Bruce Lee wore the thickest contacts ever? His eyesight was well bad."

"Yeah well most Chinese have crap eyesight anyway."

"Well my dad says it's some kinda genetic flaw 'cos our ancestors studied too hard in bad lighting. You know bad stuff gets passed down from generation to generation and all that?"

"What do you mean?"

"Like generational curses. Like Bruce Lee died young 'cos his father had a curse and then later his son died 'cos of the same curse. It's real scary stuff."

"How's it scary?"

"Well it's like if something is mucked up with your parents or grandparents you could get mucked up too. Like my granddad drank a lot. So, when my old man missed on a job with the Royal Philharmonic orchestra, he started on the Jack Daniels. But we broke the curse 'cos my mum and I prayed so hard and he got better."

"How about good stuff? Can that be passed on too?"

"Yeah works both ways, good stuff can be passed on too."

I think of Lai Ker and his *CHM*. Maybe 'cos we share the same blood and all, some of his power will be transferred to me and I can stand up to Shils.

"How about bros? Like what if my bro has good stuff, could it be transferred to me too?"

"Yeah I guess. I don't know 'cos I don't have any brothers or sisters. But I don't see why not. I guess bad stuff usually gets passed down more 'cos most people notice the bad stuff more."

I hope that I get more of the good stuff 'cos I don't want to be strange like Uncle Ho or mean like Grandma. I want to be strong like Lai Ker and pretty like Auntie Mei.

When I get home, Lai Ker is dancing in his room and he's well funny. He's bobbing his head backwards and forwards and flapping his arms like a chicken. He's grinning a super huge grin and I can see this black poppy seed right in between his front teeth.

"What's up?"

"The old Jimster is returning. The old Jimster IS RETURNING."

"What, Jimmy Tang is coming back to the UK?"

"Yup, his dad couldn't hack the slave drivers in Hong Kong. They work like double the hours."

"So, they decided to come back just like that?"

"Yeah, his dad got sacked."

"I can't believe they sacked him 'cos he couldn't hack the hours. That's harsh."

"Well that was part of the reason. Jimmy Tang's dad was also nicking company secrets and selling them. But what is Hong Kong's loss is England's gain."

Before I can ask Lai Ker any more about Jimmy Tang, Auntie Mei calls us for dinner. She looks tired today, maybe it's 'cos Grandma has been extra mean to her this week.

"Why you cut hair look like boy?"

"Why you eat so much? You not just come from prison."

"Why you eat so little? You too skinny."

"When you get married? You get too old for baby."

"Why acting job so late? When you get proper job not finish same time as bar girl?"

TICK TOCK TICK TOCK TICK TOCK TICK TOCK

Everyone is eating without saying a peep as usual. Auntie Mei is taking very, very small portions of food. Half a prawn, five runner beans, one piece of tofu, six black beans and three tablespoons of rice. She keeps looking at Grandma and is wiggling in her chair like she needs the toilet or something. Auntie Mei smiles the biggest smile I've ever seen on her porcelain face. Her teeth look so shiny and pearly and perfect.

"Ma, I have a BIG audition tomorrow."

Grandma gives a massive sniff like a giant whale coming up for air.

"Pah, when she get BIG money, then we call big audition huh?"

"But Ma it really is a BIG audition."

"Always BIG audition. Never BIG career. You know I never understand why you choose become actor. I gave you best education, best clothes, best food, best advice. Yet you choose sell your body to *gweilo*."

"Ma this time is different. My agent says I have a good chance as the director has seen my work before."

"Yes, yes, of course he SEE your work. He SEE you open legs to white man on screen. He SEE you speak bad Chinese as refugee. He SEE you dress in stupid kung fu monkey suit."

"Ma please don't spoil it. We've been through this over and over again. I can't change what I do. I've tried."

Grandma points her silver chopstick at Auntie Mei as if she is going to poke her eye out.

"YOU can't change or won't change. I change every day. I want do Chinese dance class, my father say NO. I want go America study, my father say NO. I want move back

Singapore. I beg my father, he say NO. YOU excuses every day, can change but won't."

"Ma I know some of the roles I've done haven't been great. But you know how hard it is being a Chinese actor. If we don't accept the stereotypical roles, we don't get work."

"NEVER listen to me. I want what best. Not for you be actor, no life, no husband, no PRIDE. You say YES to everything. YES SIR NO SIR. Take everything they give you. You suffer for what? Nothing. I waste my money on rearing disappointment. I rear stupid girl who make stupid decisions, who chose stupid career. Stupid, stupid, STUPID."

I feel awful, Auntie Mei takes her lace handkerchief out and tears start to pour down her face. When she cries she looks a bit like Mama. Actually she looks A LOT like Mama. Same lopsided frown, same biting of lip, same broken eyes like her heart has been split into two. Maybe if Mama had carried on living with Grandma, she would have turned out like Auntie Mei. I don't want Auntie Mei to be sad; I want her to stop crying. I want her to stop feeling sad, I want her to know that she is okay. She isn't as bad as Grandma thinks; she's kind and nice just like Mama. Grandma is just a stupid old woman who likes to bully people. How dare she bully Auntie Mei? HOW DARE SHE BULLY MAMA?

"AUNTIE MEI IS NOT STUPID. YOU STUPID OLD COW."

My voice echoes off the metallic cupboards. It's so loud and high pitched and weird. My heart is racing and my face feels all cold and tingly. I can't believe I just did that. Lai Ker opens his mouth and half a chunk of tofu drops out of his mouth and onto the floor. But Auntie Mei gives me a grateful look and I see her lips curling into a tiny smile. Grandma jumps slightly at my shrieking voice. She looks at me and narrows her eyes into tiny slits.

"You think you smart to speak rude to Grandma. Your mother spoil you too much."

She then carries on eating her dinner in slow motion

and in silence. Each morsel of food is chewed slowly and then chewed some more. Meat is rolled around the gravy on her dish in an anti-clockwise motion and then a clockwise motion. Like a spider playing with its prey, the long wait is really messing with my mind. After an hour of this she sends Lai Ker and me to our rooms to do our homework.

I'm in the middle of writing my history essay when the fifteen stone Uncle Ho bursts into my room and grabs me. His clammy hands hold me tightly like a wrestler about to do the Heimlich manoeuvre. Grandma comes in and locks the door. She hits me over and over and over again with the feather duster. Uncle Ho tightly closes his eyes. There are feathers everywhere; I can hear the feather duster whipping against the backs of my legs. It hurts SO MUCH - my legs feel like they are being hit with a hot fire poker. I want to call for Lai Ker but I know he is in the shower. Grandma knows this too. She hits me twenty-one times. Each hit is precise, painful and done in complete silence. I don't want to cry. I try to imagine what Mama felt when Grandma hit her with the feather duster. Mama would be brave. Mama would not cry. I tightly clench my hands. I want to be strong like Mama. I refuse to cry.

Chapter 14
The Portrait of an Old Man

"You not show respect to me. I not show respect to you."

Grandma's sentence for shouting at her is two weeks in my room. I have to eat all my meals by myself, I cannot watch TV, I cannot play computer games and I cannot listen to any music. The music one sucks 'cos Jay has really got me into the German composer Wagger. His songs make me smile every time I hear them. Also Handle's violin sad songs are really good too. I like it when the violins get extra sad and really high pitched 'cos they make the hairs on my skin stand up and salute.

The highlight of my day is my lunch break with Jay. He's my best friend in the world and my heart starts to get real quick when the lunch bell goes. I've never felt this excited about spending time with anyone. After the Bruce Lee incident with Shils we eat in the library every day. I like lunch breaks 'cos once I'm home it's straight to my room, lock the door and do homework. Grandma has even got the maids to take turns to guard the door. I don't like it when maid two is guarding 'cos sometimes she falls asleep and snores louder than Lai Ker.

RRRRINGGGGGGGGGGGGGGGG

The lunch bell has gone off and we're rushing down the corridor and straight to the Science corner in the library.

Running during lunch breaks is also a new thing. We run to the library, we run to the toilet and back and we run especially fast if we see Shils. Mama said exercise is good, so I guess the running bit is okay if it stops me from getting a heart attack when I'm older. The library has become our "safe house". It's not like we haven't tried eating lunch in the canteen, we have. One Wednesday we sat at the far corner of the canteen just to "see". Shils gave me a bloody nose after "accidently" throwing a tray in my direction. My blood went all over my mash like a bottle of ketchup had exploded. Jay got REALLY mad and he never ever EVER gets mad. He grabbed a tray as if he wanted to smash Shils with it. But she had about ten people with her including some huge rugby guys, so I pulled Jay away.

The library is much better than the lunch room. Jay is creeping silently amongst the books - he reminds me of Meow Meow who used to prowl a lot. We take turns to keep a look out in the library while one of us eats our lunch. Food is banned in the library so I gobble my lunch in seconds. Hope I don't get heartburn when I grow up.

"Quick Xing, eat up your sandwiches, the librarian is walking towards us. Hurry up, she's in her flat shoes today. Man you've got to eat faster, she'll be in our corner in fifteen and a half seconds."

"I'm trying to chew as fast as I can."

"Okay she's gone now."

Jay tells me about a special house guest his parents have at the moment. It's a famous Burmese artist called Aung Htwe Khin. Jay's parents always make it their business to help people in need 'cos their church helped them when they fell in love and their parents cut them out of their lives. Aung Htwe Khin has been persecuted for his political artwork and his faith. He spent a week hidden in a rice bank before he was smuggled out of the country. When his enemies bulldozed his art studio down, Htwe Khin knew he had to flee. Jay said Htwe Khin would rather they chopped his arm off than destroy his artwork. Jay tells me his parents added another line to their marriage vow.

"I vow that together we will always stick to our guns and help others to do so."

I think Jay is trying to stick to his guns by ignoring Shils and not hitting her. Today he really almost came close but I know that's not him. I ask Jay if he doesn't like violence 'cos he wants to be a pacifist like Jesus.

"Nah, Jesus weren't a pacifist or some soppy wuss with brown hair and blue eyes like they show on stained glass windows. Jesus drove people out of the temple with a whip when they were cussing God. We have to pick our battles - be wise. Sometimes being quiet is wiser than saying a hundred words."

I think Jay is a bit of a Jamaican Yoda sometimes. I don't really get everything he says, but I know he has my back.

"I think I get what you mean, like my mum used to keep quiet when my grandma cussed her, she was… "

I realise this is the first time I've talked about Mama to Jay. I bite my lip and continue.

"Yeah… she always knew when to keep quiet and when to shout. She was good like that."

"She sounds cool. Wish I could have met her."

I think of Mama doing her funny eighties dance moves to pop music and I smile.

"No, she was very uncool. But she was my mama… she was… "

I miss Mama SO much.

I miss Mama's strange cooking, her loud laugh, her long-winded stories, her warm hugs, her feisty spirit, her stupid jokes, her brave soul. I miss EVERYTHING. Good and bad. I close my eyes and wish with all my heart for one more day to say sorry for all the times I made Mama sad and all the times Lai Ker and I were rude to her. Just one more day would be good enough. One more day to say sorry.

Sorry for not saying thank you when you made me lunch every day.

Sorry for being embarrassed by you when you couldn't pronounce words like posh white people do. Sorry for playing my computer games instead of going to the supermarket when you needed me to help carry the shopping.

I feel my eyes getting hot and teary. It's been almost three months. I don't want to cry about Mama in front of Jay so I pinch my leg real hard to stop me from crying. Then, I quickly grab some crisps from Jay and stuff my mouth. I don't want to look at him so I pretend I'm trying to eat all the crisps or something.

"Easy Xing, leave some salt and vinegar for me."

"We'd better hurry up with our lunch, don't want the librarian to catch us."

I keep chomping and chomping and chomping until my tears are forced down my throat along with the salt and vinegar.

At home, I don't have to rush my food like at school. I can eat nice and slow. But my door is locked and after I do my homework there is nothing to do but lie and stare at the ceiling. There are eight tiny stains on my ceiling. They look like squished flies from afar but they are actually bits of mould. Don't know how Grandma could have missed them. I guess no-one slept in my bed much before I moved in. Sometimes, Lai Ker slips notes under the door to check if I am still alive. He does jokey X-rated cartoons that he makes up with his colourful felt tip pens. He also tells me about what he and Jimmy Tang have got up to. He says his TF4 business at his school has gone bankrupt but Jimmy Tang has helped get him a part time job as a waiter in a Chinese restaurant Jimmy Tang works in. Lai Ker says Jimmy Tang doesn't go to school any more 'cos "He's too busy plotting to take over the world." Grandma is actually happy Lai Ker has a part time job 'cos she thinks this means he is being responsible.

As long as he keeps getting As, Lai Ker can keep his job. The job makes Lai Ker work really hard, but he likes it 'cos he says the other waiters are really cool. Like they are experts at *CHM*. They sometimes write long letters complaining to the government and hold all these secret rallies. One of them has a tattoo sleeve of Chinese characters on his right arm. Some have even been to prison. Lai Ker says he and Jimmy Tang are working on a project that is the ultimate *CHM* but he says it's a secret, which is annoying.

It's my last night in prison and I'm so excited, I can't sleep. I know it's about 12am 'cos I heard the gigantic grandfather clock chime a few minutes ago.

Dong Dong Dong Dong Dong Dong Dong Dong Dong Dong Dong Dong

Two maids have to push and heave the big, gold dongs on the clock just to wind it up. Meow Meow would hate that clock, she hated anything that dinged or bonged or banged but she liked anything smelly especially tuna and prawns. I wish she were here, I could stroke her black and white fur and she would purr on me until I fell asleep. She was a well special cat 'cos she was the last present my Papa gave to Mama before he died of cancer of the balls. Papa was too embarrassed to see the doctor about his "problem" until it was too late.

"Your Papa waited only until the last minute to see the doctor and then too late. What a silly man he was - so smart yet so proud. Chinese men are too proud, but that is who they are."

Mama told me I was "conceived" the night Papa got the bad news from the doctor and I was born exactly five months and twenty-nine days after he died. When Mama started the story, I put my fingers in my ears and shouted "La La La" 'cos I didn't want to be grossed out by imagining my parents doing it. But now I wish I had listened more. It's okay to be grossed out a little if it means you hear the truth. I wonder what life would have been like if Papa had been around. Maybe we would have lived in a bigger flat? Maybe we wouldn't have got red bills that made Mama cry? Maybe Lai Ker wouldn't have been cussed so much for not knowing the off-side rule when all the other boys did? Maybe I wouldn't hate Father's Day so much? Like I hated it when school made me do stupid father's day cards with pictures of footballs and boats for Mama. Maybe, maybe, maybe - I guess I'll never know.

Knock Knock Knock

CLICK

I sit up in bed, I bet Lai Ker's FINALLY stolen the key from Grandma.

"Xing Li, are you awake?"

It's Auntie Mei!

"Xing Li, are you awake?"

"I'm awake."

Auntie Mei tightens the belt on her kimono and perches awkwardly at the corner of my bed.

"I couldn't sleep - haven't been able to sleep for two weeks."

"Why?"

"I wanted to thank you for what you said to Grandma the other day."

"It's okay."

"You don't understand. I've never dared to shout at Ma that way. I didn't think you would ever do something like that. You're becoming extraordinarily brave, just like your mother always was."

I'm smiling when I hear this, maybe soon I will be like Mama and not have to be scared of anything any more.

"Auntie Mei, Grandma hit me with the feather duster but I didn't cry."

"I know, I felt really awful when I heard about it. You must understand, Grandma despises it when you show disrespect to her or to the family. She hates losing face. Apart from your mother, only your grandfather knew how to stand up to her."

"You mean Grandpa would shout at her?"

"Sometimes, when pushed he could shout really loudly too."

My ears prick up at the mention of Grandpa. Mama said Grandpa was not with us 'cos he "ran out of luck". Whenever I asked her to tell me more she would change the subject. She kept a faded photograph of him in her red purse with the tatty edges. He's small and round like the shape of a bowling pin with a thick black moustache. Grandma says it is bad luck to keep a dead person's photo in your wallet. I keep a photo of Mama in my wallet, maybe that's why Shils keeps picking on me. But I can't throw it away; it's one of the only photos I've got.

I beg Auntie Mei to tell me everything she knows about Grandpa. After all, doesn't she owe me for the feather duster special I received from Grandma? I'm desperate to find out about the mysterious man who Grandma hated, yet who gave the Wus their millions. Auntie Mei sighs and begins to tell me the story of Grandpa.

Grandpa Wu

"Your grandfather was a very charming man. He could make the strictest traffic warden smile and if that didn't work, he would slip them a crisp ten-pound note. That was in the days when bribery could get you anything. Ten pounds was a lot of money in that time. However, he was terribly generous. Every time your grandpa visited friends he would bring the most expensive whiskey or a rare exotic plant. I never knew exactly what he worked as but I knew he had a lot of money. Grandma used to complain about his gambling. She would scream and throw furniture at him. I heard them behind the doors. It was AWFUL - really awful. I hated it so much! It could get really vicious - the room would be left in a shambles. Everyone knew, the maids all knew but of course they would clear everything away before Uncle Ho got up.

He didn't know a thing.

His friends called him in Chinese "The Lucky Eight Man". As you know, eight is an auspicious number for Chinese people. He was lucky - very, very lucky. He once made half a million by betting on a horse called Princess Monaco. For your grandpa everything he touched turned into money - property, shares, ships... even the melon he grew in his greenhouse won the top prize of £100 at our local vegetable fair."

"But Mama said his luck ran out?"

"Yes, his luck ran out. I don't know why it happened or how."

"He died?"

"No, he changed. He lost his mind."

"Like Uncle Ho?"

"Not the way Uncle Ho is strange. He was more like a clown on steroids."

"What do you mean?"

"When I was about twelve he started to become, how can I explain it? Well, he became a little bit peculiar. He would find everything hilarious and would spend many hours of the day laughing at his own jokes. He was gifted in humour, I'll give him that. The jokes were funny, but only for five minutes, not for two hours. He would roll on the settee laughing and laughing. His laugh sometimes sounded like the Joker from *Batman*. It was a bit unnerving at times. Then he became addicted, but not to drinking or drugs or anything like that. No, that would be too normal for a Wu. His addiction was to practical jokes."

"What like whoopee cushions and stuff?"

"Well, it started with little things. For example, your grandma would cook a stew and he would swap the salt with the sugar. Or he would sneak a red sock into the wash so Uncle Ho would have to wear a pink T-shirt for PE. Of course your Uncle Ho didn't think it was funny when the whole class laughed at him. Sometimes I wonder whether your grandpa cared about Uncle Ho. He liked to tease Ho a lot. Your grandpa filled Ho's drawers with whoopee cushions and fart spray instead of clothes. When you are dealing with a fifty-year-old practical joker that acts like a naughty schoolboy, you start to question whether he is right in the head. Your mother defended him to the hilt - said he was having a midlife crisis. She was his favourite you see. In many ways she shared his sense of humour.

"The last straw was when Grandpa got a huge black and white cow into our back garden. Looking back, it must have been no easy feat to arrange for it to arrive in our garden in the middle of the night. Miraculously, we slept through and didn't hear anything until late morning. Your grandfather wanted it to be a big surprise and had put sleeping pills into our evening hot chocolate. He was so sneaky like that.

"With a big animal comes big deposits - I almost fainted from the stench. Your grandmother was livid and through a contact at the hospital she arranged for the men in white coats to come. When they arrived, your grandfather was rolling on the floor in his own urine. He had wet himself from laughter and was not the picture of sanity. They took him away immediately. He thought it was all a big joke that your grandma had played on him and found the whole thing hilarious. He even insisted they put a straightjacket on him.

"The psychiatrists could not find anything technically wrong with him. He was too happy by normal standards so they gave him medication that would calm him down. He wasn't a specific threat to society but they thought his practical jokes had a dangerous element to them. They were very concerned someone would get hurt. During his time in hospital, your grandpa managed to set fire to an armchair in his room. He said it was a stink bomb that went very wrong. The doctors were convinced he had more sinister intentions and had actually planned to burn down the hospital and everyone in it. After that fire incident, Grandma decided to move him to an institution in Singapore. She believed the stricter society would not pander to his inappropriate jolliness. I think she was also tired of him."

Auntie Mei's voice sounds all croaky and tired. She looks out of the window as if she can see Grandpa standing outside.

"Did Grandpa end up dying in an institute in Singapore?"

"No he didn't. He stayed in the institute for ten years before he moved to a home."

"Then he died in Singapore?"

"No, didn't your mother ever tell you? Your grandfather didn't die in Singapore."

"Then how did he die?"

I can see Auntie Mei's face in the morning light. She has no make-up on and her eyes look so sad but I am desperate for her to continue. Mama never ever told me how Grandpa died. Yet, hearing about the man who Mama had loved so much makes me feel closer to Mama.

"Auntie Mei, how did he die?"

Auntie Mei places her soft hand gently on my arm like a tiny butterfly. She bites her lip and takes a deep breath.

"Xing Li. Your grandfather is not dead. He is still alive."

Chapter 15
Elementary My Dear Wu

I've tried everything I can to get answers from Auntie Mei. I've begged and begged and asked her over and over again, but her gob has been sealed with super glue. Maybe if I can meet Grandpa it will help me to answer questions about who I really am? Did he party all the time or did he do his Maths homework like a good boy? Does he have *CHM* like Lai Ker or is he a wuss like me? Also, does he still cry when he thinks of Mama?

Auntie Mei is a spoilsport and refuses to tell me more. She says I'm too young to deal with grown up problems and Grandma would be annoyed if she knew how much she's already told me. I ask her the same questions over and over again, hoping I can wear her down. WHERE is Grandpa? WHY is he not living with Grandma? HOW can I contact him? Auntie Mei insists she doesn't know his whereabouts. No matter how many times I ask her, she always gives the same answer.

"I don't know. Please stop asking me."

I've got Lai Ker to help me and we tag team Auntie Mei, asking her question after question, hoping to break her Grandma-glued lips.

"Please stop asking me. I DON'T KNOW. I CAN'T TELL YOU."

Lai Ker tells me Jimmy Tang told him that when the police want to break the silence of a criminal they twist every word they say. I let Lai Ker take the lead, he quite fancies himself as a Chinese Sherlock Holmes.

"So, Auntie Mei, you say you don't know. Do you really not know or do you really *know not?*"

"I said it before and I'll say it again I DON'T KNOW."

"Hmmm, that is quite, quite interesting 'cos two minutes and thirty-seven seconds ago you said *I don't know*. Followed by *I can't tell you*. That little slip of the tongue suggests you know NOT."

"What? What do you mean by know not?"

"You *know not* what you are talking about. Which suggests to me you know. You KNOW where he is, so don't lie any more and tell us the whereabouts of the old man."

Auntie Mei smiles, maybe if Lai Ker gets her laughing her guard will go down and something might slip out.

"I know you want me to tell you and I appreciate you trying. However, the answer is still the same as always. I don't know and maybe one day when Grandma feels ready she will tell you. But until then, you will just have to be patient."

"Patience is not a virtue my mum passed to me. What if my dear lil sis and I choose not to be patient? What if we hassle you day and night until you tell us? What if we hound you until you see us in your dreams? What do you say to THAT dear Auntie?"

"Well, I don't know. But I DO know that if you choose to carry on with your behaviour, I WILL tell Grandma and she will bring her feather duster out."

"Well enuff said. Thank you for your time."

With Lai Ker's plan not going as well as we hoped, the chance of ever meeting my grandfather is starting to fade away. He may as well be dead.

I asked Jay if he ever wants to meet his grandparents and he says no.

Grandma thinks I'm doing my history project with Jay. But

actually I'm sitting in his room and he is carefully cleaning his old, silver flute. Jay has never played his flute in public. He has a grade eight distinction, but he says his music is way too personal to share with the world. To get the grade eight distinction, Jay practised for thousands of hours, sometimes getting up at 5am. But 'cos of his flute the older, sporty boys used to call him a "black fag". When he first started at West Hill he had to hide his flute in the cleaner's cupboard just so he wouldn't get beaten up.

"You mean you never, ever, EVER want to meet your grandparents?"

"Nope."

"But don't you want to know where you come from?"

"Watcha mean?"

"Like aren't you curious to find out about your Jamaican side or your Chinese side? Like whether you're like your grandparents?"

"I guess when you put it like that, maybe it would be cool. But it ain't gonna happen. They'll never accept my parents being happy, so best not to think about it. I'm half of my father and half of my mother and that's enough for me."

"But what if you had to pick and you only had to be one."

"What do you mean?"

"I dunno like… like say there was a war between China and Jamaica, which side would you take?"

"Neither. I guess whatever side the UK's on."

"No, no, say the UK don't exist any more and you HAD to pick one. Which one would you pick?"

"Man that's tough. I really dunno. Like I get some parts from my mum and some parts from my dad. I dunno, it would be hard. I guess I'm just half and half."

"Well I guess two halves make a whole?"

"Yeah, I guess so."

Jay's mind is ticking; I know from the frown on his forehead he is looking through his massive brain for one of his random facts.

"You know Xing, during World War Two when the Japanese attacked Pearl Harbour, they rounded up all the Japanese Americans and put them in concentration camps."

I leaned in closer to listen - this is not something we learnt in our history lessons with Mr Wool. Jay starts cleaning his glasses and continues.

"It didn't matter whether they were American or their grandparents were American or even their great grandparents were American. All they saw was how they looked and that was that."

"What happened to them?"

"They were rounded up like animals and taken to the middle of the desert and held as prisoners in places called Japanese Inter... Internment Camps. Not just adults, but kids too. Some younger than us."

"That sounds well scary. It would never happen today."

"I guess so."

"With human rights and all, they wouldn't let that happen... would... they?"

"Guess we don't know unless China or Jamaica attacks the UK."

"Nah, they wouldn't let it happen. We're all modern now."

"I guess you're right, the government might protect us. But you never know. My dad says wars make people do some crazy stuff."

"Like what?"

"Like people don't think right. Like they do anything to survive. My dad told me how in Jamaica there were these wars called The Maroon Wars. "

"What like the colour maroon?"

"Yeah, all these black slaves couldn't take it no more so they fought the white people to be free. But some real crazy stuff happened."

"Like what?"

"Like in order to catch the slaves that were hiding, some of the white people got hundreds of bloodhounds to hunt them down. The ones that got caught were whipped in public, some naked."

I think of my new neighbour Mr Holmes - he has a bloodhound that is really cute and wouldn't hurt a fly. Guess how dogs act depends on what their owners teach them. Maybe people are kinda like dogs - they only act the way they do 'cos of what they are taught. Jay starts putting his flute carefully into its case like it's the crown jewels. I watch him in silence.

"Xing, all this talk of wars is making me well depressed."

"Me too… "

Jay slams the flute case shut and locks it very slowly. His brain is ticking, I hope he doesn't come up with another scary random fact - though I kind of want him to. He frowns and pauses for ages.

"Yeah. Let's go see if the tortoise is awake."

"Okay, I've got some bananas I know he will gobble up in no time."

Chapter 16
The Island

It's the last day of school! Christmas holidays here I come! Four weeks off from Shils and horrible swimming lessons and boring history lessons and eating in the library. But I'm kinda sad 'cos Jay's family are going to Jamaica and we're not gonna hang out for ages. Jay's packing up his locker, he never leaves anything in his locker over the holidays.

"My Jamaican grandparents wanna meet me, but they don't wanna meet my mum. My dad said to them it's all or nothing."

"What did they say?"

"They chose nothing."

"Are you going to visit them anyway?"

"Nah, as my dad says, all or nothing. Don't want to meet anyone who don't like my mum, just won't be right. We're a tight trio you see."

A tight trio just like Mama, Lai Ker and me were. But now Mama's gone and Lai Ker is super busy with rugby practice or hanging out with Jimmy Tang. Lai Ker and Jimmy Tang have been best friends since Jimmy Tang hit Lai Ker with a giant, pink rubber on our first day at St George's. I didn't have a Jimmy Tang at St George's, but I had Poona, Lee, Debs and Shevon. They were my best friends in the world who said they would never forget me and we would be BFFs forever. When

I left to stay with Grandma, they vowed to email me every day and told me I could visit "any time, any day, anywhere". But as the days and weeks passed their emails became shorter and their text messages less juicy. Now they don't contact me no more. I asked Jay what he thought.

"Talk is cheap man. What's the point in saying one hundred words and not doing nothing. Beethoven wasn't a talker - he just let his music do the talking."

"I suppose, actions speak louder than words and all that."

"Yeah my dad says you should always, 'Let your yes be a yes and your no be a no.' Don't talk rubbish if you don't mean it."

"Yeah, if not you're talking cock."

"What?"

"Talking cock, it's a Singapore slang word my mum used to use."

"What does it mean?"

"Well, she said it meant you were talking rubbish. Wait, I'll show you what it says when I look it up online."

I look it up on my phone. I tell people I type slow 'cos I'm left handed, but actually it's 'cos my thumbs are too small. Guess I'm *talking cock*.

"Here it is: Talking cock: *a Singaporean saying when someone has spoken nonsense/senselessly. Probably originated from the English expression 'cock and bull story'.*"

"Cock and bull story, eh?"

"Yeah. You know when I read it out to my bro he laughed so hard he cried, then he said the meaning's got nothing to do with talking rubbish or a cock and bull story. He said it's to do with a Chinese bloke who liked to lie all the time about the size of his thing. But then he got found out and so they said he was talking cock. That's how it started."

"Are you sure?"

"I swear my bro knows these kind of random things."

"Weird! We should change the description on Wiki then. Okay then… my dad says you can't talk… 'talk cock'. Your words gotta be expensive like solid gold - never cheap."

We walk past Mr Chan's chippie and the smell of his soggy chips makes my stomach growl. If there was a prize for best tasting soggy chips I'm sure Mr Chan would get it.

"I guess so. Guess you don't want your words to be as cheap as Mr Chan's chips."

"Yup that would be a SERIOUS problem. Are we going to eat or what? I'm starving."

"Yeah I want sausage and chips today with mushy peas on the side."

"Okay since we aren't gonna hang out for a while, it's ALL on me today."

"You talking cock?"

"Nope."

"Promise?"

"Promise."

I get home and Lai Ker, Auntie Mei, Uncle Ho and Grandma are all sitting in the lounge as if they are having some kind of family therapy session. Uncle Ho is sprawled on his back across the sofa and is impatiently shaking his leg. Lai Ker is smiling which isn't always a good thing. Turns out, Grandma has booked us all return business class tickets to Singapore and we're spending the whole holiday there. Grandma says she could have easily afforded first class tickets but she thinks being around rich BUSINESS people might influence Lai Ker and I in our career "aspilations".

"First class people are rich people, no need work for money. Just go cruise, play black jack and drink cocktail. Business class got rat race people. Work hard still not waste time casino."

I'm super nervous but super excited too. We're going to Singapore, we're going to Singapore! Grandma points at me again.

"Also, you two becoming too like English children. Don't know how speak Chinese, eat too much sausages and worse

107

speak back to older people. No respect. Next thing I hear you want study Art and live with squatters in dirty bedsit. No, you need go Singapore. Need know where you come from."

Grandma tells me I've got one hour to pack, "If not we lock you in and leave behind." Lai Ker told me she decided to go on the trip only last night. He thinks its 'cos he told her he got ninety-six percent in English Literature and ninety-eight percent in Maths.

What do I pack for a trip like this? I've never been further than Bath.

I knew Lai Ker shouldn't have drunk that super large banana milkshake at the airport. He said he had an iron bladder and tried to get me to punch him in the stomach after he drank it. It's about thirty seconds before take off 'cos the aeroplane pilot made the announcement.

"I'm not gonna get up, if you wanna take a piss, you've gotta to wait until the plane has left."

"Okay lil sis, have it your way. But desperate times call for desperate measures."

Lai Ker takes an empty bottle out and starts undoing his belt in a *melodramama* manner. I get up and give him a sharp karate chop on his back as he passes.

"Next time you had better get your bottle ready. I won't give you respect next time."

"Next time I won't even give you the option of the bottle."

Lai Ker grins and walks to the toilet in a wiggly line. He returns from the toilet with his pockets stuffed with shavers, toothbrushes and combs.

"Hey lil sis, gotta get the good stuff before it's gone."

I bolt out of my seat to the toilet and pick up a comb, toothbrush and a couple of sanitary towels. I haven't had my first period yet, but the towels are free and Mama taught me to never turn my nose up at free stuff. Lai Ker sees my bulging pockets and chuckles.

"Xing, can you believe they play classical music to help

108

you piss?"

"Yeah and did you see how ginormous the mirrors in the toilet were?"

"I sure did. I sure did. They really make sure you get a bloody good view of your butt. We're going up in the world - I ain't going back to cattle class after this."

"Yeah me too!"

Lai Ker and I press the call button over and over again to order snacks, drinks, games and children's colouring books. They have special colour pencils that don't need a sharpener, you unwrap them and the lead becomes longer and longer. We have three course meals like we're in a posh restaurant. You are meant to put napkins on your lap not under your chin. Lai Ker keeps putting on a phoney accent when he orders from the pretty air stewardesses who tiptoe around in their uncomfortable high heels. I jab him in the ribs 'cos he keeps trying to look down their blouses as they bend down to clear away my tray.

"Can I help you, Sir?"

"Yes, *Sir* would like to have a wonderful Singapore Sling and *Sir* would like the cherry to be put on a small separate plate. Thank you, kind stewardess lady."

"Would that be all, Sir?"

"Erm, *Sir* would like some nuts to be put on a separate plate. But only ma-ca-da-mi-na nuts."

"Pardon me, but does Sir mean macadamia nuts?"

"Yes, kind lady. Bring me the nuts."

As the plane touches down into Singapore airport, I see the air stewardesses breathe a collective sigh of relief. In twelve hours, Lai Ker and I have eaten four packets of instant noodles, five cans of nuts, six packets of crisps and nine bars of chocolate. Lai Ker pats his stomach and gives me a wink as he tries to stuff the aeroplane headphones into the free sick bag.

Singapore is an island, but not in the way I imagined. There are tall, white, freshly painted blocks of flats and silver-coloured skyscrapers everywhere. The shiny high-rise buildings look as if they are giant diamonds in the hot sun. The large airport is beautiful with lots of flowers and trees and feels like someone has put cleaning stuff over everything. Lai Ker skates along the slippery floors in his worn, leather shoes and does a spin like those ballerinas. He is about to start a figure of eight but Grandma gives him an icy stare. We pass designer boutiques, duty free stations and souvenir shops selling T-shirts that say: *Singapore is a FINE city*.

I learn the laws of the land from a twenty-dollar T-shirt:

It is illegal to urinate in an elevator.
You may not walk around your home nude.
Failure to flush a public toilet after use may result in hefty fines.
Jaywalking is illegal.
If you are convicted of littering three times, you will have to clean the streets on Sundays with a bib on saying, "I am a litterer."
The sale of gum is prohibited.

I tear out a page from an old newspaper from the plane and make notes in the margins. When going to public toilets, I will have to be careful to close my legs. Who knows where they hide the secret cameras that capture you not flushing the loo. To save time, Uncle Ho usually walks from his bedroom to the bathroom naked when Grandma gives him a bath. I have to warn Grandma before the police accuse her of running a nudist colony. Lai Ker told me on the plane that Singapore canes criminals. He described how prisoners are stripped naked and "shackled" by strong, leather straps to a frame. They're held down in a bent-over position with their butts sticking out. A stocky warden carries a four-foot stick called a "rattan" that has been soaked in water. On the plane, Lai Ker re-enacted the caning using a stuffed lion, chopsticks and half a plastic cup. He added his own sound effects, yelping each time the lion got whacked. I had giggled and begged him to stop. But judging by the security guards with their big guns, they mean business. I quickly rush to the toilet to flush my gum down the loo.

Grandma and Auntie Mei want to look at the designer boutiques, while Lai Ker has found a computer games store to occupy him. That means I have to bring Uncle Ho to the food court. His hair is ruffled from sleeping on the plane and he looks well suspicious. Grandma says I HAVE to look after Uncle Ho and gives me fifty dollars to buy food. Uncle Ho starts to drool and herds me along with his stomach. Through a massive ball of smoke, I see little hawker stores selling delicious yummy food. Satay, beef ball noodles, chicken rice, prawn laksa and duck rice. My mouth waters and Uncle Ho pushes past people. He eyes all the stores like a child who hasn't eaten for a week. This is the first time I have been properly left alone with him. Apart from sometimes grunting, I've never really chatted with Uncle Ho. Lai Ker says the meds make him all quiet and for him every word has to count. A Chinese hawker store owner with the darkest tan I had seen on a Chinese man starts speaking to me in Mandarin. I go red 'cos I don't understand a word he is saying. I smile and nod. To the hawker seller, I look Chinese so there is no reason why I wouldn't know my own language. As he continues to jabber on in a foreign tongue, I nod rather than tell him my Chinese is limited to swear words and counting from one to twenty.

The man takes two steaming plates of chicken rice with chilli and places them in front of me. I wanted prawn noodles without chilli but that would mean admitting I don't speak the language. That would tell the man I am an outsider and what Chinese people call a banana: white on the inside, yellow on the outside.

Uncle Ho looks at my chicken rice as if I have just bought a steaming plate of maggots. But then he changes his mind and eats it anyway. The yellow, plastic stool he sits on groans under his weight. I look across at Uncle Ho. He has dry skin, dandruff is flaking from his hair and he does not notice the chilli sauce dripping from his chin. Uncle Ho has spent the majority of his life sleeping and eating with occasional fits of violence in between. Apart from his family and seeing Dr Lincoln twice a week, he doesn't do much with the outside world. He doesn't commute on the train or go to friends' birthday parties or visit the cinema. Also, Grandma stops him from cooking, cleaning and even bathing himself. Mama once told me that Uncle Ho was a talented tennis player. She said he was shy and quiet off the courts, but then on the courts he was super fit and would thrash his opponents. I find it hard to imagine, but he does have giant hands so maybe that helps.

Uncle Ho stares at me; I notice the white parts of his eyes have a faint yellow tinge to them. He reaches for my chicken rice and starts gobbling it up. I watch him with my mouth wide open and he doesn't look up. He just concentrates real hard on spoonful after spoonful after spoonful, like if he were to miss one bit of rice the world would end. After swallowing the last grain, Uncle Ho closes his eyes. I see a frown in the centre of his forehead; Mama had a deep frown there too. For some reason, he makes me feel really stressed and grip my stool tightly. After five minutes, I can hear soft snores coming from Uncle Ho. A teenage girl in a green and yellow school uniform on the next table starts to titter. My hands are shaking as I collect the cutlery and put it in the massive tub with dirty dishes.

I don't think I like Uncle Ho and I feel bad 'cos Mama would have wanted me to.

Chapter 17
Geoffrey's Adventures in Wonderland

My cousin Geoffrey Joo Chiat Wu is fat - REALLY fat. He's like a Chinese version of that ginormous boy in *Charlie and The Chocolate Factory* that falls into the chocolate river and gets sucked into the pipe. Oh yeah, his name was Augustus Gloop; Geoffrey is a Singaporean version of Augustus Gloop. We arrive at his HDB (Housing Development Board) flat in Bedok, and he is munching a half-eaten pandan cake. There is a trail of neon green crumbs on his chest. He offers us some cake when his mum Auntie Sarah tells him off for being rude to "your special guests from London". As soon as we've entered the flat and barely taken off our shoes, Auntie Sarah has offered us drinks.

"Would you like Coke? Lemonade? Bandung rose drink? Apple juice with aloe vera?"

We are dripping with sweat and anything cold would be good. But Grandma acts all embarrassed.

"Sarah, no need to trouble."

"No trouble, what do you want to drink?"

"Just water will do."

"Don't be silly, it is no problem at all. What you want to drink? Some juice maybe?"

"Aiyah, so much trouble. *Paiseh* you also got so many desserts."

Grandma opts for bandung and Auntie Mei copies her. Lai Ker has a coke and I try bandung 'cos I've never drank anything with squashed flowers in it. It's very sugary and pink and tastes delicious like a mixture of strawberries and Calpol, but in a nice way.

A spread of cakes are lined precisely on the coffee table. Mango cake, Japanese cheesecake, Chinese kuehs and the half-eaten pandan cake our cousin is scoffing. Geoffrey finishes off his piece of cake and wipes the crumbs from his mouth before licking his fingers.

"Hey cuz, you got a hole in your sock. Careful you don't slip on the floor."

Geoffrey is Cantonese Chinese like us and shares the same great grandfather. He is like those flame-boy-ant fashion designers except he likes girls 'cos he has a huge poster of Lucy Liu in a bikini on his wall. Lai Ker has no interest in chatting with Geoffrey, so for the first time ever I take the lead.

"Geoffrey, what do you study at university?"

"I study Me-di-cine. Quite hard work, you know?"

"Do you like what you are studying?"

"It's ok lah. If I don't become doctor, my mother say can do work in medical lab. And you?"

"I'm still in Year Seven - first year in secondary school."

"I mean what you want to study when you go to uni?"

"I have no idea."

Lai Ker decides to join in at this point.

"I want to be a doctor."

"DO you? Well then maybe me and you can set up business together. What you want to specialise?"

"Gynaecology."

Geoffrey gives a huge laugh and nudges Lai Ker so hard he almost topples to the floor.

"Yah me too!"

Lai Ker wiggles his eyebrows and Geoffrey does the same. They've got the same thick, caterpillar eyebrows.

Geoffrey says he is twenty-one and has just started uni after spending the last two years serving his country through national service.

"Yah was damn tough doing army. But what can I do? Spent two years doing touch typing and boring admin tasks."

"But didn't you get to play with guns and stuff?"

"No, my flat feet stopped me. They flat like pancakes. Their loss."

Geoffrey shows Lai Ker his gigantic collection of computer games from Japan with a booming "ta-da". I think Lai Ker will want to be mates with him now.

"So wanna go party and meet girls? I bring you to see some *chio bus*?"

Geoffrey rules the party scene in Singapore and his favourite nightclub is Zoo. His nickname is "GIP" short for Geoffrey Is Partying. I think Geoffr… GIP is really cool 'cos he goes clubbing three times a week and picks up his mates in a red open top car. The car belongs to his mother, but he pimps it out with tinted windows and sprays it with this really nice pinewood smell. If Mama had been alive she would have immediately banned us from seeing him. He is what she would call a *pai kia* which is slang for gangster. But 'cos GIP is studying to be a doctor, Grandma says he can look after us in Singapore.

"You can learn from your smart cousin."

We arrive in Singapore on a Friday and on Saturday night we're partying with GIP in Zoo. Grandma let us stay over at GIP's house 'cos he convinced her he was taking us to an evening lecture at his uni on Chinese culture.

"Yes Geoffrey, good you look after your cousins. Good Chinese influence on them."

GIP's best friend works part time as a bouncer and he lets us sneak in for free. On Saturdays, Zoo has "Retro Foam Party Night" with an extended happy hour. We enter the club by climbing through a looking glass with a hole in the middle, I feel like Alice arriving in a warped wonderland.

Strobe lights, glittered mirrors, giant rabbits, plastic silver coloured sunflowers and diamante top hats. On the "Z" shaped dance floor students stand in rows doing hand movements to eighties music. Every thirty minutes, a tattooed man with LOADS of piercings sprays foam on the crowd. They scream in excitement and chant to the guy: "Soak us more! Soak us more! Soak us more!"

GIP knows all the retro dance moves and teaches us his best ones - "The Catwalk" and "Walk like a mad Egyptian". He struts up and down the dance floor like a supermodel at London Fashion Week. Lai Ker catches onto the moves super fast and adds a smooth spin to some of them. He learnt his dance moves from watching Michael Jackson videos. Several pretty girls stop to watch and clap. Lai Ker is channelling his inner James Bond and loving every minute of it. But I'm super nervous about making a fool of myself and not being cool. What if people think I'm sad and a crap dancer? Everyone looks so cool and confident. I think of Shils and how in gym class she said I wouldn't be able to do a cartwheel even if someone gave me a million quid. I did half a cartwheel before falling flat on my face.

I stayed perched on top of a large speaker, the music is so loud I can feel it going right through my body.

BOOM SHAKE SHAKE SHAKE THE ROOM BOOM SHAKE SHAKE SHAKE THE ROOM TIC TIC TIC TIC BOOM.

GIP gives a whooping massive laugh and pulls me onto the dance floor.

"COME ON! Show the people YOUR moves."

"I can't… "

"It doesn't matter what people think. JUST HAVE FUN LAH."

I jerk my hands from side to side to the beat of the music. I watch everyone twisting and moving their heads as if they were in a Saturday Night Fever themed party. GIP insists on buying us drinks. He waves his hand into my face when I offer to pay. He pays for EVERYTHING from our dinner to the mints I got at the door. He says it's the Singaporean way 'cos we are guests so we don't pay a penny. I'm not used to people being nice like that. I wonder what GIP would think of the BYO BBQs in London where everyone brings their own meat to cook on the grill. You have to be very careful at BYO BBQs, people have been known to get into fist fights when you pick up their sausage from the grill by mistake.

"So, decided what you wanna drink?"

Lai Ker looks at the girls next to him and wiggles his eyebrows.

"Cuz, I'd like a martini - shaken not stirred."

GIP grins and looks at me.

"And you little Cuz?"

"Erm... can I have a Ribena?"

GIP gives me a wink and fights his way through the wet haired mob at the bar - using his pointy elbows to nudge people out of the way. When he returns, he hands me a large jug of Ribena mixed with vodka with a stripy straw.

"All for me?"

"Yah ALL for you. Drink up."

I feel all grown up. Auntie Mei gave me a makeover before I left, she straightened my hair with hair straighteners, put on a ton of foundation, mascara and lipstick. Also, I'm wearing her tight white Chanel dress and there's an okay looking guy checking me out.

I put my fingers through my hair and stare at Lai Ker, he's wriggling on the floor like a worm.

What the heck!

I take a big swig from my Ribena jug and go on the dance floor. My heart is pounding and everything is blurry. The room starts to spin a little. I close my eyes, so all I feel is the music going up and down my body. I start to move quicker and quicker and soon I'm dancing like a mad chicken on steroids. This isn't West Hill, this is Singapore! I can be who I want and no-one knows me. I do my chicken moves, my Egyptian moves, my Saturday Night Fever moves, GIP's catwalk moves and some weird moves of my own.

I dance and dance and dance and dance.

The room starts spinning and I start to laugh. This is great! Stuff what everyone thinks, stuff West Hill, stuff Shils. I'm having fun. I have so much fun I don't notice for ages that people on the dance floor have formed a circle and are cat calling. GIP and Lai Ker have to carry me off the dance floor.

We walk out of the club into the humid night air. Couples are snogging and there is a drunken slugging match near the entrance. GIP's voice has risen to alarming heights.

"WAH - LAU YOU SURE KNOW HOW TO PARTY."

GIP drives out of the car park and almost knocks over a drunk, Indian couple.

"SORRY! FORGOT TO CHECK SIDE MIRROR."

GIP puts the music to full volume and starts to sing along to his personal mix that consists of Kylie, Shania Twain and Madonna. I close my eyes, and put the window down. Everything is spinning less now. Lai Ker looks at me and shrugs his shoulders. We start to laugh and join in with our mad cousin's loud rendition of "Man! I feel like a woman!".

"Duh, Duh, Duh, DUH, DUH - Man! I FEELO like a WO-MAN… "

As we zoom down the PIE, singing our hearts out, I feel free. This is the first time I have stayed out late since Mama died. This is the first time I have stayed out late - ever.

Chapter 18
Through the Cooking Glass

We join GIP's uni friends at Abdul's Cheese Prata store:
OPEN 24 HOURS, 7 DAYS A WEEK, 365 DAYS A YEAR.

Through the smoke, I see groups of students, Indian construction workers and lobster coloured white people eating Indian-style pancakes with cheese. It's well hot and noisy and crowded and I'm finding it hard to walk in a straight line. The air is so thick with oil, when I get home I'll have to wash my hair twice. GIP's friends wear designer glasses and are dressed in T-shirts, tank tops and jeans. GIP orders four cheese and mushroom pratas and three Milo Godzillas. GIP says the owner came up with the name for the DELICIOUS chocolate drink with strawberry ice cream and whipped cream while watching *Jurassic Park*. I sit next to a friendly girl who chain-smokes and chats A LOT between her mouthfuls of cheese prata.

"So, you from London? That's damn cool."

"I guess."

"I wanna go there for post grad, can't wait to leave this place. So damn boring."

The chain-smoking girl is actually called Ting-Ting but she tells me to call her Tracy. She's studying mass com at uni and wants to be a high flying journalist. She speaks with a Singaporean accent that has American bits - like her words all go up at end of the sentence. She does go on a bit like the MPs you see on the BBC.

"... the weather too hot, nothing to do and worst of all no freedom at all. You say one thing bad about the government and that is the end of your journalism career. Kaput! I want to be a proper journalist, you know? At least in London, I can write what I want. Your journalists are so free."

I think of the journalists that hacked into famous people's phones and the paparazzi that chased Princess Diana to her grave.

Tracy takes a big gulp of her Milo Godzilla. A bit of the chocolate powder stays on the edge of her mouth, she licks it off and I notice the pink crystal stud on her tongue. She carries on with her political rant. I wonder if her Milo Godzilla has had a little something extra added to it. She gives Lai Ker a naughty grin and licks her lips with her studded tongue.

"Guys sleeping with guys is illegal you know. But girls sleeping with guys is fine."

Lai Ker almost chokes on his cheese prata and I have to karate chop him on his back.

Everything Tracy talks about, I've heard it all before. Mama sometimes would go on a bit too. She said in London, Lai Ker and me were free from "Asian pressure".

"I didn't want you to be one of the little kids separated into groups according to their grades - to feel your worth is whether you get an A, B or C on your report card."

In Singapore, primary school kids are divided into classes according to their grade. So, I'd probably be in the dummy class and Lai Ker would be in something called the "Gifted Programme". Kids in this programme get smaller classes and special trips overseas. Once you get into the gifted programme your whole life is set up for you. Gifted kids go on to be super smart scholars and are sent overseas to the best unis.

It's weird 'cos even though Mama complained a lot about

Singapore, she still called Singapore her home - right up until the day she died. Like when Mama read in the newspapers of teenagers violently mugging people for their iPhone or twelve-year-olds getting pregnant or drunk people pissing in the tube she would sigh and say, "That would never happen back home." Also, once Mama came back from work looking furious. When we asked her what was wrong, she said it was 'cos she didn't get promoted at work. She said she had been working for longer and harder than this other helper at the nursing home, but they didn't promote her. I asked her why she didn't say something and she said she did, "But these things are so hard to prove. When you grow up you will understand. Aiyah, at times like this I wish I were back home."

Mama said London is a cosmo-politican country and 'cos of that it's okay to be an "ethnic minority" 'cos there are quite a few of us. But then it gets weird 'cos I'm neither here nor there. Like I'm not totally white and I'm not Singaporean either. I love Sunday roasts and Chinese food too, but I can't speak fluent Chinese and the only Chinese word I can write is my name. None of my friends have ever been Chinese apart from when I met Jay, but he's half. Kilburn was where I grew up - whereas Singapore is a strange land where people sound and act different. They use words like *wah lau*, *kena*, and *meh*. But most of the people here look like me and my name is just normal, not strange. Also, I blur into the crowds of black haired people and, if I wanted to, I could be like Where's Wally. I could disappear and people would struggle to find me. Mama said I should be proud to be a BBC - British Born Chinese (when I was little I thought it meant that Chinese people were owned by the BBC). Mama said being a BBC makes me special. But I don't feel special. Most of the time I feel strange.

Tracy is still talking and talking and talking. She orders another Milo Godzilla.

YUM!

GIP sees me staring at it and orders one for me too. He gives me a thumbs up sign and winks. I really like GIP, he's like all confident and friendly. Also, he pays for everything even though I know his family ain't rich. Tracy smiles and talks to me like I totally get her even though I haven't said more than two words.

"Yah, so annoying. They stop our fun. When I get to London, I will go cra-a-azy! I will party like anything and write stories about the Singapore government."

Tracy pauses and frowns. She's got a huge mole next to her right eyebrow. Actually when I look closer it's not a mole, it's another piercing.

"Hmmmm… but if I write bad stories about government, they will ban me and I can never return to my home. That will be REALLY very bad? That would be the worst… "

Tracy bites her red lips and then stubs out her final cigarette.

"Anyways, I guess I will party like anything and I will be free… "

Chapter 19
Taxi Jiver

Auntie Mei tells me Singapore has three seasons:

Summer
Monsoon
Shopping

"Xing Li, you spend too much on shopping. Auntie Mei go herself. You come with me."

"Where are we going Grandma?"

"No time talk small. We need go now."

"How about Lai Ker?"

"Lai Ker learning good, Chinese values from your older cousin so not coming. You talk too much. They say children should be seen not *herd*. You see, you chat too much you become like *herd* of cows. Just eat grass and make noise. Moo, moo, moo, all day do nothing."

I keep quiet, just like Mama did all those times Grandma came to visit us. The aircon is at full blast and my back keeps sliding down the shiny, leather seats of the taxi cab. Grandma keeps silent. Her awkward silence is an art form. We pass row after row of HDB flats, their walls painted in white or cream. GIP told me more than eighty percent of the population live in these high rise towers while ninety-nine percent of white expats live in condos or houses. The taxi speeds past several blocks of new condos with black slated roofs that are all glisteny like the black onyx bracelet Auntie Mei has. Grandma is leaning on the window, her small eyes staring at all the new buildings.

"Aiyah, so many new buildings. So much change."

The taxi driver sighs and shakes his head.

"Auntie, Singapore changing so fast. Everything so different - more and more not like my home anymore. Too crowded with people. Wait in ten years time we become like Hong Kong and nowhere to move without people left right centre."

Grandma shakes her head and keeps staring and staring at all the new buildings. I want to ask Grandma about how she feels about being in the country where she grew up. Does she find it weird or does she like being back in her hometown? But she is super busy looking at all the giant buildings and shaking her head.

We are stuck in a HUGE traffic jam snaking down a crowded road. The taxi driver says the road is called Gaylung. It's getting dark and queues of locals are waiting in the heat for their dinner. People have travelled from across the country; they are happy to wait for hours just to get the "best chicken rice in Singapore", or the "number one chilli crab". I read in the papers about chicken rice millionaires who made their pile just by owning a tiny, oily hawker store. Maybe I'll open a fish and chip shop here and become a millionaire, then I won't have to see Shils ever again. That would be super cool!

This part of town is super run down. The walls of the shops are dirty and loads of people have hung their towels on the windows to shut the world out. On the side of the road there's rows of old men sitting selling tons of different types of pills. Some look like they're wearing stripy PJ bottoms to go with their dirty, white tops.

"Grandma, I thought drugs were illegal in Singapore."

"They not real drugs. Only pills to make old men strong."

"You mean like the pills Uncle Ho takes?"

"NO."

SILENCE.

Grandma looks away and I know the conversation is over. We pass another road and I see rows and rows of beautiful, young girls in tight mini dresses just standing and smiling. They are wearing loads of make-up and they look like they are auditioning for a rapper's music video. Sometimes men old enough to be their granddads follow them up dark staircases. The taxi driver notices I'm staring and gives me a sad shake of his head.

"Xiao Mei you so lucky your grandmother look after you. Some of these girls not so lucky. They got no choice like you."

"Where are they from? How do they get here?"

"Thailand, Philippines, China, some already got families, even husband also. Some maybe as young as my granddaughter."

"How old are they?"

"Some fifteen, some fourteen. No-one knows, only their big boss know. He lock away their passport so no-one can see."

Grandma gives the taxi driver a dirty look.

"BE QUIET. I never pay you for speak to granddaughter. Only pay to drive."

The taxi driver shakes his head and sighs; he keeps quiet for the rest of the journey. When we are finally out of the jam, the taxi driver drives over the speed limit and a bell goes off in his car.

DING-DONG

DING-DONG

DING-DONG

DING-DONG

We zoom past large houses with gardens and seesaws and swimming pools. Maids chat on the corner of streets while they wait for their owner's tiny, fluffy, white dogs to poo. We stop in front of a huge, white building with beautiful gardens. There's a giant fountain with a massive horse in the middle. Grandma gives the taxi driver a hundred dollars and tells him to keep the change. He thanks her loads and rushes to open her door. Grandma takes a tissue out of her bag and wipes the buzzer on the gate before pressing it.

"Mrs Wu here. Let me in."

Grandma glances at me and in an ever so casual way says, "Xing Li you meet Grandpa today."

She speaks as if she has just said, "Xing Li, you are going to school today," or "Xing Li, we are having lunch today."

"Xing Li, you meet Grandpa today."

Chapter 20
Send in the Clowns

Grandma looks at her watch and rolls her eyes.

"Your grandfather want meet you. He call me every day until I tell him I change phone line. Then he call your Auntie Mei over, over again. So I say okay, but only fifteen minutes."

"How about Lai Ker?"

"Pah, he only want meet you. He crazy you see. Just like before, he only care for girls not Uncle Ho. Stupid man. I bring you so he can shut up."

I have arrived in the planet of the oldies - women playing mahjong, men reading newspapers and a quiet few watching the soaps on TV. There's an old lady with red, curly, dyed hair sitting next to the window. She looks well sad. The nurse tells us her daughter-in-law had chased her out of their house 'cos they couldn't deal with a "crazy woman with dementia". When Grandma and me walk in, every single resident lifts their head up in excitement and then down again.

An old man in red, silk PJs bounds into the room and a few of the Chinese grannies smile. He starts doing a little jig next to a pretty, moon-faced Malay woman. She playfully hits him and pleads with him to stop teasing her. Grandma purses her lips. The old man is seventy going on sixteen and dances like the penguins in *Mary Poppins*. His legs are super flexi for his age - they stretch out like worn out rubber bands.

After a sweaty performance, the dancing man gives a bow. There are a few nods and a couple of claps. He spins around; his fat belly and small head remind me of a top.

Grandma nods at me, "She your granddaughter."

Grandpa gives me a gigantic smile and with his large false teeth then takes my hand and kisses it. His lips are very wet and I wipe my hand on my jeans. My heart starts to beat at an alarming rate and I put my hand on my chest.

THUMP-THUMP THUMP-THUMP THUMP-THUMP

"Very charmed to meet you. I see you have the good looks from my side of the family."

Grandpa sounds like a British actor from an old Hollywood movie, there is not a hint of a Chinese accent; his petite nose that flicks out at the end is exactly the same as mine. He picks up an empty saucer and balances it on his head.

"If money hadn't got in the way, I would have made it as a tightrope walker. My sense of balance is phenomenal, don't you think?"

Grandma rolls her eyes and sits heavily onto a sofa.

"Balance in life is important. 'All work and no play makes Jack a dull boy.'"

There were so many questions I wanted to ask him, but with guard dog Grandma looking at her watch, it was unlikely I'd get a chance.

"How about you go out for supper and I spend some time with my only granddaughter?"

Grandpa should add mind reader to his list of circus tricks. "No."

"Come on, don't be a party pooper."

He sticks his tongue out at her, it's fat and long like Mama's used to be. Then he gets on his knees and I hear them crack. With his hands clasped together he starts talking in an over-the-top manner.

"I'll give you fifty thousand."

"Don't speak ridiculous. She don't need spend time with silly man."

"How about a hundred thousand?"

Grandpa gets up and takes a cheque book and gold pen out of his pocket.

"Mrs… "

"Wu… "

"Yi… "

"Ling… "

"One… "

"Hundred… "

"Thousand… "

"Dollars… "

"Only… "

He signs the cheque and waves it in front of Grandma's nose. Grandma gives him a dirty look, sighs and snatches the cheque out of his hands.

"Two hours, I come back. No stupid dancing, no stupid ideas."

Grandpa watches Grandma walk slowly down the corridor. When her tiny frame turns round the corner, he thrusts his arm in the air and sings a super happy song.

"Ding dong, the witch is gone. Ding dong, the witch is gone. Ding dong, the bitch is gone."

Grandpa bows to me and gives me his arm. I take it and he pats my hand in a comforting way.

"Would you like to join me for tea? Perhaps some scones and cake will whet my beautiful granddaughter's palate?"

We skip to a small bedroom with an enormous window. Tall piles of neatly pressed silk PJs are stacked on a floral chair with its stuffing coming out. There's also a small fridge, a single bed and a teeny-tiny bedside table. There are cracks on the ceiling and outside the window is a huge palm tree version of the giant beanstalk in "Jack and the Beanstalk".

"Have a seat, young, enchanting lady and let me put the order through. Darling, Nurse Ning could you please bring my special tea? You know the one that I save for royalty and special guests. Yes. Yes. Thank you. Bye bye."

"So, Xing Li, what can I do for you during our short time on this earth? Time is ticking and alas we have to say adieu in a few hours."

Grandpa's round face is lined and flaky from spending too many days in the sun. Or in his case, too many days digging for shells in the sea with his plastic bucket and spade. He tells me he's been in the home for more than ten years and has not returned to the UK for ages and ages. Not for Auntie Mei's graduation, not for Grandma's seventieth birthday, not for Mama's funeral. I remember the empty chair next to Auntie Mei at the funeral, every time the door opened Auntie Mei would look up with hope.

I'm honest with Grandpa and tell him about my problems at West Hill and how I hate living with Grandma. Everything pours out of me. I'm like a Coke bottle that's been rolling in the car for days until someone opens it and all the crazy, fizzy stuff just whooshes and whooshes out. Grandpa sits in silence and pats my back every so often.

"Yes, yes, life is tough. But when life throws you lemons, you make lemonade, when life throws you oranges, you make orange juice, when life throws you banana peels, you make banana milkshake. Do you get my point child?"

"Yes, but Grandpa I hate West Hill so much. I hate it!"

"My child there is a fine line between love and hate. You just have to choose which one you want."

"What do you mean?"

"Let's put it this way. When life is tough, you have a choice. You have a choice to curl up in a ball and wither away like the crocuses in winter. Or you can fight like the fir trees that grow come snow or rain."

"Fight? You mean like *Chinks Have Mouths?*"

"I beg your pardon young lady."

"Well Lai Ker says that Chi... Chinese people have to fight to be heard and all that. So he says Chinese people have to have mouths and we have to fight for this."

Grandpa frowns and scratches his head. He doesn't scratch

130

it like once, he scratches it lots and lots like he has nits.

"That is quite a curious observation from your older brother. It is not wrong and it is not right. Who am I to judge the decisions of a young man? However, I can tell you from experience that fighting fire with fire rarely works. I mean look what happened between your mother and grandmother. It was such a never-ending battle."

"What were they fighting about?"

"Everything I suppose, World War One was the battle over your father and World War Two was the battle over Ho."

Auntie Mei said she never got to meet Papa 'cos Grandma banned him from the house. When she wanted to meet him, it was too late - she looked really sad when I asked her this. I tried to ask more but she said she needed to learn her lines for a film.

"Grandpa, what was my papa like?"

"He was a handsome chap, very quiet but a decent sort. That's what your mother told me anyway. You see, by the time your parents were dating, I had scooted off to Singapore. I never got to meet him."

Grandpa talks quite quickly, I have to use extra brain cells to catch up.

"How about Grandma, what did she think of my Dad?"

"Well, she wanted to know whether he was suitable for our family. So, she grilled him good and proper. How much he earned, where he went to university and even who his ancestors were."

"She didn't like it that he was a crew-pier did she? I know she thinks casinos are full of germs."

"Of course she wasn't happy with that, but that wasn't the problem."

"He didn't go to university, did he?"

"That is a valid point my clever girl. However, it was not the deal breaker so to speak."

"What was it then?"

Grandpa looks out of the window and starts humming

softly to himself. The tune sounds like it's from a Disney movie but I can't quite remember which one.

"What was it Grandpa?"

"It was his blood. The blood flowing through his veins was his downfall."

"His blood?"

"I don't know if you are aware of it Xing Li… "

Grandpa starts scratching his head again in super speed.

"Xing Li, your other grandfather was Japanese."

"What?! How did that happen?"

"I don't know the full details. But during the war there were many Japanese soldiers in Singapore. They did some horrible things to our women. But from what I know, your Japanese grandfather's relationship with your grandmother wasn't like that."

"But then why couldn't Papa marry Mama?"

"It was because he was Japanese."

"But I don't understand why. Like Japanese people look like us. They're nice and they have black hair and brown eyes and most white people can't tell us apart."

"I understand young lady, but there are some complications in life I cannot explain."

Grandpa makes a big sigh and puts his hand on my knee. His fingers look all red and swollen like sausages about to pop out of their skins.

"Xing Li, sometimes there are… there are some hurts that run so deep it takes more than one generation to erase them."

Grandpa stares at me and just shakes his head over and over again. He starts to talk real slow and soft.

"Some of the things I experienced during the war are things I will never forget for as long as I live."

"What kinds of things?"

"Awful, awful things… like the ache in your belly when you are so hungry you think you are going to die, the smell of rotten flesh outside your doorstep; feeling too terrified to sleep at night. I only have to close my eyes and I'm back there again."

"So, you and Grandma hate Japanese people 'cos of the war?"

"No, I certainly don't hate Japanese people... because what can more hate bring? But let's put it this way, I would not willingly touch sushi even if you paid me. To date, I have not bought a single Japanese product."

I think of the German brands in Grandma's kitchen.

"When the Japanese attacked Singapore, they took everything. My father lost his arm, one brother died, another brother disappeared and for many years I couldn't sleep through the night. You learn to train yourself to not have any deep sleep because a knock in the middle of the night could change your life. It could mean that your brother was found dead or alive. You know, your grandmother's auntie almost starved to death."

"Did Mama know all this?"

"Yes, but she... she still chose your father."

I thought of the tears in Mama's eyes every time I asked her about Papa.

"That's 'cos she loved Papa."

"Yes, she did. Very much."

"But you never met him?"

"No, but she wrote to me about him. She said she was going to marry him despite everything. She hadn't written to me for years and then, suddenly, she told me she wanted to get married and that was that."

"But if you loved Mama, you could have at least gone to the wedding?"

Grandpa ignores my question and carries on as if I hadn't said a word.

"Look, I told your mother I washed my hands over the matter. Yes, I washed my hands with soap and water. But your grandmother couldn't do that, she was too busy trying to win the fight with your mother to back down. Their fighting was not the way, too much shouting wastes time."

I think of Lai Ker and *CHM* and how he said I needed to shout if I wanted to be heard. But then Mama and Grandma shouted a lot and it got them nowhere.

"Xing Li, there is an old Chinese saying: 'You cannot fight a fire with water from far away.'"

"What does that mean? Like do you need a really long hose or something?"

"No, no, the saying means your problems cannot be fought from afar, you have to find the resolution there and then. For you, that means staying in London and dealing with the problems head on. Running away will not be the answer. It never is. One day you wake up and you realise it is too late. The time has gone and you are old."

Grandpa stares out of the window at the palm tree beanstalk. He stares for ages and ages. Then he takes a small recorder out of his drawer and plays the song from *Beauty and the Beast*.

"Grandpa, will I get to see you again? Like can we keep in touch?"

He puts his recorder down and starts scratching his head again. I see some dandruff fall like a tiny blizzard on his red PJs.

"I suppose we could write. But I'm terrible at replying to mail. Reading makes me extremely bored and I'm not great at all the soppy stuff. I think your two hour visit is quite enough for you."

He smiles at me and then suddenly he sniggers like he is making fun of me or something.

"Yes, I can't look after Lai Xing and I certainly can't look after you! Just the thought of it, what a crazy idea! Your grandma would have my head."

"What do you mean?"

His eyes suddenly look different like they belong to another man. They look cold and faraway.

"What I mean, my dear granddaughter, is I suppose this is goodbye. Yes, it has to be goodbye because I have no more to give, no more to say, no more to share… so I hope you find your path and I bid you adieu."

I want the nice, serious man I was talking to to come back. I want to talk to him more and for him to be nice and offer me more scones. Most important of all, I want him to want me to stay. But instead Grandpa kisses my hand - it's more sloppy than the first time. He suddenly gets up like he is about to start a race or something and he gives me a little wave. Then he skips down the corridor as if he is going to a tea party in a fairy tale.

He doesn't look back.

Chapter 21
Love You Wrong Time

Auntie Mei comes to collect me from the nursing home. She says Grandma has dragged Lai Ker to the hairdressers to get his ears cleaned.

"What do you mean he's getting his ears cleaned? Are they gonna wash them out with a special shampoo or something?"

"No, Xing Li dear, it is an old procedure. You get a haircut, followed by a massage and finally you have your ear wax taken out."

"That's gross, how do they take the ear wax out?"

"They use a special ear-pick to take it out. It's actually quite therapeutic, like a tiny massage to the inner cavities of your ears."

Auntie Mei opens her designer handbag and shows me her ear-pick. It's a long stick, about four toothpicks long, with a tiny spoon at the end. She says they are usually metal but hers is solid gold. The image of Auntie Mei leaning sideways in her fur coat while someone picks her ears with diamond earrings makes me smile.

"Xing Li, did you have a nice time with your grandfather?"

I tell Auntie Mei about what we talked about. She keeps very, very quiet.

"Auntie Mei, can I ask you a question?"

"Yes?"

"Why didn't you ever meet my father?"

Auntie Mei's lips tremble and I'm worried she's going to start crying again like when I caught her behind the bins at Mama's funeral.

"Xing Li, I... I... wanted to meet your father. Believe me I did. But Grandma said she would disown me if I did. I was completely helpless - she was my mother after all."

"But couldn't you have sneaked it? Like couldn't you have like... I dunno like... tried harder?"

"You're right, I could have tried harder. I should have tried harder... it was a difficult period for me too. I had problems of my own."

"What type of problems?"

"There was someone... how can I put this? It was an extremely challenging time. I was in a terribly difficult situation with someone."

"Someone like a boyfriend?"

"Yes... I know... I know nothing excuses the fact that I did not try to fight for my relationship with your mother or your father. But please understand that I could not see straight at the time."

"Is it because your heart was broken by some bloke?"

"Yes it was."

I look at Auntie Mei with her perfect skin that's never spotty and her natural, kick-ass curves that Chinese women never get unless they get a boob job. How could any guy want to break her heart?

"I'm sorry Xing Li. I'm sorry I did not try harder with your parents."

"It's...it's okay. I guess you had stuff going on."

Auntie Mei's voice goes all sad and tiny.

"I'm really sorry Xing Li."

I want to link arms with Auntie Mei or give her a hug or something. I wish I could tell her that it's really, really okay and I do like her lots. Not as much as Jay or Lai Ker but still enough to be good friends one day. But she's standing super straight and looks all prim and proper again. I'm scared if I hug her, I might crease her dress. So instead, I ask her if she needs help with her shopping and we chat about normal stuff all the way to the taxi stand.

Chapter 22
Roses Are Red, Grandma Is Blue

Grandma is acting a bit weird. Like we have to be at the airport in three hours and instead of her usual morning Chinese tea, she asks the con-see-age person for black coffee.

"Two and half sugars, if more I throw in toilet."

She does not read the newspapers from cover to cover but flicks through the pages quickly. Uncle Ho is staring at her too. He puts his hands on his ears, but she still carries on. The front page story is about an Indonesian maid who jumped from a flat on the twentieth floor. This was after her employers made her sleep on the balcony and use a rusty, dripping tap to wash herself. Grandma turns the newspaper upside down, then sideways, then upside down again. Lai Ker looks up from his lads' magazine and whispers, "Looks like old age is finally getting its grip on the old bird."

Grandma paces up and down our hotel room with a stressed look like she's about to do a Maths exam. She stops and points at me with her yellowing fingernails.

"Xing Li need haircut. We go now."

Auntie Mei ALREADY brought me to her super nice childhood hairdresser Graca Wong yesterday.

"Grandma, I had a haircut already. Auntie Mei brought me… "

"Your haircut look like monkey head. You need proper

139

haircut, proper lady will make better."

"But we need to go to the airport in a few hours."

"WE GO NOW."

I do not want to start World War Three over a haircut and quickly put my new red flip flops on. Lai Ker looks at me and uses his fingers as if he is letting an imaginary gun shoot his head.

Grandma pushes me to the front of the taxi queue. Being a senior citizen in Singapore gives you certain rights such as queue jumping.

"We go 115 Bukit Timah Road. Hairdresser called Lin, she give proper haircut. Then all friends West Hill be jealous. They wish they got such nice Grandma."

She gives me a smile that lasts for a quarter of a second and sits back on her seat. I can't see my only friend Jay turning green over my multiple haircuts. Judging from his messy dreadlocks, he probably wouldn't notice a thing. Thinking of Jay makes me smile. I kinda miss his long speeches about Viv-Audi. I wonder whether he's having a good time in Jamaica with his family.

The taxi driver whistles as he drives down the motorway.

"Stop your whistle, whistle. People paying money for you drive, not make musical."

The taxi driver glances at Grandma in his rear view mirror and stops whistling. We pass worn out 1960s-style houses with colourful shutters and outdoor coffee shops with loud blaring TVs and even louder blaring old men with Guinness. Grandma starts to twist the handle on her leather bag. The taxi stops outside a ghetto-type hair salon. A pink neon sign says, "Lin's Hair Place".

"Auntie, that will be $20.80."

Grandma has twisted the handle on her bag until it looks like a curly telephone coil. She looks at the coil as if she were a brain surgeon inspecting a difficult operation and slowly starts to unwind it. The taxi driver SIGHS. With the handle loose, Grandma unzips her bag and takes out her crocodile skin purse. She takes AGES to count her wad of fifty-dollar notes and then stuffs them back into her purse.

"We go to 108 Bukit Basah Drive."

"Now Madam?"

"No, tomorrow - OF COURSE now. I pay good money."

Grandma waves some fifty-dollar notes in the air. The taxi driver puts his foot on the accelerator and the car lunges forward. I bump my head on the seat in front.

OW!

We arrive in front of a cream bungalow with blue worn out shutters. Loads of rose bushes grow wildly around the tiny front garden. They're not like Grandma's tidy bushes; they're more like weeds than grass. Grandma gives the taxi driver fifty dollars for his time.

"Xing Li, Grandma visit sick friend for five minutes."

Grandma rushes up the garden path as if an imaginary five-minute clock timer has started in her head. The brass door knocker is shaped like a frog and Grandma cleans it with a wet wipe. She lets her hand hover over the door knob for a few seconds before knocking it.

KNOCK KNOCK KNOCK

A young Malay nurse dressed in a pale, green uniform opens the door.

"Can I help you?"

"I here see Mr Tan."

"I'm really sorry Madam, Mr Tan is asleep, and he gave me strict instructions that he's not to be disturbed."

"Ah, he sleep. Okay, you wake him up."

"Madam, I'm really sorry but the captain needs his rest. He hasn't been well recently you see."

"I understand he sleep, but I am very, very old friend. I leaving Singapore TODAY. Best see him now."

"Madam, how about you come back in a few hours?"

"Aiyah! Few hours plane already leave. You wake captain now. I leaving TODAY. Captain will be angry he missed me. If you want sack you let him sleep. I KNOW he SACK you

141

if he find out."

"Okay, I will go and check. You wait here. No promises, but I will check with Mr Tan."

The nurse shuts the door a little louder than needed. I lean against the white walls of the bungalow; being in the heat is s-o-o-o-o-o tiring. Grandma mops her brow with tissue paper and starts fanning herself with a two for one pizza flyer from her handbag. The hot air is so thick with the smell of lavender and roses. We stand for what feels like hours with a silence I'm used to. Grandma starts to twist the handle on her bag into a telephone coil again. The door opens and it feels as if the door is an opening to a giant fridge.

"Madam, Mr Tan will see you."

We follow the nurse down the spacious corridor with old photographs of British army generals. Grandma's breathing starts to quicken with every step. She looks like a nervous, little girl in her tiny, green, silk jumpsuit. Auntie Mei told me Grandpa had lots of important friends from Singapore. They would visit him at home and swap stories late into the night over well expensive whisky. She'd secretly sit on the stairs and listen as they chatted about war scars and beautiful women. Grandma disliked Grandpa's friends; she found their stories crude. That was probably why Grandma said we were only staying for five minutes.

An old, bald, Chinese guy with a coffee brown dressing gown that matches the colour of his eyes gets out of his bed when we enter the room. His tanned skin looks kind of pale like the colour of peeled apples when they go brown. I can see the veins through his skin. He reaches for his oval glasses with trembling hands.

"Rose ah!"

Grandma is smiling - like a real one with teeth and all. She gestures for him to sit down but he insists on standing until she pulls up a chair. He starts to cough and Grandma thwacks him on the back.

"So, the bird has finally flown home?"

"Never fly home. I go today."

"Today? So quick? If you stay longer I'll get my dancing shoes out just for you."

He smiles weakly and starts to cough again. Grandma gives him another two sharp thwacks.

"Don't speak stupid. What dancing? You know I bad dancer."

I imagine Grandma doing the tango with Mr Tan and her thwacking him for stepping on her toes.

"It is so good to see you. It has been too long."

"Yes long time. Time passed quick."

"I didn't know if you were ever going to come. I was hoping you would."

"I always know I make it. Keep promise good thing."

Mr Tan looks at me and smiles. He's missing the bottom half of his teeth.

"So, who is this young lady you have brought to visit me?"

"She my…. she my granddaughter."

"Well she's quite a looker. Her grandmother must be beautiful."

"You talk too much rubbish."

"Well, apparently I eat too much rubbish too. That's what the doctors say anyway."

Mr Tan takes s-l-o-w, shallow breaths. He looks like he is in pain but doesn't wanna show it.

"Rose, I've got… "

He looks down and I notice that his oversized dressing gown makes him look like a child trying on his father's dressing gown for the first time.

"Rose… I've, I've got stomach cancer."

Grandma nods and starts to grip the sheets on the bed. Her voice goes all low and soft. I've never heard Grandma whisper before.

"I know. Your sister call me few weeks ago. But you good fighter. We know you get better soon. Of course you get better soon."

Mr Tan and Grandma stay silent.

I can hear the swirling sound of the old ceiling fan. It swirls round and round and round. It's Friday afternoon, the happiest time of the week. I hear the laughter of excited school kids as they run past Mr Tan's window. Grandma gets up from her chair so quickly the chair almost topples over. Mr Tan tries to catch her eye but she won't look at him. She looks to the floor.

"Well, my granddaughter need get haircut and you need sleep. So, I go now."

"So soon?"

"Yes have to move if not too late for her."

The captain looks sad and puts his hand out. Grandma first holds his hand gently, as if it is made of glass. Then she grips it so firmly I can see the veins pop up on her hands.

"Goodbye Rose. You take good, good care okay?"

"Goodbye."

Grandma hurries me along the corridor as if spending another minute in Mr Tan's house is going to suffocate her. As Grandma is about to step out of the front door, she turns back and looks at the nurse.

"How long he have?"

"About two months Madam. Four months if he is lucky."

Grandma closes her eyes shut for a few seconds and then nods. Without a word, she walks quickly into the street and hails a taxi by sticking her umbrella out. As the taxi drives down the tree-lined street, Grandma leans her head against the window. Her fast breath makes small patches of steam on the glass. I see a tear roll down the side of her face. The tear stays halfway down her powdered cheek and she does not wipe it away. I reach over and hold her hand - it feels hot to the touch. She does not let go of my hand for the entire journey to the airport.

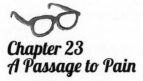

Chapter 23
A Passage to Pain

We arrive at the airport and Grandma suddenly lets go of my hand. Then she demands that I don't tell anyone about her meeting 'cos she says it's private. I want to tell everyone, especially Jay and Lai Ker. But then I remember when I was eight years old and my mate Shevon told me her parents were getting divorced. Shevon wanted me to keep it as a secret; she said I couldn't tell a soul. I asked Mama if it was okay if I only told people who were nice. Mama said it wasn't okay 'cos "Other people's secrets are never for you to tell. If you tell people's secrets, it will hurt them and it's never good to hurt anyone."

Grandma's spending ages in the toilet in the plane. Auntie Mei says she has a tummy upset, but when Grandma passes me, I see her eyes are all puffy. Grandma doesn't eat anything for the whole journey home. She only has some Chinese tea. When we are about to land, I turn around and see her curled up against the window, staring at it as if she is watching a film.

It's strange being back in London. No more sunshine and yummy food and people that all look like me. Instead, there are clouds and school and yucky homework. First days back at school after the holidays should be banned.

BUT there's Jay!

Jay's grown taller, he's now five foot five inches tall - half an inch taller than me and he's got more freckles on his nose. He taps me on the shoulder and my heart flips round and round.

"Alright Xing?"

He gives me a half hug, one arm on my shoulder and one arm to the side.

"Alright Jay! How was Jamaica? Did you go to the beach in the end?"

"I didn't touch the beach. Burning to a crisp just ain't for me. I spent most of my time in the library listening to my iPod. How was Singapore?"

"Was pretty cool. Got to party lots. I also got to meet my grandpa."

"That's crazy!"

I tell him everything that Grandpa told me. It's weird thinking that a small part of me has ancestors in Japan. I'm gonna read up about Japanese culture - maybe I need to watch more Quentin Tarantino films or something. I dunno. It's crazy but, at the same time, it don't change the fact that I still have to go to West Hill and I still have to stay with Grandma and I still have to deal with Shils.

"How about you Jay? Did you meet your grandparents in the end?"

"Nope, but we passed by their house. Zoomed round the block a couple of times. Didn't want to go in or nothing. My dad just wanted me to see the house he grew up in."

"What was it like?"

"It was all wooden and was painted bright blue like my glasses. They had a small yard and this large brown dog. I got to spy on them a bit."

"Wow! What do they look like?"

"Well didn't see my grandma, but my granddad was in the garden sleeping. Couldn't see him proper 'cos my dad was driving well fast. But he looked alright - just a normal, old Jamaican guy with black rimmed glasses and white hair. Think he was gardening - must have fallen asleep or something."

"Well at least you got to see him I guess. Maybe one day you'll get to meet proper. But only if you want to I guess."

"Yeah maybe. But it was weird… "

"Like how?

"Well, he just looked so… so normal."

"What do you mean?"

"Like I don't know like… maybe 'cos of all the crap he gave my mum and dad I thought he'd look evil or something. But he looked normal. Just an old man having a nap."

"Did your dad say anything?"

"No he didn't. But I could see he was upset. He starts shaking his leg real hard when he's upset."

"How about your mum?"

"Yeah I could see my mum was a bit teary. She put her hand on his shaking knee and asked if he was sure and he just nodded and put his foot on the accelerator."

Jay suddenly looks at my hair and I start to feel well self-conscious.

"By the way, nice haircut Xing."

"Thanks, my auntie got a cool lady to chop it off."

We grin at each other and then Evil Barbie and her wicked witches arrive.

"Sing-Song, did your grandma cut your hair for you? It looks like she took a bowl and cut around the edges. I heard that is what Chinese people do."

Jay stands between Shils and me. He hisses, "Don't listen to her. She don't know nothing."

"What's wrong Sing-Song, did the cat get your tongue? Or should I say dog? Oh no, of course not, I forgot your mother cooked the dog for your tea."

Shils gives me a fake smile. She looks like a demonic Miss World contestant.

"Oh, but your mother's not here any more is she? You poor

little chinky bitch, you must miss HER cooking so much."

Shils gives a big SIGH and takes a step closer. I see Jay gripping his fists tightly.

"How sad Sing-Song. I bet your mother is looking down wishing she never had such a loser - bet she's glad she's gone."

Mama is gone.

Tears start to sting my eyes and I can barely make out Jay's shape in front of me.

"She's never coming back and I bet she's glad she doesn't have to deal with such an ugly bitch of a daughter. "

Mama is gone.

Jay takes out his headphones ready to put them over my ears but I swipe them away so rough his mouth opens. I suddenly feel really sick like someone lit some fireworks and they exploded in my heart.

MAMA IS GONE AND I AM STUCK HERE. I'M BACK AND I'M STUCK. MAMA IS GONE.

I HATE IT. I HATE IT. I HATE IT.

I push past Shils and start to run really fast, gulping down tears with each step. The world looks blurry and I can't see clearly, but I continue to run.

I'm running and running and running.

My heart hurts so much but I don't care, I just keep running. My legs are carrying me past the perfect tennis courts with perfect students, the giant grey statues, the tall trees naked and bare and sad like me. I run out of the gates that Mama once entered, the gates that had been her prison just as they are to me. I run past buses, cyclists, single mothers, dogs and screaming babies. I run past restaurants, dustmen, pizza delivery scooters, stray cats and a blind guy with a Labrador. The cold air hurts my lungs and I gasp and gasp for breath until I collapse in an alleyway behind a bakery. My tears fall down, slowly at first - then loads and loads of tears and heavy breathing. A pain pounds in my heart and the sadness has exploded into sobs. For the first time ever I let my tears fall lots and don't hold back. I'm not scared of drowning in my tears no more.

I whisper over and over again,

"Mama is gone."

"Mama is gone."

"Mama is gone."

"Mama is gone."

I feel a knot squeezing tightly in my stomach as memories of Mama flash through my head.

Mama singing to me when I had nightmares, Mama picking me up when I fell into the drain, Mama helping me make plasticine animals, Mama wiping my forehead when I was sick, Mama smiling on her birthday.

Then, I think of future memories that should have been. Memories that I will never have. Things that should have happened but didn't.

Mama explaining to me about my first period, Mama looking proud at my graduation, Mama smiling at my wedding, Mama crying and holding my first child.

I don't know how long I've been lying in the alleyway. I've just been crying and crying. But Jay's found me. He doesn't make a fuss or say anything. The tears keep rushing down my cheek and my neck. Jay squats next to me and takes out his piano handkerchief. I blow loudly on the handkerchief and Jay gently puts his hand on my shoulder and closes his eyes. His hands feel clammy and he starts to whisper under his breath. I can barely hear what he's saying. There's like a rhythm to his whispers. He is praying. He's desperate for his God to heal me. The prayers are repeated over and over again, his eyes are kept firmly closed. He is frowning, deep in concentration. I close my eyes and focus on his words. He keeps repeating his prayers over and over again. His hand grips me a little more tightly. With each rhythm-like chant I feel the knot in my stomach slowly being unwound. We stay in the alleyway until it becomes dark, Jay with his prayers and me with my pain.

Chapter 24
The Music of the Fight

Jay insists I follow him home for dinner.

"My mum is a pretty good cook, you need some Chinese-Jamaican food in your belly, then you'll feel lots better."

I tell Grandma I'm working on a Science project and need the "advice" of Jay's father. Grandma thinks Jay's father is a physicist who lectures at Imperial College and his mother is a Chinese translator for the British Ambassador. Lai Ker helped me think up those jobs. If Grandma knew Jay's parents were musicians she would ban me from having Jay as my friend. Musicians, artists and fashion designers are all on Grandma's "list" of people she thinks will be a bad influence on me.

"Creative people no good. You feel sorry for them and be their friend. Then next you know, you on drugs and live on street with one leg begging for money."

When I brought up Auntie Mei's job, Grandma sighed and shook her head.

"Auntie Mei lost cause. You follow Grandma and have good chance reach far. Not like Auntie Mei, she give in peer pressure too much. Too much magazines brainwash her. They tell you sell house and follow dream. You chase and chase dream then next you know you on dole and run out money and no-one want employ you because big fat gap in CV. Auntie Mei too weak, listen to *Vogue* writers too much."

Jay's house is in a mess or as he says, "a well structured mess". Worn out plastic bags and mismatched shoes line the entrance hallway. In the kitchen, stacks of unwashed dishes, empty plastic cartons and pieces of paper with musical notes cover the table. His mother, a petite, fair-skinned Chinese beauty with green glasses looks well embarrassed by the mess. Jay told me there would be a mad cleaning frenzy the day before any visitors. Guests would see a clean, sparkling, house, not the daily mess he's used to.

"Jay, you never told me your friend was coming today."

"I DID Mum, remember I told you yesterday when we were watching the docu on TV *Mozart and His Women*?"

Jay's dad laughs as he walks into the kitchen. At six foot four inches with a bald head and a massive smile he reminds me of a retired basketball player for the NBA. When it comes to the tall genes, Jay has definitely taken after his mum.

"I guess old age is catching up with me lovely wife."

He grabs Jay's mother into a bear hug and she squeals. Jay rolls his eyes and shakes his head in disgust.

"Get a room man! We have company."

His mum smiles at me and struggles out of her husband's grip.

"It is lovely to meet you Xing Li, we've heard so much about you. You must excuse my husband. He has the worst manners."

Jay's father opens his mouth in mock surprise, smiles and gives me a welcome hug. I go red, Chinese kids ain't huggers. Jay's dad takes out several black bin liners from a kitchen cupboard. With the help of his wife the mess from the kitchen disappears within minutes. They hum the same tune and remind me of the scene in *Snow White and the Seven Dwarves* when Snow White cleans up the cottage. Two bin liners are filled to the brim and Jay's dad gives me a satisfied grin.

"Easy come, easy go - just remind me wife not to throw these bags out by mistake."

"Yeah Dad, remember the time you threw out my Geography homework by mistake? I don't want a repeat of that fiasco."

Jay's mum joins in with the family joke.

"Yes, don't throw out the hit musical I wrote last week."

"You mean the one that makes us thousands?"

"No, the one that makes us ten quid."

The family laugh.

Jay's mum starts to dish out the mouth watering curried goat that has been stewing on a low heat for over three hours. She smiles at me and gives me the largest portion and then pours me some Coke into a chipped mug with penguins on it.

"Jay tells me you like computer games. Is designing computer games something you want to get into?"

I almost choke on my food, talking at the dinner table is not something I'm used to any more.

"I don't know, maybe. But my grandma wants me to be a doctor, lawyer or banker. She can be quite scary, so maybe I'll stick to that. Not worth fighting for."

Jay's father bites into a humungous spoonful of rice and curry and shakes his head. He only has a tiny, tiny bit of a Jamaican accent and is kind of cool for an old person.

"You know Xing Li, sometimes there're fights worth fighting for."

"What do you mean?"

Jay's dad tells me how when he first got married they could only afford a small flat in a tiny village up north. They'd walk hand in hand down the street and people would do a double take. Seeing a tall black man with a tiny Chinese woman gave their neighbours enough gossip fodder for the year. Sometimes strangers would shout crude remarks such as, "Fancy a bit of Chinese?" or "Hey, there's Martin Luther King with Suzy Wong". For the most part he would ignore the taunts, but Jay's dad found it super hard to walk away when the insults were at his wife.

When Jay was born, the staring and finger pointing grew

152

to greater heights. Locals would look at his lanky, black father, do a double take at his petite Chinese mother, and then stop and stare at the Chinese-black child. Some would even take pictures of Jay as if he were an animal in a zoo. When Jay's dad worked as a classical musician in London, it got bad again.

"You know I was the only black musician in my school and later on when I met me lovely wife I was the only black musician in the orchestra for the musical *South Pacific*."

Jay's mum's eyes start to mist up and she takes her glasses off to wipe them. She speaks with a British accent that becomes Chinese every so often.

"He had to ignore the jealous whispers that he was the 'token black man' so the company could tick the boxes for equal opportunities. For my husband, music was something he would never give up, even if the whole musical world were against him. It was his greatest love, it still is."

"Well it was me greatest love until I met a feisty, Chinese girl who left China with the equivalent of ten quid in her pocket to find fame and fortune in London."

Jay's mum laughs and squeezes her husband's arm.

"It was love at first fight."

"Yes, sometimes there are fights worth fighting for."

Jay don't remember any of this, but he told me his parents told him the stories to remind him of where he came from. After dinner, Jay makes his parents play me some music.

"Just show her man, show her what you can do."

His mum looks all red and squirmy. "I'm sure Xing Li doesn't want two old fuddy duddies playing Beethoven for her."

"It's alright Mum. Xing Li quite digs classical stuff now. Not the hardcore stuff but she don't mind most of it."

"Its true Mrs Anderson, I don't mind."

"Okay, what's your favourite song?"

"The animal one by St Sands."

Jay's dad smiles. "Ah-ha that is one of me favourites too."

Jay's mum takes out her violin, it's got shiny strings but the body looks like it's hundreds of years old. His dad opens a pretty, wooden piano, it's so polished and clean like Grandma's kitchen. They smile at me and then they screw their eyes tightly shut and smile the secret kind of smile when you are just smiling to yourself and no-one else.

Jay stands all straight like a soldier who's gonna announce something important.

"Ladies and gentleman the Andersons would like to present to their special guest Xing Li Wu... 'The animal one by St Sands'."

I look at Jay with his secret smile and his dreadlocks that look like little swinging worms and decide that he is my favourite person in the whole world.

Chapter 25
Law and Disorder

Grandma's driver has come to pick me up. He says we have to leave NOW 'cos there's been an incident at home. It's well awkward 'cos he parked the white Mercedes right in the middle of the car park. People from Jay's estate are beeping their cars when we pass and one fat bloke with a ciggie hanging from his mouth winds down his window.

"NICE WHEELS CHAIRMAN MAO."

The driver ignores him and starts driving super fast. He looks really stressed 'cos Grandma put an alarm clock in his car. We get home in fourteen minutes and as he is parking the car the alarm goes off and makes him swerve funny.

There's a police car parked right outside our house, you don't see many in this area. I run into the house and two policemen are talking to Grandma and Auntie Mei. One is a lady policeman.

"Thank you Mrs Wu for your assistance. We're really sorry that you had to hear it from us. All the best now."

The lady policeman looks like the blonde lady from the film *Psycho*. She gives me a little smile as she leaves.

"Grandma, what's going on? Is Uncle Ho okay?"

Grandma is red and shaky. She ignores me and rushes up the stairs.

"Auntie Mei, what is going on? Where's Uncle Ho?"

"Uncle Ho is fine, he's sleeping upstairs."

"What's going on?"

"It's Lai Xing… "

LAI KER?!

I push past Auntie Mei and run upstairs two steps at a time. Grandma is in Lai Ker's room; she's digging through his drawers and throwing his clothes on the floor. She keeps looking and digging and throwing. She finds a book, it has *Chinks Have Mouths* on it in Tipp-Ex, and she takes it and throws it hard across the room.

CRASH

It hits a lamp and it falls to the floor but Grandma doesn't care; she is opening all Lai Ker's cupboards. She's taking his shoes out and throwing them on the floor, she's ripping his bed sheets from the bed.

"Grandma what's going on? Where is Lai Ker? WHAT'S going on?"

"Your brother not welcome here any more."

"WHY? What's going on?"

"He choose… "

Grandma stops short like she is almost going to cry, then she looks really furious.

"He choose break law. He not coming back."

Grandma takes Lai Ker's computer games and I try to pull on her arms to stop her.

"Grandma PLEASE STOP."

She pushes me away and throws them out of the window. Then she throws his trainers and his rugby ball and his favourite Nike T-shirt that Mama spent lots of money on. I'm scared, my eyes are getting all teary. Where is Lai Ker? Grandma then looks at me and speaks really quiet.

"Your brother never coming back. He no longer a Wu."

She walks out of the room and slams the door so hard Lai Ker's picture of Mama falls to the floor. I pick up Mama's picture and run down to Auntie Mei. Mama's picture is broken and I cut myself and it hurts and I'm dizzy and I can't see anything. Mama's gone and now Lai Ker's gone. For the first time ever, Auntie Mei gives me a proper hug. Then she sits me on the sofa and puts a plaster on my finger.

"Xing Li, your brother is in hospital but he is okay."

"WHAT?!"

"Don't worry, he is fine. He will be fine. He just needed a couple of stitches for his eyebrow and his arm... "

"What happened to his arm?"

"It's broken."

"HOW?!"

"He got beaten up."

"What like by a gang?"

"No, it was more a fight. He got into a fight with some guys and his friend Jimmy Tang."

I KNEW IT! I've never trusted Jimmy Tang. When I was eight he nicked my orange squash and blamed it on the blind kid in our school.

"What was the fight about? Bet it was Jimmy Tang's fault."

"Well, it could well have been Jimmy Tang's influence. But all I know is your brother thought it would be a wonderful idea to spray the letters *CHM* at the back of his classmate's father's restaurant. It's a very expensive restaurant in Mayfair."

"What happened then?"

"Unfortunately, his classmate caught him and things got nasty."

"So he got beaten up?"

"From the sound of it, everyone got beaten up."

"So is Lai Ker in big trouble? Is he going to prison now?"

"Well, because of Lai Xing's age they've decided to just give him a warning so to speak. He will be fine but if he gets into trouble again, they won't be so lenient."

"I want to see Lai Ker. Where is he?"

"I'm afraid you will have to ask Grandma. But I have to warn you she's terribly annoyed. So perhaps it would be wise to speak to her tomorrow."

I go outside and put all of Lai Ker's computer games in

the emergency green plastic bag that Mama put in my school bag. She used to say that it is always good to have a spare, clean, strong plastic bag handy just in case you need it. Most of Lai Ker's games are okay but Death Star 5 has been smashed beyond repair. Lai Ker will be well upset. I'm going to hide the games underneath the newspapers in the tortoise box in the shed. Hope he doesn't eat them.

The tortoise is chomping on a pink rose I took from Grandma's garden. I stroke the tortoise shell, just like how I used to stroke Meow Meow. It's not the same but it is still quite nice like with each stroke my heart beat gets slower. The tortoise closes his eyes and pops his head back into his shell. The tortoise looks all snug and warm. I wonder if Lai Ker is all snug and warm. I hope he's okay.

I call Jimmy Tang like ten times before he picks up.

"What's... upppp?"

"This is Xing Li."

"Who?"

"Lai Xing's younger sister."

"Ah the Lai-ster's lil sis."

"Yeah, where is my brother?"

"I ain't telling you nothing. Stay out of this, it's your bro's business not yours."

"It's not just his business, it's YOUR business too. You told him to graffiti his classmate's shop. I bet it was your idea, not his."

"Look that white git deserved to be punished. He was the one that got his minion to dob your brother in to Mr Haywood about our business deals. He also spread the rumour round that chinks have small dicks. I wish I'd roughed him up more."

"I want to know where Lai Ker is."

"I ain't telling you nothing LITTLE GIRL."

I'm SO mad at Jimmy Tang, WHO DOES HE THINK HE IS? I decide to speak all psycho calm like Grandma does when she is about to shout.

"You're going to tell me where my brother is."

"And why would I do that?"

"'cos if you don't, I'm… I'm… I'm going to call the police and tell them you're… you're selling illegal substances."

I'm not sure if he is but I can hear Jimmy Tang starting to breathe really hard on the phone.

GOTCHA.

"He's at Kensington & Chelsea hospital, Ward C. Don't you bloody contact me again."

I slam the phone down and write the details down but my hands are so shaky I can't write. Then I smile. That was for the blind kid that Jimmy Tang accused of stealing my squash.

"Why you smile? You brother in hospital because he break law is so ha-ha?"

My legs are starting to tremble, but I move them apart to balance my shaky body.

"I want to go and see Lai Ker in the hospital."

"You want to go to hospital? You think you help?"

"Yes. I want to go."

Grandma stares up at me, and folds her skinny arms across her flat chest. Lai Ker needs me, yes he was stupid but he is hurt and Mama's not here so I have to go. We stare at each other for a good ten seconds. It's like we're playing Street Fighter and Grandma is thinking how to do a triple combo with a finisher on me.

"So Xing Li, you want go hospital? Go ahead."

That was easy!

She sweeps her hand towards the door like a tour guide showing Big Ben to a group of tourists.

"O-K-A-Y then. Let me pack a few things first."

Grandma sits all mute on my bed and watches me as I pack an old satchel with my mobile and items that Lai Ker may need. A clean flannel, a packet of chocolates and the limited edition comic book I recently nicked when he was in the shower. She doesn't move and I try my best not to look in her direction.

"Okay Grandma, I'm going to get the driver to take me

now."

"Where?"

"Where… where… Lai Ker is."

I'm not falling for it; I'm never going to tell her where he is. Grandma gives me her best poo under her nose look.

"SURE, S-U-R-E! You go Kensington Chelsea hospital. You ask reception for Lai Xing Wu. Then reception say he not here. You ask her 'He where?' She don't know. You say BYE-BYE you come home here."

"You're lying."

"Of course, I lying… I lying because I 'bad' person. I so 'bad' I move your brother out of Kensington Chelsea ghetto hospital to nice private hospital. I make sure he get best doctor for his broken arm, I pay all fees up front. You brother think he so clever, *Chinks Have Mouths* this *Chinks Have Mouths* that. Let see how far *Chinks Have Mouths* get him after money in hospital run out - he on own without family?"

"I think Lai Ker's learnt his lesson. I think it's okay for him to come home now."

"No, he not coming home. He want destroy his life and end go prison he end up do it himself."

"I want to see him. I want to make sure he's okay."

"NO."

I think of when Lai Ker shared with me the last chicken wing at Mama's funeral lunch. He told me that now Mama was gone we had to stick together no matter what. We made a promise that he would have my back and I would have his. Then we spat on our hands and shook on it.

"Please Grandma, I beg you. I need to help Lai Ker."

"NO, your stupid brother never coming back. I give everything and he throw it all away. As long he carry on like this and I alive he NEVER coming back."

Grandma has won and she knows it. She walks out of my room as if she has just won The Battle of Trial-vulgar.

Chapter 26
The Good, the Bad and the Exam

Our mid-term Maths exam is a killer. In the silent exam room, you can hear children groaning and sighing. The West Hillites are tapping super fast on their calculators as the clock ticks away. I can't concentrate, I keep thinking about Lai Ker. I hope he's okay and he's safe and doesn't become homeless. I've never seen a homeless Chinese person, but there's always a first. Please Lai Ker, try and survive until I find you.

I read the first question:

Tom invited 20 more boys than girls to a party. 3/4 of the boys and 2/3 of the girls came. 19 people didn't come. How many people did he invite?

Apart from it being strange that Tom invites more boys than girls, the question seems okay. Mrs Wing drilled fractions into me until I got a headache. The next question is a bit trickier.

Of the visitors at the zoo, 40% are children, 3/4 of the adults are women.

a) What is the ratio of children: men: women.

b) The second day, the amount of children increased by 20%, the amount of adults remains the same but women make up 3/5 of the adults. If there are 336 more children than women, how many visitors were there on the second day?

My mind goes blank after I read "increased by 20%".

Percentages are my arch-chillis heel. I shift uncomfortably in my seat and pray to Jay's God that the answer will appear in my head. Grandma expects me to get at least ninety percent in this Maths test. I look around the room, everyone is scribbling away. Rich, white people are the same as all Chinese people 'cos they also want their children to be good at Maths. That way their children can count all the money they will be earning in the future. The future net worth of my classmates probably comes into the billions.

Shils is sitting diagonally in front of me. Her glossy hair has been newly highlighted with honey tones to suit her sweet nature. Before our exam, she told me with a smirk to, "break a leg, arm and head". Shils' pink, diamante pen is lying neatly next to the list of Maths questions. She is the only student not writing.

Wait a second!

Why is she staring like crazy at her tanned right thigh? Shils' thigh looks like it has a large scripted tattoo on it, the marks look like those tiny Jewish symbols that Hollywood actresses like to plaster on their bodies. She's copying the tiny symbols onto a blank piece of A4 paper. She does this swiftly, while keeping an eye out for our watchful Maths teacher Mr Moyles. Sometimes she flashes him a smile with her white teeth and he looks down shyly. All our male teachers are secretly in lust with Shils.

I try to concentrate on answering the Maths questions about Tom and other strange children who spend their lives working out fractions and percentages. It's difficult to keep my eyes off Shils. At one point she flicks her long, honeyed locks and glances behind her.

OH NO!

She's caught me staring at her thigh! A look of horror creeps across her face before she gives me a look like that hungry shark in *Jaws*. Using her right hand she quickly gestures her finger slitting her throat. I look back at my Maths paper. She's seen me, but I've also seen her.

I can't sleep.

I keep replaying the Maths exam in my head over and over again.

Should I tell someone?

Who?

Jay?

No I can't tell Jay, I don't want him to be hurt by Shils. But then I've got no-one to tell. I can't tell a grown up like Auntie Mei 'cos she won't understand. Then Lai Ker is not here any more. Man, he would know what to do. When I was little and Uncle Ho pulled the head off my Barbie, Lai Ker fixed it with paper clips and a rubber band. When I had a tummy ache from eating some out of date ice cream, Lai Ker nicked a lump of coal from the fake fireplace in a department store. He cut a tiny piece of the coal and gave it to me with water. It did the trick. So, it really sucks that I had to be the one to see Shils and her secret without sharing it with Lai Ker. This is just the kind of hard problem he'd know how to fix.

I close my eyes.

ZZZZZZZZZZZZ

HELP HELP HELP

I'm screaming and I'm sweaty and my heart is beating super fast. I had a nightmare of Shils slitting my throat mixed with dreams of zoos with forty percent children, sixty percent psychotic parents.

"Xing Li dear, are you alright?"

Auntie Mei sits next to me and starts stroking my head in the dark. It's nice, if I close my eyes it feels as if Mama is right next to me.

"I'm okay… I had a nightmare."

"Why? Is something bothering you?"

I don't want to tell Auntie Mei. Mostly 'cos I'm twelve and nine months now and I'm old enough to deal with my own problems. But also 'cos if I tell anyone and Shils finds out she will probably hurt me more.

"It's nothing, it's just… I don't know… "

"Why don't you try me? Maybe I can help?"

"Well… it's like… say you… "

"Carry on… "

"Well, like, say you knew someone had done something wrong, but it's really not for you to say, should you get involved or not?"

"Well, it really depends, has that person done something terrible?"

"I suppose."

"Will getting involved harm you?"

"Maybe."

Auntie Mei sighs the longest sigh in the world.

"If you are going to get hurt, I would recommend walking away."

"You mean not doing anything?"

"No, walking away from a hurtful situation actually means you are doing something. In life, there are circumstances where staying means that you will be hurt more. I've learnt to walk away."

"Why, what do you mean? When did you walk away from something bad?"

Auntie Mei keeps quiet, she's sitting so near I can hear her heart.

Thump Thump Thump Thump

"Auntie Mei, are you talking about that guy that broke your heart?"

Auntie Mei goes silent; I can hear her heart beating faster like she is in the gym or something.

"Yes, I chose to walk away."

"But how did you meet the bloke?"

I squint my eyes and can just about see her face in the dark, I think her eyes are closed but I'm not sure.

"We met when he was studying a Business degree and I was in my final year of drama school."

"Then what?"

"Well, every day we'd glance at each other secretly and not say a word. You see, I thought he was a pretentious Chinese guy who was aiming for a big city job. Whereas he thought I was a stuck-up acting student that dreamt of making films that only elite, creative minds would understand."

"But you were wrong about each other, right?"

"No, no, we were both completely right about each other. Yet, for some reason there was a strange attraction between us."

"When did you first talk to each other?"

"Well, he made the first move during a particularly crowded, wet rush hour. You see, just like most of the people in the carriage I was rain soaked and desperate to get home. But, there he was, standing right in front of me - our noses almost touching."

"What happened next?"

"He stared directly at me as if to challenge me to look down. I stared back. Then he stared back harder. I could feel the warmth from his body. It was terribly exciting… my eyes started to sting and become watery but I refused to look down. He became a blur, but I could hear him laughing."

"Then what?"

"Well, it annoyed me so I stepped down hard on his foot with my stiletto. The shock on his face made me giggle and he started to smile. Eventually, we were hysterical."

"People must have thought you were both nuts."

"Yes, I'm sure they did, but we didn't care. We were young."

"How long were you together?"

"I was with him for five years."

"Wow, you must have really loved him."

"I did, I loved too much."

"Then what was the problem?"

"The problem was we argued almost every day since the day we met."

"What about?"

"Most were silly bickers, but every week or so we would have full-blown tirades. This was when things became ugly and his tongue would slice through me like a jagged knife. You know Xing Li; the tongue is like the rudder of a ship. It's such a small part of the body, yet it controls everything that comes out. You can really destroy someone with your words. The poison can linger long after they have been released."

I think of Shils, every day her words echo in my head.

Stupid chinky bitch.

"Yes, we argued so much. Most of the major arguments we had were about me giving up my career for him. His family wanted him to be with someone who would be a supportive wife, the sort of lady that only appears on the arm of millionaires at business functions. Not some modern, British actress. They wanted him to move back to Hong Kong and enjoy the lifestyle they had brought him up in. He loved me, but he agreed with them and was vicious to me about it. When he was annoyed, he would call me "useless", "stupid", "ugly", "a wh… ", anything to hurt me. I hated him for this. It would have been easier if he was always intolerable, but he wasn't. He would be loving and affectionate one day and an absolute snake the next. That was the internal struggle I had. I loved him but I hated him too. How could I be with someone who I hated so much? I really loved him but I knew it couldn't carry on. I had to leave him."

"Then how did you leave him?"

"One day, after a particularly bad argument he threw a vase at me. It almost hit me and he didn't apologise. Instead he left our flat because he said he needed to cool off. As I sat next to the shattered porcelain, I knew I had to leave. It could never be me and him against the world, it would always be me and him against each other."

"So you told him you were leaving?"

"No, while he was out, I wrote him a note explaining that I was leaving him and walked out of the door. I didn't even pack any of my possessions. I just picked up my handbag and left. It was the first time I had properly stood up to anyone. I could have stayed, but I chose to break my own heart."

"You just left like that?"

"Yes, I didn't even say goodbye. I just walked out of the door. You see - I chose to step away from a terrible situation because it was the right thing to do."

"It's been so long now Auntie Mei, don't you think you will ever find someone else to love?"

Auntie Mei doesn't even need a millisecond to think.

"No."

"Not ever?"

"Not ever, I never want to love someone like that again. Loving someone like that means that you end up doing foolish things like shutting everyone out and saying goodbye to your self esteem and… and… losing your sister."

Auntie Mei suddenly sits up and pats me on my shoulder.

"Anyway, what's past is past. It's getting late now; you need to go to school tomorrow. You should get some sleep."

Just as she's reaching the door, Auntie Mei turns around.

"Xing Li, I know that I told you that it's good to walk away sometimes. But I want you to know, I never walked away from your mother… not in my heart."

"Okay Auntie Mei."

I hear her padding down the hallway like a giant cat.

Then it's quiet again.

What am I supposed to do?!

Auntie Mei says I should walk away but then maybe Lai Ker would tell me to have *CHM* and dob Shils in. But if Shils finds out it's me, she'll probably kill me. But then Jay's always with me, so I think I'll be okay. I hate not knowing what to do.

What would Mama do?

She always fought for what was right. Like when Mrs Alsanea broke her leg, Mama told one of our neighbours off for nicking Mrs Alsanea's newspapers. Also, when someone didn't give an old woman a seat on a bus Mama kept clearing her throat and pointing at the special sign above their seat. I don't know, my head is starting to hurt and I have to go to school in four hours.

As I lie in the dark, I hear a voice in my head.

It's Jay's dad.

Sometimes there are fights worth fighting for.

Chapter 27
Flight or Fight

We're halfway through our music lesson and Shils has been summoned to Mr Lewis' office. The class carries on banging on their mini keyboards while Shils gets escorted out of the music room. I'm desperate to catch Jay's eye, but he's clanging away with his eyes closed. If this were Physics class, a hair falling on the floor would be enough to distract him. But in Music class, I can wave a red stop sign above my head and Jay won't even notice.

Shils doesn't return to our music lesson or to any of the other lessons. Rumours about her whereabouts are already swirling around. Her good mates think she's in hospital visiting her father 'cos he works long hours and drinks like a fish. They say, "It was only a matter of time before his heart or liver gave way." The Cliff Richard lookalike dated Shils for two months, but said he got tired of her lies. He's positive she's faking an illness and has gone out shopping in the sales. His theory was shot down 'cos Shils had been "summoned" to Mr Lewis' office rather than leaving herself. Jay's reaction is, "Don't know and don't care."

I know exactly where she is and why she's there.

As the class whisper and create more and more crazy stories, I keep my trap shut. When the final bell goes off, I grab my school bag and rush out of the door right into the

169

belly of Mr Lewis. He is a short man with dyed ginger hair that is greying at the roots. He stares at me with his tiny blue eyes; a grim look on his face.

"Xing Li Wu, I would like you to come with me to my office."

I sit in the messy headmaster's office - it's the first time I have been in any headmaster's office. I'm not like Lai Ker who's made himself at home in his headmaster's office. He kept to Mr Haywood's terms of visiting his office once a week. Lai Ker said the visits were unlike any detention he's had. Mr Haywood and Lai Ker spent their weekly meetings chatting lots. Sometimes they ate a special kind of posh pizza that's really flat and has got super thin crust without any of the cheese in it. Lai Ker told me Mr Haywood taught him how to play all the games from the olden days - chess, dominos and checkers. I wonder if Mr Haywood is worried about Lai Ker too. He must have noticed Lai Ker's gone, even if the rest of the world don't care.

I shake my leg and lean back in my chair, acting all cool and casual the way Lai Ker would.

Mr Lewis leans forward in his leather chair and puts his elbows on his gigantic wooden desk. He reminds me of a doctor on TV about to break bad news.

"Xing Li Wu, I would like to talk to you about your allegations against Shirley Teddingham."

"Yes, Mr Lewis."

"I have spoken to Shirley Teddingham and she has vehemently denied the allegations. She says you are a compulsive liar."

The blood rushes from my face and my leg isn't the only thing shaking now. I KNEW Shils would not give up without a fight. With a swish of her hair, she could turn black into white and night into day. I have been so stupid to think I could win against the queen of West Hill. I wanted to have *CHM* but maybe I'm not so strong. Mr Lewis notices me shifting in my seat and speaks with a softer tone.

"Shirley Teddingham says you are a liar. Telling lies is a serious matter. But cheating is just as abominable. I would like to hear your side of the story."

I slowly explain to him step by step what I saw during our Maths exam. No details are left out from her pink, diamante pen to the radioactive glow of her tanned thigh. Mr Lewis stares at my face until I go red.

"Xing Li Wu."

Jay says Mr Lewis likes calling students by their full name. When you call someone by their full name it makes things more scary. I imagine his mum probably did the same when he was naughty. *John Gerald Lewis, stop looking at birds and do your homework.*

"Xing Li Wu, I have heard Shirley Teddingham's story and I have heard your story. There will have to be further investigations before we get to the bottom of who is the liar and who is the cheat. Until then, Shirley Teddingham will be staying at home and I would like you to do the same. Xing Li Wu, I am a fair man and I will get to the bottom of this. Make no mistake, the liar in this situation will be found out and will be punished."

Mr Lewis gives me a firm nod as if to say he knows exactly what's going on. If he's true to his word, Shils will be expelled and I will be fine. He must know that she's a liar. Why would he "investigate further"? I walk out of the school into the biting, winter air. It's the first time I've ever left West Hill with hope in my heart.

Chapter 28
Uncle Ho's Cabin

Grandma is angry about what Mr Lewis refers to as my "rest days". She hates people missing school. When Uncle Ho was little he was sent home with the mumps, Grandma was furious and rang his school nurse.

"Why my son go home? He good boy, never do anything naughty."

"Mrs Wu, he has mumps and needs to rest. We also don't want the other children to get sick."

"What this mumps?"

"It's an infection that mostly affects children. Their face swells up and they need to rest."

"His face just get bit more chubby from eating too many sweets. I bring him back tomorrow."

I try explaining to Grandma about Shils and the exam. But she just shakes her head and wags her finger at me.

"Why you don't concentrate on your exam? So nosey looking around class. How you can get one hundred percent when you looksee looksee at your classmate and her pink pen?"

"But Grandma she was cheating, I could not NOT look at her."

"She cheat now, one day when she older and can't count money she get found out. But YOU, when you older and

172

cannot get to university because failed Maths test, what you do then? You lucky Mr Lewis call me explain it's "rest day" not suspension. You don't go school. But you better still study. If not end up like your mother, make bad choice with her life."

Grandma is stopped mid-lecture by Uncle Ho. For once, I'm grateful for his strangeness.

Uncle Ho is dragging the spare futon from under the stairs, across the lawn, past the perfect rows of roses and into the garden shed where the tortoise lives. We follow him.

"Ho, what you doing?"

"I am sleeping in the shed."

"Don't be silly. Why you want sleep in shed, so cold, so dirty?"

"It's a lot safer than my room where the ceiling is cracking and so are the walls."

"Yes, but so dirty in shed with smelly tortoise."

"Dirt can be good sometimes. I'm moving here."

If Uncle Ho's gonna use the shed like a cabin in the woods, I'm gonna move the tortoise. I reach for his box and Uncle Ho grabs my wrist really tightly. His grip is a lot more painful than when Lai Ker gives me Chinese burns. Uncle Ho grips my wrist even tighter; I can feel his nails digging into my bone.

"Don't touch ANYTHING."

He lets go suddenly and there is a bizarre, sad look on his face.

"Please don't touch anything."

I look at Grandma for help. Maybe she will talk some sense into Uncle Ho, all I want is my tortoise to be okay.

"Grandma can I please move my tortoise?"

"Xing Li leave tortoise, don't disturb Uncle Ho. You enough trouble already."

I think of when Uncle Ho grabbed me while Grandma hit me with the feather duster. I don't want Uncle Ho to stay with the tortoise even if he does like it.

While Uncle Ho eats his dinner next to the tortoise, Grandma gives strict instructions to the maids to "detoxic shed" and put two fan heaters inside. This is the first time Uncle Ho has changed his routine. His life is practically the same every day.

8.00am Eat breakfast in bedroom.

9.00am Walk downstairs and sit in the garden on the green bench.

10.00 - 10.15am Lie down on futon under the stairs for mid morning nap.

12.00 - 12.15pm Have lunch in bedroom.

1:30pm Either lie in the lounge looking at the ceiling or lie on the futon on the landing.

3:30pm Have a mid-afternoon snack.

4:30pm Have daily shower.

6:00pm Watch the six o'clock news.

7:00pm Have dinner in bedroom.

8:00pm - 8:15pm Lie down on the futon under the stairs.

9:00pm - Tea in bed.

10:00pm Go to bed.

I tell Auntie Mei about Uncle Ho and she keeps real quiet.

"Auntie Mei, do you think Uncle Ho will ever become normal again?"

Auntie Mei frowns really hard and I see all the lines on her forehead. I wish Lai Ker were here, then I could tell him that I won our bet over whether Auntie Mei had Botox or not. I know she's not meant to talk about Uncle Ho, but I can see she wants to 'cos her eyebrows are so frowny; her face is about to explode.

"Auntie Mei, please tell me. I can't take all these secrets any more. Do you think he will ever be normal again?"

Auntie Mei sighs like she's kept the sigh inside her for hundreds of years.

"I don't know, Xing Li. I used to think maybe he would be

fine again. But that was a long time ago."

"When was that?"

"A long time ago, before you were born. You see in the beginning, we were all hopeful about Uncle Ho's treatment."

"Including Mama?

"Especially your mother… "

Auntie Mei starts talking really fast now.

"She was so adamant that with proper treatment we would get our brother back. You see, the doctors said many people go on to have normal or at least semi-normal lives. In fact, in the second year after his diagnosis, he did show big signs of getting better."

"So he got okay?"

"Yes, he was looking into applying to universities and moving out. Your mama was so excited, she said that maybe one day after treatment Uncle Ho could even get married and have a family."

"But then what happened?"

"Grandma stopped him."

"It was Grandma's fault?"

"No, it wasn't her fault, she wanted to do what she thought was best for him. She wanted him to stay with her - wanted him to be safe. She told him that he wasn't ready for university, not just yet."

"What did he do then?"

"Well, what can you do? Of course he obeyed Grandma's wishes and stayed with her. But then… then… for whatever reason, little by little, he shut everyone out. He shut the world out."

"He became bad again?"

"Every year I could see him slipping away. Four years passed, and he became even worse than before. So, Grandma decided to bring him to Singapore."

Auntie Mei pauses like she don't want to go on. But I shake her shoulder softly.

"Then what happened?"

"Your mother used to write long letters to me about Uncle Ho. She told me about his progress."

"Mama? I thought Grandma didn't want her near the family after she married Papa?"

"Yes, for the first four years of your parents' marriage, Grandma shut your mother out. However, your mother did something very brave."

"What did she do?"

"She apologised to Grandma even though it wasn't her fault. She said sorry for the sake of Uncle Ho."

"She said she was sorry for marrying Papa? She was sorry for marrying Papa?"

"Yes and no. Yes, she told your grandma she was sorry but no, I know your mother, in her heart she was never sorry for marrying your father."

"So, what happened then?"

"Well, Grandma finally relented. She said they could move to Singapore on the basis that she would never cross your father's path."

Mama wrote to Auntie Mei every week, it must have been tough hiding Papa away while being there for Uncle Ho. Mama's big heart must have had to split into two, one half for Papa, one half for Uncle Ho. How did Mama do it? She was always splitting her heart for everyone. Once Mama's best friend Mrs Alsanea told me, "Your mother's heart splits in all directions, if someone asks for help she never knows when to say no. She takes on too much, sometimes I'm worried that your mother's heart will explode." Mrs Alsanea was right, when the oven exploded and killed Mama her heart exploded too.

Auntie Mei asks a maid to bring us some tea. With honey and milk for her, one sugar and milk for me.

"You know I wanted to write back to your mother so many times. I started hundreds of letters, but did not finish them."

"Why didn't you?"

"I was having my heart broken at the time and didn't know

176

where to start. When Grandma told me they were bringing Uncle Ho back to the UK, I was overjoyed. Then your mother wrote and said it was because hospital workers in his ward had been beating him. The pain in my heart was unbearable. In those days, beating mental patients to keep them in check happened a lot. I don't think it would happen today, I don't know… "

I don't know either. I don't know what to say. Like what do you say when someone has just told you that your sick uncle was beaten up by hospital people that you are meant to trust? I don't know if I want to hear any more. People always say it's good to hear the truth. But what if the truth keeps you up at night? What if the truth is so bad that you wish you had never asked?

"… the doctors blamed the bruises on him - for fighting with the patients. But a nurse at the hospital told Grandma the truth. When your mother sent me pictures of the bruises on his arms and legs, I cried for days. Then I threw the photos away. What reason did I have to keep the photographs? Why keep something if all it does is bring you pain?

Your grandma refused to let Uncle Ho return to any psychiatric ward. She told us she would rather die than let that happen. She said, *The day he go back to hospital ward is the day you take knife and slit my wrists.*

"How about Mama, what happened with Mama? Why did she stop seeing Uncle Ho?"

"She began arguing with Grandma again. This time it wasn't over your father, it was about Uncle Ho. She blamed Grandma for everything that was wrong with Uncle Ho. She said Uncle Ho was the way he was because Grandma was an unfit mother. She was angry, she couldn't see that Grandma's heart was just as broken as hers. The arguments were affecting Uncle Ho, he was getting all upset and becoming terribly anti-social. In the end, the doctor stepped in and said the arguments had to stop or Uncle Ho would get worse. Your mother left because Grandma said she was not welcome in our house any more. They only saw each other again when you were born. I begged your mother to let us visit, but she told us we were too toxic to be around you both. I begged her until she said I could see you and Lai Xing, but only once a year."

"Did Mama see Uncle Ho after everything?"

"She sent him birthday cards and Christmas cards and tried to call him all the time. But by then he was too gone. He refused to talk to her. Poor Ho said she had abandoned him and was no longer his family. Just like that, he decided something and that was that. You see, once Uncle Ho decides something, he doesn't back down, ever."

Chapter 29
Hollywood Creams

Uncle Ho has stayed in the shed for most of the weekend. He only comes out for his bath or to nap under the stairs. The tortoise is okay. When Uncle Ho is sleeping, I feed him. I think Uncle Ho's been feeding him too 'cos I found some half-eaten roses and prawns. His head looks fatter than ever. I can't tell Jay about this 'cos Grandma has taken away my mobile phone and my computer games as my punishment for my "rest days".

I've spent all weekend working on my essay for English coursework. I've got four weeks to write it, but I've got nothing better to do so might as well start now. The topic is quite hardcore, "Write a 500-word article debating the pros and cons of euthanasia." I had to look up the meaning of the word on Wiki. Mrs Wilkins never picks easy stuff, like last term we had to write about stem cell research. A month ago, she wanted us to write about whether guns should be legalised. She says we need to think about these issues 'cos if we don't think about them the world will always be a bad place without any changes. She said, "Children, the future of the UK lies in your hands. It is up to you whether the society you live in is a place that future generations can be proud of. You must be well read and well rounded in your education as it prepares you for university and later the working world."

I ask Auntie Mei whether she thinks it's important to have a round brain to go to uni.

"I wouldn't know Xing Li, I've never been to university. I went to drama school instead."

"Really? I thought Grandma would make you go for sure."

"Well, I did try one and a half years of university, then I dropped out. By then, Grandma was too busy with Uncle Ho to bother me. Anyway, she gave up on me a long time ago. The day I decided to be an actress was the day she decided to wash her hands over my career."

I get Auntie Mei to tell me stories about her life as an actress. There are enough stories to make a trilogy of films plus a prequel. I like listening to her stories 'cos it reminds me of Mama, she liked telling me funny stories too.

"What was your first role?"

"Let me see, my first paid role was when I was seventeen. It was over the summer holidays for one month. It wasn't proper acting, but more as a background artist for a Hollywood film. I got £30 for a nine-hour day plus overtime. The village in our scene got blown up by the Americans."

"Americans like to blow up everything in films."

"They certainly do, there were so many bombs and explosions."

"What did you do every day?"

"Well… every day I would sit for hours in a makeshift, giant tent with hundreds of Korean, Vietnamese, Japanese and Chinese people of all ages. You see, the production crew had struggled to find enough Chinese people and they took anyone who was remotely South East Asian. There were plenty of illegal, underage, non-English speaking people on the set. A real colourful mix of people from post-operation Thai ladyboys to retired Japanese chefs. I saw there was a whole crazy world of people out there. It was a real eye opener for me."

I wonder what a post-op Thai ladyboy really looks like down there. Like everyone says post-op this and post-op that, but does anyone really know what goes on? Like where does their wee come out of if they don't have any more bits?

"What was it like being in the tent? Did you chat to lots of cool people?"

"Well, the days were long and the tents were like being imprisoned in a sauna. We would sit on the dirty floor playing cards and gossiping about which crew member was a friend or a foe. We got to eat last which did not go down well with the Chinese folk. The food order was crew first, principal actors, supporting actors, runners, film student lackeys, water carriers and then us."

"That's harsh, you should never let a Chinese person wait for their dinner."

"Indeed. Food was the highlight of our day as it was a buffet. Roasted pork, beef burgers, smoky ribs, cous cous salad, ham joints, baked potatoes, fresh yogurt and honey. Oh, the cream cakes were to die for. Many of the extras sneaked the creamy goodness home for their families.

"Free cream cakes, that's REALLY cool. Who was the director?"

"It was an Italian director, I can't remember his name. But I remember he'd won an Oscar. Though he refused to make eye contact with us. He was very intimidating and even sacked a few of the Filipino boys because they looked too happy on camera. But to be honest, people didn't mind how they were treated. Earning about £200 a week in those days was a lot of money. At seventeen, I felt grown up making my own money. But it's a tough industry, I've fought the negativity every day of my life since I was seventeen."

"Did you ever think of giving up?"

"Give up acting?"

Auntie Mei snorts and arches her eyebrows that get threaded by maid three once a week.

"Of course, I would think about it all the time. Sometimes I'd go through the long process of recall auditions, get to the last two and then be told, "Sorry, goodbye, you are too 'exotic' for us." The thing that affected me the most was when I was limited by my race. Times have certainly changed, but not as much as you would think. Even today, Chinese people on British TV speak in broken English and are ridiculed for their accent. There are so few characters of well-spoken Chinese doctors, Chinese lawyers or heaven forbid a Chinese politician on British TV."

I'm trying to think of famous British Chinese people on the telly and all I can think of is Gok Wan and that girl who was the red Teletubby.

"You know Xing Li, I once met a famous, black actor who worked in Hollywood in the fifties. That was when black actors had roles as maids, cooks, nannies and slaves. She said, 'Mei, you are one of the pioneers; you have got to keep going. It took us fifty years to reach where we are and look, now we even have a black president.' This is the main reason why I have stayed in the acting industry. I hope in some small way I can contribute to the stereotypes being overturned. But sometimes I wonder if I am naïve and should just walk away."

"But Auntie Mei, you can't give up now. You've been doing it for twenty years. You have to keep fighting."

"I suppose… maybe it won't happen in my lifetime, maybe in the next generation."

Auntie Mei's story time is over 'cos she has to go and learn a script for a big corporate film about money laundering. For once she gets to speak in her own accent, so she's quite excited about this one. You know I always thought Auntie Mei was this delicate lady who was all la-dee-dah. But 'cos she's survived so long in acting, I think she has *CHM* in her own way. Like Lai Ker, just more classy.

Chapter 30
Bye Bye Beauty

It's been four days since I met with Mr Lewis and six days
since I've seen Lai Ker. Grandma says I am not to think or talk
about Lai Ker any more. I hate all this waiting. I'm waiting
for Mr Lewis to ring, waiting for Lai Ker to contact me.

Waiting

Waiting

Waiting

Sleeping

Waiting

Waiting

Waiting

"Xing Li, Mr Lewis call."

Grandma has slipped into my room without me noticing.
Her feet are well soft.

"What did he say?"

"He say you can come back to school tomorrow."

"Does that mean Shils has been found guilty?"

"She found cheating, someone else tell Mr Lewis. So, you
return to school tomorrow and stop all nonsense."

"Is Shils going to be there?"

"No. But all I know you go back school tomorrow and
that is good."

SHILS IS GONE SHILS IS GONE SHILS IS GONE

My first day back at school is one MASSIVE joyous blur. Shils has been found GUILTY of cheating 'cos the Cliff Richard lookalike told Mr Lewis he saw Shils cheating. The fact that Shils had got ninety-five percent in the Maths exam when she had scored forty percent in her last exam did not help her case. Mr Lewis is using Shils as an example to students about what happens when you cheat and she's been expelled.

Shils is gone and I am free!!!

FREE!!!

My life of torture is over. There are no warning bells or sounds of trumpets. Just a short slip of paper from Mr Lewis to say:

> *Thank you for alerting us about*
> *Shirley Teddingham's indiscretion.*

The first thing I'm gonna do when I find Lai Ker is tell him I've got *CHM* 'cos I spoke up and now Shils is gone. He'll be well proud. I smile the biggest smile since Mama's death.

Jay and I are SUPER happy. We eat a S-L-O-W lunch in the canteen. No more sitting in the library EVER again. We walk down the hallway and we don't run. Nope, no more lunchtime exercise for us. We look up rather than at the floor. With Queen Shils gone, her subjects walk around the school like sheep without a shepherd. Their "baas" are now tiny bleats that no longer hurt us. During our lunch break the Cliff lookalike comes up to Jay and me. He smiles and offers to shake Jay's hand.

"No hard feelings friend. You know we were just messing around right?"

Jay s-l-o-w-l-y shakes his hand and the Cliff lookalike seems a little relieved.

After school, Jay wants to go out and celebrate Shils'

departure, but I'm well tired from being joyous all day. Being super happy is not an emotion I'm used to and I want to go home and rest. There will be no more crying or nightmares, I've taken a chance and it has paid off.

I walk down the road and there's a bit of a skip in my step. It's only 4:30pm, but it's already dark and the rain has started to pelt down like crazy. Usually, in gloomy weather I run home, but today's rain is not gonna get me down. I feel as if Mama is watching me and she's so happy she's crying down rain. I wish Mama were here - she said she likes it the most when Lai Ker and me are happy. I take my usual short cut through the alleyway between Smith Street and Holmes Place. It's starting to fog and the rain makes it hard to see. Typical London weather, always foggy and grey and rainy and cold.

UH-OH.

There's a scary, tall figure in a dark, hooded coat following me, he's walking faster and faster. Grandma warned me about muggers in London, that's why she gave me pepper spray to keep in my bag. "When they come, you spray their eyes. That will teach them from trying mug Chinese girl."

I start to run and the tall person chases me. I fumble in my satchel, desperate to find the pepper spray, it's started to rain really heavy and the raindrops are clouding my eyes.

Where is the spray?

The tall figure rushes towards me as I try to run as fast as I can. Before I'm out of the alleyway the tall figure has pushed me roughly to the pavement. I skid on the wet concrete and hear a rip in my tights.

"Don't even think of running, Sing-Song. Stupid bitch."

It's Shils, her coat collar has been turned up and the lower part of her face is covered with her white scarf. I can smell the alcohol on her. She pins me to the ground and hits my face several times, cursing me with each punch. I can taste blood in my mouth. She's put her whole body on me and her knee is crushing my chest. The icy air is cutting through my lungs with each breath and I try to break free. Shils' long limbs overpower me; she grips me tightly and spits in my face. Her eyes are manic and crazy and can't seem to focus on anything.

"See if you're so clever now. You lying chink. You Chinese people think you can get away with anything."

As I lie on the wet pavement it feels like time is going really slow. I'm wet and cold and scared. I need to escape but she's so strong. I try to scream but all I can taste is blood.

"You ruined my life, you little bitch. All you chinks swarm in and ruin people's lives. I'm going to kill you."

I feel her long nails scrape against my right cheek.

"Let me go, please let me go."

"Who do you think you are? You're just a stupid chink whose grandma paid to get her into school."

My rain-soaked coat feels like it's loaded with weights, it gets heavier with each drop.

"You think you're so clever telling on me. See if your grandma is going to help you now."

Shils is breathing very quickly and she smells of a sickly mix of alcohol and vanilla and lavender. I try to struggle some more, but she slaps me across my face and a bit of her nail cuts into my cheek again. I'm starting to cry, I've never been so scared in my life.

Please let me go. Please let me go. Please let me go.

I hear faint footsteps coming from behind Shils. She takes her scarf off and stuffs it into my mouth. I start to choke and she pulls it out slightly. The footsteps get closer and closer and I try to wiggle and kick as much as I can. Shils looks alarmed, but keeps her iron grip on me.

"Stop struggling you stupid chink."

The footsteps get louder and more urgent. The people are coming in my direction. I give a muffled scream. A light is shining on my face, it's so bright. I can make out three figures. They are wearing the West Hill uniform.

"What are you doing Shils?"

I know the high-pitched voice, it belongs to one of Shils' followers - the girl with the D-cup and wavy brown hair. She looks more terrified than me. I stare at her, pleading at her and she looks down at her feet.

"Well, don't just stand there, help me hold onto the bitch."

Another girl with a blonde bob and her ginger-mane friend look uneasily at each other.

"GRAB-HOLD-OF-HER-NOW."

The three girls drag me up from the ground. Ginger at the right, blonde at the left and brunette at the back. My nose has stopped bleeding, but the bruises on my head have started to swell. The girls glance at me, trying their best not to catch my eye. Shils takes a small kitchen knife out of her handbag.

"Let's teach this chink a lesson, once and for all."

I can feel the girls trembling as they hold me. But I'm shaking more than them. The brunette speaks; her voice is a nervous whisper.

"Shils, what are you going to do?"

Shils ignores her and holds the knife over my leg. I feel her looking at me and hating me and wishing I were dead. She roughly pulls the scarf out of my mouth and I start to cough. I feel like I'm going to cough and cough until I vomit. My stomach starts to retch and Shils slaps me across the face again. She opens up the scarf, it's become like a mosaic print made of blood and rain water.

"I'm going to cover her mouth with this. Don't let her go, no matter what."

"Shils, what are you going to do to her?"

"Please talk to us."

"Shils, this isn't right."

"SHUT UP and do what I say."

Shils covers my mouth with the scarf and ties a double knot at the back. The ginger haired girl starts to cry. Shils takes her knife and cuts into my leg. Blood oozes out and trickles down my leg.

C
H
I
N
K

The pain from each letter sends shock waves through my body and I try to scream. But the rain soaked scarf causes me to gag. I don't want to choke on my own vomit. I don't want to be sick, I don't want to die.

"See if this teaches you a lesson, stupid chink."

Chapter 31
The Flautist

Grandma's posh doctor has given me two weeks' bed rest along with fresh bandages for my leg. He arrived in his silver Ferrari five minutes after Grandma found me lying on the stairs in my vomit. I was all blurry and crying and being sick. I don't remember much, but I remember getting blood on the carpet and Auntie Mei wailing and Grandma getting the maids to throw the carpet out. After I was all bandaged and drugged up, I slept a couple of hours. Grandma told me the Wus' official statement to the outside world is I have slipped on a puddle and hit a cyclist. She doesn't want ANYONE to know about *The Incident* as she calls it. I know it's 'cos some kind of deal has been made with Shils' dad and step-mum. Grandma didn't mention the deal, but I know a deal has been made 'cos Auntie Mei told me Grandma's three lawyers were there when the Teddinghams came round with their lawyer. They came with a massive gift basket and Grandma shut herself in the living room with them and the lawyers. They were in there for about an hour. Auntie Mei keeps saying she's sorry over and over again like *The Incident* was her fault. She keeps telling me everything will be okay 'cos I'm strong just like Mama, then she tears up and has to leave the room. But I don't feel strong, I feel really weak and shaky and frightened and confused. Grandma says by keeping my mouth shut, it will protect my future. She gives me a massive box of Panadol and doesn't mention *The Incident* again.

I hate her for that.

Jay tries calling me over fifty times. I let the phone ring and ring. Sometimes I pick up the phone and put it to my ear. When he says hello I open my mouth to speak, but the words just don't come out, so I hang up. How can I keep my mouth shut about something like this?

But how can I tell Jay the truth?

How can I describe to him the horrible pain in my leg as Shils cut into it and the smell of my blood mixed with the grit and rain? How can I explain to him the sound of my heart pounding non-stop for ten minutes after she ran off? How can I tell him that as Shils hit me, I thought I was going to die, and in that moment part of me didn't mind 'cos that would have meant I would now be with Mama.

I've been spending all week in bed just staring and staring out of the window. I can walk okay now and my leg doesn't hurt as much. But I don't want to leave my bed. I want to lie here and never wake up. I wish I were like the sparrows that fly round and round. I wish I were like them, all free and whistley and soaring across the sky. My broken body is resting, but my mind is moving in super speed. Whenever I close my eyes I see Shils and the night she *got* me. It's like I'm there and it plays over and over again like a cinema projector on auto. I see her with the knife cutting into my leg. Even though I'm crying, she doesn't care. All the girls are crying too. I see her punching me on my head and my breathing gets heavy as I hear her voice in my ears.

Stupid bitch.

Stupid chink.

Was there anything I could have done to stop Shils?

Maybe if I had run away faster? Maybe if I had shouted louder? Maybe if I had kicked quicker? Maybe if I had not joined West Hill? Maybe if Mama did not die? Maybe if I didn't live in London? Maybe if I hadn't been Chinese?

It's 'cos I'm Chinese.

If I weren't Chinese, Shils would have left me alone. If I hadn't done *CHM* and kept my trap shut to Mr Lewis, I would be okay.

Stupid *CHM*.

If Lai Ker did not graffiti his white classmate's dad's restaurant with *CHM* he would be here too.

Stupid *CHM*.

But then Auntie Mei has *CHM* and keeps fighting in the acting industry and she's okay. She's got loads of admirers and friends. She said that when you fight for something that is worth it, it don't matter if it takes years. What matters is that the outcome is good.

I dunno, it's so confusing.

Like Jay's parents are okay too. They fight for what's right too. Like his Dad keeps going with his classical music and his parents got married even though their parents hate them for it. But then they don't get to see Jay's grandparents. Yet, they seem happy and are super talented in music too.

I don't know.

My mind is spinning with thoughts after thoughts. I'm confused again and I feel crap and horrible and I want to cry lots, but I've no more energy. I just want to lie here in my bed and never go out and never go back to West Hill. What if I left London? What if I left Shils and West Hill and Grandma - then I wouldn't feel this way. I could run away and live with Grandpa in his retirement home in Singapore. We could eat delicious scones and drink Earl Grey tea. But I've already written nine letters since we met. He didn't reply to any of them, so he doesn't want me around.

What do I do?

Maybe I can just stay in bed and just wait and wait. Maybe if I wait long enough I'll be as old as Grandma and I can go to heaven and be with Mama, Papa and Meow Meow sooner.

I must have dozed off 'cos when I open my eyes, Jay is peering at me as if I were at death's door.

"You alright Xing?"

I go all red and pull my fingers through my hair.

"How did you get in?"

"Your auntie told me your grandma's playing mahjong. She sneaked me in. Are you okay?"

I keep quiet.

"Your grandma told the school what happened. Being hit by a crazy cyclist must have been well scary."

I think of Shils spitting in my face and then bashing my head on the ground.

"Yes… it… it was very scary."

"When the school said you'd been in an accident, I tried calling you again and again. But I think something's wrong with your phone."

I speak through gritted teeth. The lies keep coming and I don't know how to stop.

"Yeah, my stupid phone is… is… is broken. But it's all fixed now. I'm all fixed now… I'm… I'm okay."

"That's good. I was well worried."

He looks down when he says this and then starts digging around in his blue sports bag like a mole.

"I got you some stuff 'cos your aunt said you might need cheering up. They're all as cheap as Mr Chan's chips. So, don't worry about me wasting money and all that. My mum also has some chocolates for you too. She never buys me chocolates, so I'm well jealous."

Jay puts a gigantic box of chocolates on the bed, followed by several worn-out comics, a cat purse and a black notebook with gold musical notes on it. I like his pressies lots. He also carefully puts a slim black leather case on the bed. It feels heavy next to my legs.

"Auntie Mei said you were listening to pop songs on the radio every day, I thought you might like to listen to some real music. I know when I'm sick too much Britney does

192

my head in."

Jay opens the black case and I can see his hands are
starting to shake. The three pieces of his silver flute lie snug
in purple, velvet padding. They're so shiny - more shiny than
the silver cutlery Grandma's maids polish every day. Jay fits
the flute together as if each piece is worth a million quid. To
the side of the mouthpiece bit I see a long word Ge-mein-
hardt in old fashioned joined up writing. Jay lifts the flute up
to his mouth and it gives out a sharp sound. With a wrinkled
nose and a short shake of the head he starts twisting the top
part of the flute before testing the note again. Then he takes
a deep breath and begins to play "The Swan" by St Sands.

♩♩♩ ♩♩♩ ♩ ♫ ♩ ♪ ♫ ♬♬♬ ♩ ♩

The music is really low and slow like a sad swan swimming
on the river. It's so beautiful, every note is perfect and sad and
wonderful. Jay's eyes are closed, he looks all serious like a
proper concert musician.

I close my eyes.

As each note plays, I feel like my broken body is being
mended by the music. I see the swan going up the river in the
middle of the night - the water is black, the air is quiet but the
swan keeps on going. My heart is floating among the notes;
I'm like the sad swan swimming up and down, up and down,
not knowing where to go. I feel my eyes tearing up; the tears
force themselves down my nose and onto my lips.

Jay stops playing.

"What's wrong Xing?"

I'm crying real proper now and I can't stop. I'm crying so
hard, it feels like my heart is breaking into millions of pieces.

"It… it… was Shils… she… she… said I was a… stupid…
ch… "

I can't say it. I can't look at him. I'm a mess. I can hear
her in my mind. My mind flashes with Shils holding the knife
and I can almost smell my blood that was washed in the rain.

Stupid chink.

Jay puts his hand on my hand. It feels like his hand has been wrapped for hours in a warm quilt. He looks at me and squeezes my hand real tight. When I see his eyes through my tears I suddenly realise I don't have to tell him everything 'cos he gets it. He really, *really* gets it.

"Xing, you're not stupid. Shils is stupid. You know that right?"

My voice comes out all tiny.

"… but maybe I could have done something different?"

"Xing, Shils is bloody messed up. Her step-mum is Chinese; her mother shacked up with multiple younger men. She had to repeat our year twice 'cos of her problems. She's messed up and it was nothing to do with you. You have to know that okay?"

I slowly nod and my throat feels sore like I've swallowed a stone.

We sit in silence for a while but it doesn't feel awkward or anything. Jay picks up his flute and starts playing another pretty song. He plays song after song after song until I finally shut my eyes and fall asleep.

Chapter 32
Much Ado About Dumb Things

I miss the old Xing Li, the one that lived in 187C Kilburn Road with Mama and Lai Ker. The Xing Li who was not sad. The Xing Li who had not started to grow up.

It's my first day back at West Hill and everything looks the same. The noisy kids with their touch screen phones, the huge hallways with their slippery floors and the Cliff Richard lookalike strumming his guitar by the window. Yet, the day feels longer and greyer and sadder. I feel like I have this gloomy feeling with me all the time and I can't get rid of it. Like it's so much trouble to do anything and everything. When I speak I have to remind myself to finish a sentence even though I don't want to.

While I was away, Jay was paired in Music class with Milly Bridgeman. She's a small, frizzy haired girl with thick glasses and a grade eight in piano and violin. Together, they composed a cool jazzy version of "Old MacDonald Had a Farm". While I was resting at home, Jay and mousy Milly spent lunch breaks talking about how cool Beethoven, Wagger and Bart are.

"Alright Jay."

"Alright Xing. You know Milly, right?"

Milly stares a bit too long at the scratches on my face. Her large brown eyes remind me of an owl.

"Hi Xing Li, I hope you are feeling better. Sorry to hear about your accident."

"It's alright. Pain killers helped to keep me high."

Milly giggles at my comment - she laughs like a horse with a bad cold.

"Jay was right, you're funny."

I wonder what else Jay's told his new pal Milly. Doesn't he know hanging out as a three never works? Someone always gets left out; threesomes never work. I don't have to worry though 'cos Preema Singh comes to join us and she's part of our new gang too. Her father owns a massive steel corporation and she always talks like she's in a rush.

"Hi-Xing-Li-hope-you-are-better.-You-know-it-is-absolutely-freezing-in-here.-They-should-switch-on-the-radiator-so-cold-in-here.-Jay-how-is-the-stupid-music-assignment-going?-I-suck-at-music. My-mum-tried-to-get-me-to-learn-the-piano-and-then-the-trumpet-and-then… "

And so on, my mind's stopped listening. The sad feeling is taking over me and the world is being shut out.

Just before the bell rings, three of Shils' ex-followers come to our end of the classroom. Ginger at the right, blonde at the left and brunette at the back. I haven't seen them since *The Incident*. After Shils ran off they started crying lots as if Shils had hurt them too. Then they helped me home. But they didn't wait with me until Grandma came home, they just left me at the bottom of the stairs.

The brunette with the D-cup turns tomato red.

"Erm, Shing Li. We just thought we'd come over and say we're sorry. I mean we're erm… sorry for the accident that happened."

They are shifting lots and nudging each other to say something more.

"Yeah, we're like REALLY sorry about your accident Shing Li. Like really, really sorry."

"Yeah, like we wish we could have done something. We were scared of… we wish we… we're just really, really sorry about everything."

I don't want them near me, I don't want to talk to them or look at them or be in the same room as them. I want them to disappear and never come back. The redhead fiddles with her hair while the brunette and blondie with the bob look red faced at their toes. They look all strange, like they're scared I'm going to go all psycho on them. Suddenly, I feel all weird like everything around me is moving real slow and I'm seeing them for the first time for who they are. They're just scared little girls who were just as terrified of Shils as I was. They're no different from me. I look them in the eye for the first time since I joined West Hill.

"What's done is done. I'll be… I'll be… okay."

The girls look well happy and give me their toothpaste commercial smiles before walking away. Before they reach their desks, I shout REALLY loudly so everyone can hear.

"BY THE WAY MY NAME IS XING LI NOT SHING-LI."

Everyone is quiet and then I shout again.

"MY NAME IS XING LI. DON'T YOU EVER GET IT WRONG AGAIN."

At lunchtime, Milly and Preema are still part of our gang. Jay told me that he doesn't like them around.

"Those giggling girls annoy me so much, wish they'd leave us alone. But what can you do? Can't skank them."

When Preema starts her long speeches (which is like all the time), Jay puts headphones in his ears and turns the music on at full blast. But, when Milly and Jay get into really l-o-o-o-n-g chats about the latest classical CD, I wonder if he really means what he says. Like does he like Milly more than me? I don't want Milly around all the time. I mean it's cool to have new friends, but it's not the same as when it was just Jay and me.

It's been a tiring day.

I need Auntie Mei's golden ear-pick to prop up my eyes.

It's the last lesson of the day, Chemistry. I usually don't mind Chemistry 'cos Jay and me get to make little Bunsen burner bonfires and torch things like old rubbers and hairs. Jay's hair takes longer to burn than mine, but today I'm just sleepy and want to go home to bed. I receive a note from Milly.

In pink capitals, she writes:

GOTTA TALK TO YOU AFTER SCHOOL ALONE.
VERY URGENT.

I look over and she's grinning from ear to ear and gives me a thumbs up. As Jay says, we don't wanna skank her so I give her a nod before putting the note on the mini bonfire that Jay made in the corner of our heat mat. I feel well satisfied seeing it puff into flames. As soon as the bell rings, Milly gallops over to me like a horse

She grabs my arm and gives Jay a knowing look.

"Girl talk Jay, not for you."

"Xing don't do girl talk."

"Yes, well she does now!"

It's starting to rain again. Luckily, Grandma now makes sure the driver picks me up.

"So, Milly, what's the urgent news? I've got to go 'cos my grandma's car is waiting."

"Well, it's no big deal really. Actually, it's a little bit of a big deal. Well, maybe a medium big deal."

It's drizzling outside and I really want to get home.

"Hmmmm, I guess it's sort of a big deal."

"What's up?"

"Well, there is this guy... you see, there is this guy who I like. I think he likes me too. But I'm not sure if he likes me. Like the other day, he got a test tube out of the cupboard and then he asked me if I wanted one too. He didn't ask anyone else you see. So, I don't know what to do."

"Maybe he doesn't like you, maybe he's just being nice?"

"Maybe, but I don't think so. Like last week he chatted to

me for ages and he also gave me one of the sticks of his gum. So, he can't like NOT like me. At least he must like me a little bit? I mean it was so nice of him to offer me his gum."

Milly and Preema could write a thousand-word essay about the pros and cons of a guy's text message.

"I guess he likes you then."

"You really think so?"

"Erm. I guess… "

"Are you sure?"

"Yes?"

Milly smiles and gives me a hug. She stands up and puts her bag on her shoulder and then she frowns and sits heavily down again.

"Why?"

"Why what?"

"Why does he like me?"

"Erm - the gum?"

Milly frowns and stares across the playground as if she's working out what the cure to cancer might be. Then she looks at me with a gigantic smile.

"Yes, I knew it! You are like so right. I knew you were the right person to talk to. Preema said you had no idea about these things. But she was wrong. Like SO wrong!"

She gets up for the second time and gives me a hug. I stand with my hands swinging from side to side like a monkey. Most Chinese families have allergic reactions to PDAs. I watch her skip across the playground and shout to her.

"So, Milly who's the lucky guy?"

She pauses mid-skip and swings around; her cheeks are flushed and her frizzy hair bounces around her face. She smiles at me with her white, horse-like teeth.

"Jay."

I'm not smiling when I wave goodbye.

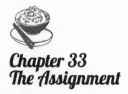

Chapter 33
The Assignment

Uncle Ho has actually left the shed. Like, moved all his stuff out. It's the first time in weeks. He's sitting at the kitchen table eating some prawn noodles and reading the first draft for my English coursework on Eutha-nay-sia. I wish I didn't leave it on the table.

Please don't take my essay with you.

I stand almost hidden behind the kitchen door as he reads through the essay. I can't face writing another boring essay, not when doing everything these days seems to take me double the time. Uncle Ho puts the essay back on the table and stares at me a bit longer than normal. Then he picks it up, screws it into a ball and throws it to the corner of the kitchen. My knees start to tremble and I zoom upstairs to my room, climbing the steps three at a time. When I come down for dinner he's already returned to his shed with my tortoise.

The nightmares have started again.

I see the tall figure with the knife standing in the rain. It's so dark I can't see her face. I can only hear her voice and smell the stench of alcohol.

"Stay still, you stupid chink."

She grabs me and starts slashing at my leg.

"Stop, please, stop."

"SHUT UP, you stupid bitch."

I wake suddenly.

My back and face are soaked in sweat and my PJs are wet. I can taste the saltiness on my lips. I reach for my leg and with the tips of my fingers trace the letter-shaped scars. They will always be a reminder of what happened. Even when I'm grown up they will still be there.

C H I N K

In the dark, I can see a figure standing at the foot of my bed. I shake my head super quickly to check if I'm still dreaming. The figure stays completely still. I panic and grip my quilt tightly.

How did she find me?

How did she get in?

I hear heavy breathing.

It's Uncle Ho.

I squint and see his big belly shadow. He's watching me. How long has he been watching me? I hold my breath and try not to move, terrified that if I make any sudden movements, he may turn on me just like he turned on Auntie Mei when Grandma and me came home late that time.

Uncle Ho stands in the dark staring at me for a good ten minutes. My eyes are used to the dark now and I can see him. We eye each other up like two animals ready to pounce. If I call for Auntie Mei, by the time she runs from her bedroom to my room, Uncle Ho could smash the table lamp over my head. Grandma wears ear plugs to sleep - she would probably take Uncle Ho's side anyway.

Uncle Ho moves towards the edge of the bed like a giant bear. I slowly move the quilt off me, ready to make a run for it. The meds and extra pounds mean he's quite unfit. I'm sure he won't be able to beat me in a race. But if he catches hold of my leg, or I trip, he could easily push me to the ground. I remember his tight grip when Grandma taught me the lesson with the feather duster. With his fingers locked and eyes closed, he held me so tightly I struggled to breathe.

Uncle Ho reaches deep into his pocket.

I hear a rustling. He pulls out a supermarket carrier bag and starts to untie the knots he's carefully done. One of the knots has been tied together a little bit too tightly. Using his teeth, he bites into the knot and rips open the carrier bag. Inside the bag is another plastic bag filled with some white sweets. He throws the bag on the bed. I can see the white sweets all shiny in the moonlight. I pick them up and inspect them. Close up, they look like circular shaped mints. Uncle Ho is watching me, waiting for me to accept his gift. I put one of the mints in my mouth and spit it out. It's horrible and bitter, they're not sweets. There's hundreds of them, he must have been storing them up for ages.

"I want you to do me a favour."

His breathing is loud and even. It feels like he is standing closer to me than at the foot of the bed.

"What favour do you want me to do?"

"I know you loved your mother, she would want you to help me. You have to help me."

I think of Mama, how she loved Uncle Ho lots.

"What do you want?"

"I want you to do what you wrote about in your essay."

Chapter 34
Secrets and Limes

Mama once told me the story of when Uncle Ho got lost in Hamleys. He was four years old and the gigantic toy store was his most favourite place on earth. Uncle Ho saw an electric aeroplane whizzing around the store. He was terrified 'cos he thought it was a bird trapped inside the building and he didn't want the bird to run out of air and die. When Grandma's back was turned, he ran after the buzzing aeroplane.

Mama said, "Your Uncle Ho passed the giant stuffed teddy bear, the pirate Lego display, the sweet factory, all items that would cause any child to stop and stare. But he was focused on saving the "bird". Helping the bird to safety was all he wanted. Round and round the aeroplane flew; it was fixed to a wire that took it from the bottom of the store right to the top and back again. Uncle Ho ran up the escalator - determined to not let it out of his sight. He disappeared so quickly; Grandma didn't have time to stop him. After shouting at the security guards and threatening to sue the toy shop, Grandma found Uncle Ho lying exhausted on top of the stuffed animals on the top floor. He had been chasing the aeroplane non-stop for two hours and his stubborn tiny legs had given way."

After his night visit, Uncle Ho has started to follow me with his eyes. I know he's staring at me, and most of the time I feel weirded out. I try to imagine what Lai Ker would say about my night visit, about Uncle Ho. Making up chats with Lai Ker in my mind helps me miss him less. I think the conversation would go something like this:

"Uncle Ho visited me last night. He wants me to help put him to sleep."

"He's nuts innit, just give him a chocolate bar and everything will be okay. He won't remember what he said."

"You don't understand, he was dead serious."

"Yeah, well I don't blame him. What kind of life does he have anyway? At least if he were in prison he could talk to the inmates."

"Are you saying I should do it?"

"Of course not. I'm just saying you should feel sorry for him. Imagine having no friends and no life and having your mother washing your underwear at the age of forty-two."

"What am I supposed to do? He creeps me out."

"Why don't you just give him thirty mints and then when he doesn't kick the bucket tell him that if you survive after eating so many pills, it's God's will you've survived and nothing to do with you. He can't argue with that. Look he's mental, you can't take ANYTHING he says seriously. He has good days and bad days. You just got him on a bad day."

That's what Lai Ker would say. It would be a crap idea, but at least he would know and I wouldn't be alone. Telling Jay is out of the question, he'll probably think my family are nuts and then he'll think I'm crazy too. I don't want Jay to think bad of me at all, especially since Milly keeps making it obvious she likes him. Like the other day she made him an extra lunch of ham sandwiches and prawn cocktail crisps. Jay shared the lunch with me though.

Maybe I am going loopy 'cos I haven't slept enough. Maybe what happened with Uncle Ho was all a bad dream. Maybe it didn't happen at all. These days I'm lucky if I get to sleep more than four hours. I sleep, then I wake up sweating. In the morning when I open my eyes for two seconds everything is fine. For two seconds it's bliss 'cos I'm in between the dream world and real life. But then I remember everything. How Mama is dead, how Lai Ker is gone, the scar on my leg and the night of *The Incident*.

Auntie Mei's already left for the airport to shoot a film, so I can't ask her if I'm going nuts and there's no way I'm telling Grandma. Last night when Uncle Ho ate the leftover fried noodles in the fridge and blamed it on me, I got a thirty-minute lecture from Grandma.

Uncle Ho's started to wait outside any room I'm in. When I wake up in the morning, he's sitting outside my door. I dread taking showers. As I take my clothes off, I imagine his eyes peering through the keyhole. I start hanging my towel on the door knob and bathing in my underwear. Sometimes when I open the bathroom door, he's standing right in front of me. He only says one word.

"When?"

I keep quiet and hurry past.

I'm trying to sleep but I swear he's standing in my room. I open my eyes and scan the room for his fat shadow. He's not there. I always think he is, but he never is. I don't want him to get to me. Grandma, Auntie Mei and Lai Ker accepted Uncle Ho and his ways. Mama loved him so much, she would want me to do the same. I have to accept him and ignore him and try to love him too. I must try because I don't want to be like Shils. I don't want to hate him just 'cos he's different from all the normal and cool people. But it's hard 'cos every time he looks at me, every time he's near, my hands get sweaty and my stomach gets churny and my heart beats super fast.

Jay and me are sitting cross-legged on the floor of my room as the tortoise tries to munch on the rug. Uncle Ho's out with Dr Lincoln, so we manage to carry the tortoise up the stairs. He's well heavy; he's grown quite fat and his head looks like a scaly, half-deflated balloon. It's nice chatting to Jay without Milly and Preema. A bit like old times before *The Incident*; before I felt sad all the time; before Uncle Ho started to weird me out. Jay says Milly and Preema are wusses 'cos they feed their tortoise using tongs while wearing gloves.

"They're silly, I like feeding the tortoise."

"Yeah, me too. He really likes limes you know. When I last had him, which was ages ago, I gave him two small sour ones and he gobbled them up whole."

Jay opens his mouth and mimics swallowing the limes. He makes a loud chomping sound to prove his point.

"My mum's happy you've been looking after him more now. 'Cos when he was with us, she was forced to put him on a diet 'cos the food bills were getting too high. He got so hungry, I had to sneak him my rice and carrots. He turned his nose up at the rice but liked the carrots."

"He's a proud one just like my old cat Meow Meow. She turned her nose up at a lot of foods. I miss her lots."

"Yeah, I know, it's sad your grandma made you give her to the RSPCA."

"Yeah, I liked having Meow Meow around. She didn't say nothing but it was just nice having her sitting there. Just by having her in my room it changed everything. Like everything felt more happy. It's hard to explain."

I finally pluck up the courage to ask him how he feels about Milly, I can see my hands start to shake. But I want to sound all casual like it don't matter at all.

"So, like... what do you think of... of... Milly. Like I think... I think she fancies you."

"Well... she... she knows more about music than... any... any girl I've ever met and she's got nice hair."

I feel my face getting all red and I can't look at Jay. He looks at the floor and starts pulling on the carpet before he continues.

"... but Milly's well annoying, so it'll never work. Anyway, I prefer... like... I... I prefer hanging out with... just with you."

"Me too."

I feel super duper happy! The most happy I've felt in a

really long time. I want to give him a big hug. But I feel too shy, so I just grin like a silly monkey and look at the tortoise. He's walking s-l-o-w-l-y across the room, his claws get caught in the rug and he doesn't seem to care. I untangle him.

Silly tortoise that I like so much with the fat head.

"Oh yeah Xing, he quite likes dog biscuits as well. My neighbour's dog buried one in the front garden and he sniffed and pulled it out. He was a bit stuck after that for a few weeks. Then he pooed everywhere, best not to give him any more."

I like the way Jay says things without hiding anything. When his mother asked him if she had put on weight, he answered, "Not everywhere, but your tummy makes you look a bit pregnant."

When Lai Ker told Jay that his computer skills were crap, he simply replied, "Yes that's true."

Grandma is always telling me that I have to keep things in the family. When I was four, she opened my palm so my fingers were spread out flat. She said, "This is your family." Then she put a crumpled sweet wrapper into the middle of my hand and closed my hand tightly. "Chinese families keep rubbish in and don't let rubbish out." She kept my hand closed shut even when I struggled to open it. I laughed 'cos I thought she was being funny. But now that I'm nearly grown up, I know it ain't a game.

The Wus take their rubbish to the grave.

To the outside world, Uncle Ho is a writer and works from home. That's why he sleeps at odd hours and is well strange. As for Grandpa, people don't know he's alive and living in Singapore. Instead, he passed away twenty years ago and made the family millions through working as an investment banker. Also, everyone thinks Auntie Mei does acting as a hobby, but her real job is as a plastic surgeon, that's why she travels so much. But you know what's weird? The Wus aren't the only people to "keep the rubbish in". When Mrs Alsanea's husband was on the dole, she told everyone he had found a job at the employment office. Mama caught him picking up his cheque when she was there looking for a job. Our old neighbour Mr Wang said his son studied Economics in Bristol and was dating a girl called Lesley. His son was actually studying fashion at St Martins and dating a guy called Lesley. But Jay's family is different. He gets a big telling off if he breaks the ninth commandment. He said they've seen enough lies in their life especially from other Christians. After going to a mega church for ten years, they left when one pastor had an affair and another nicked funds from the offertory box. Now they attend a small home church that don't have no rituals and keeps things simple. All they do is love God and love others. Simple - no arguments about whether communion is in a cup or glass.

The tortoise is nibbling on the edge of the rug Grandma bought in the sale for £3,500. His yellow eyes do not blink and he looks determined. He must be hungry AGAIN. I feed him some mints and he don't like them so he spits them out immediately - like within half a second. We laugh! From the tortoise there's no lying, hiding, or minding your Ps and Qs. Just a slimy, half-bitten Tic Tac on the floor.

Chapter 35
Tick Tock

Grandma is out playing mahjong and Auntie Mei is still in Croatia finishing some scenes for a Hollywood film to do with kung fu fighting aliens. As soon as the maids leave the house, I rush up the stairs to my bedroom. I lock the door, unlock it and lock it again. The rusty lock is a bit stiff at times and I don't want to take no chances.

BAM!!

The cupboard door hits me in the head.

I fall to the floor and Uncle Ho steps out.

I'm scared to breathe and my heart is galloping lots. He stares at me and offers his hand to pull me up. I don't take his hand and scoot my bum to the edge of the room near the window. My head is throbbing a bit and I rub it. Mama said rubbing bruises stops blood clots from forming. When I bruised myself she would rub my bruises until they turned from black to yellow. I begged her to stop. But she said rubbing helps with the healing 'cos sometimes pain is good.

Uncle Ho walks towards me and stops when he's about half a foot away.

"Xing, we need to talk."

I'm looking at the window wondering if the neighbours would be able to hear me if I opened it and shouted for help. They have very pricey, double-glazed windows.

"We NEED to talk."

"What do you want to talk about?"

My voice is all shaky and weird. Uncle Ho sits down next to me on the floor. He almost topples over like a drunken man losing his balance.

"I need you to help me. But you still haven't helped me. I've been waiting every day and you haven't helped me."

His pills are lying at the bottom of my drawer between old, white, cotton knickers and stripy, multi-coloured socks. I edge away from Uncle Ho bit by bit. He moves even slower towards me, making sure we're never more than half a foot away from each other.

"I'm sorry Uncle Ho, but I'm... I'm waiting... for the right time."

"Now is the right time. No-one is in. Just you and me."

The clock ticks in slow motion, only four minutes have passed. Another two hours to go. I need to think up things to chat about before he gets annoyed; before he knows I'm lying.

"Uncle Ho, why do you want to die?"

He stares at me.

"Why do you want me to help YOU to die?"

Maybe saying it out loud will make him understand how serious it is. Maybe talking about dying will scare him the way it scares me. I don't know, maybe it's a crap idea, but I don't know what else to do. He doesn't answer and I repeat my question again.

"Uncle Ho, WHY do you want to DIE?"

I can almost hear his brain ticking; maybe I've broken through the fog in his mind. He looks at the floor and starts speaking real soft.

"I want to die 'cos I am bored of my life."

His eyes look at me and I see tears forming. I've never been so close to Uncle Ho's face. His skin looks more blotchy than usual - it looks red and scaly as if it would be sore to the touch. His wrinkly face reminds me of a Chinese farmer I saw in Auntie Mei's *National Geographic*. Like the grinning farmer Uncle Ho has deep smile lines except I have never seen him smile.

"I am bored of my life."

He shakes his head from side to side like he is moving in slow motion. His words come out all whispery.

"So bored. So bored."

I see tears dripping down his face and mucus trickling from his nose, but he doesn't wipe it away.

"I am bored of my life… sometimes I feel sad. I feel sad through my whole body and it aches. I lie there waiting for it to go. But it doesn't. Every day I wake up, eat, sleep, eat, sleep, eat, sleep. I can't do it any more. I can't do IT any more."

Uncle Ho starts to breathe quicker, his tears are falling onto his red shirt and I can see dark patches forming under his armpits.

I know how he feels.

After *The Incident* that's how I feel a lot of the time. That sad feeling that he talks about, the one that goes through my whole body. Some days I wake up and the sad feeling is with me from the moment I open my eyes until the end of the day.

Uncle Ho starts talking really fast like every word is a horse galloping in a race.

"I am sick. I have been sick since I was a teenager. I bet THEY were happy when I became sick."

"THEY?"

"THEY said I was a poof because I had to wear a pink T-shirt in PE because Pa thought it was a joke putting his red sock in the wash. THEY found his joke funny. THEY called me the 'chink fag'. THEY laughed and laughed and laughed. But I showed THEM. I got sick, THEY couldn't touch me any more."

"Who are THEY?"

He keeps quiet. I can see he is shaking badly, I want to reach over and put my hand on him but I can't. Instead I edge a little bit closer. His tears keep dripping down his neck and onto his chest. He still doesn't wipe them away; he just lets them flow.

Suddenly, he crouches to the ground and starts to pound the floor with his arm. I watch him hitting the floor over and over again. He whacks the floor like a child having a tantrum. I suddenly remember the story Mama told me about Uncle Ho when he was little and how desperate he was for a packet of lemon sherbets. When Grandma refused, he threw the sweets at her and fell to the floor crying and flailing his arms.

Uncle Ho was a boy once.

I think of the picture of a young Uncle Ho on the mantelpiece holding up a fish that he caught in Devon. All smiley and dimply with messy black hair. A young boy with hopes and dreams just like all the boys in the world. He went to West Hill, loved sweets and when he grew up, he was gonna be a pilot.

Uncle Ho keeps bashing his clenched fist into the floor. His hand is turning red and is starting to bruise.

"THEY wanted me to be sick. THEY kept laughing and laughing and laughing. Ma sent me to see the expensive doctors, but I know I can never be cured. Ma hopes I will, but I know I can't. I will die one day because I am sick. Why not today? Today, tomorrow, next year, it is all the same. Every day is all the same."

I want him to stop the banging and crying. I'm desperate for him to stop. He's starting to whimper softly. Cuts have started to form on his right hand. He keeps hitting the floor over and over and over again. Blood and bruises and tears.

I think of the night of *The Incident* and feel my eyes fill with tears. I understand his pain. I understand his pain of people thinking he's crap; his pain of not fitting in; his pain of being seen as different.

Why not today? Today, tomorrow, next year, it is all the same. Every day is all the same.

I get up from the floor and open my drawer.

The banging stops.

Uncle Ho is kneeling in a praying position and his bloodshot eyes stare at me. His eyes are begging me, they're willing me to carry on. I fish out the clear plastic bag with the pills and it feels cold and heavy in my hands. I grip the pills so tightly, some of them crush in my hand. Then I unlock my door and Uncle Ho follows me in silence down the stairs. There's a joyful bounce to his step and the beginning of a smile. I could run outside and throw the pills in the bin. I could end this right now. But my legs carry me past the front door, down the corridor and into the kitchen.

Uncle Ho was a happy child.

The heating has been turned off and I feel a chill run through my body. I open the cupboard under the sink and take out the chef's pounder bowl. Uncle Ho sits down heavily on a stool and watches me all quiet and peaceful. I put a pill in the heavy bowl and crush it, then another pill, then another. My eyes fill with tears. They drop into the white powder and a glue-like paste starts to form. Uncle Ho starts to cry too. My tears are sad tears; his tears are happy ones. In my head I count each pill as I crush them.

One.

Two.

Three.

Four.

Five.

Six.

Seven.

Eight.

Eight pills have been crushed already, there's another hundred or so to go. I suddenly think of Mama. What would she say if she were standing here right now? How would she feel? Would she be proud that I was making Uncle Ho happy? She loved Uncle Ho, she would want me to be brave, she would want me to make him happy.

He has a chance to be with Mama.

Nine.

Ten.

Eleven.

All of a sudden, I hear Mama's voice. It's super clear and loud, as if she's standing behind.

Xing, what are you doing to my brother?

I drop the pounder on the marble table top.

CLANG

Uncle Ho gets up quickly from the stool and it falls to the floor. He looks furious and he narrows his eyes at me. A few seconds ago, he was sobbing lots, but it's like a switch has gone off in his brain.

"WHY HAVE YOU STOPPED?"

"I'm sorry."

I'm trembling so much I can see the bottom of my jumper shaking up and down.

"I'm sorry. I just… "

I can't do it.

Uncle Ho rushes over to where I'm standing. He's breathing very quickly and I can smell his sweat. His fist is clenched and he looks ready to punch me at any moment. I don't want to carry on. I want to leave. I want to leave forever.

"I'm sorry, I was… I was just taking a break. I will carry on."

I put another pill into the bowl and pound it as s-l-o-w-l-y as I can. The pounder feels slippery as it shakes in my sweaty hand. If I give Uncle Ho most of the pills, he'll probably fall into a coma. Maybe he won't die. If I give him all the pills he will die. If I don't give him the pills, I might die. It's him or me. I think of the night of *The Incident*. It was Shils and me. I should have run away when I could. I shouldn't have reached for my pepper spray; I should have run away faster without turning back.

Twelve.

Thirteen.

Fourteen.

If I give the pills to him, he could die. If I don't give them to him, I could die.

Him or me?

Fifteen.

Sixteen.

Seventeen.

Eighteen.

Him or me?

I could make a run for it; maybe I could run out of the back door? I could hide in the shed with the tortoise. I hear Mama's voice again; it's louder than the last time.

Xing, you need to STOP.

Uncle Ho's now sitting at the kitchen counter. He's less than two feet away. He looks like he's in a trance.

Nineteen.

Twenty.

I turn swiftly and push the handle on the kitchen door.

IT'S LOCKED.

Uncle Ho grabs my arm roughly and I trip and fall to the floor. I cover my head with my hands, he is standing right over me. His breath is hitting the back of my neck. I won't be able to fight off his large frame. I see Shils standing over me, I can hear the rain and smell the alcohol on her breath. Her voice is pounding in my head.

Stupid chink.

Stupid bitch.

"HO, WHAT YOU DOING?"

Grandma has arrived home and her face looks pale like she's about to faint. Uncle Ho doesn't say nothing to Grandma and runs out of the kitchen.

"Xing Li, what you doing on floor? Get up quick."

I grab Grandma's hand and she stands in silence as I explain EVERYTHING to her. I see her take a massive breath when I point at the crushed pills in the bowl.

"How many pills in bag?

"I don't know Grandma, maybe eighty, a hundred? I didn't count."

"First time he ask you?"

"No, he asked me many times, but I didn't know how to tell anyone."

Grandma nods and sits down on the kitchen chair. She looks furious.

"HO, COME HERE NOW."

Uncle Ho walks slowly into the kitchen; Grandma is the only person he listens to. She is the only person who really loves him. Grandma turns to me and screams the loudest I've ever heard in my life.

"XING LI, WHY YOU NEVER TELL ME HE WANT TO DIE? WHY YOU KEEP SECRET? WHY YOU NEVER TELL ME? GO TO YOUR ROOM, YOU TERRIBLE GIRL."

Uncle Ho puts his hand on her shoulder like he's comforting her or something. I run to my room and slam the door. I will never ever forgive Grandma. She chased away Lai Ker, she doesn't care about what happened with Shils, she blames me for Uncle Ho. I hate Grandma more than anyone in the world.

I hate Grandma more than Shils.

Chapter 36
The Grandma of Wrath

I wake up to the sound of the front door slamming. I look outside and see a green and white van pulling away. It's super cold today, the kind of morning you would give your right arm for thirty more minutes in bed. My bed is so snuggly and I feel like a warm polar bear all wrapped in fur. I tiptoe into the silence of the usual breakfast routine. Grandma's reading her papers; she ignores me. There's nothing strange about the silence, but it feels weird like more quiet than usual, like there's something missing. I pour the last of the cornflakes into my bowl and go to the fridge to look for the milk. That's weird, there isn't any more milk. The maids get into serious trouble when we run out of food, Grandma once sacked a maid when we ran out of eggs. Grandma walks slowly behind me. The bags under her eyes look puffy and sore. In her hand is the missing half full carton of milk. Without looking at me, she unscrews the cap and pours it down the sink. She shuffles back to her newspapers and continues to read the business section of *The Times*.

Grandma doesn't speak about Uncle Ho or where he's been taken to. I overheard one of the maids saying that they've locked him up somewhere and they became all quiet when I passed by. I feel bad 'cos even though I feel sorry for him, I'm actually secretly happy he's not around any more.

I know that makes me a terrible person 'cos Auntie Mei said he's sick and how he acts is not his fault.

Grandma dusts off some old tiffin tins and begins filling them with home cooked food that she's prepared. She starts to leave at 6am in the morning and returns pale faced and red eyed in the evening. The maids quietly take the empty containers out of her hands and wash them in super speed. This goes on for almost a week. Day after day after day, Grandma does her tiffin tin ritual. After six days, Grandma comes home really, really red eyed, like super bloodshot and puffy. The next day she stops doing her tiffin tin ritual and everything to do with Uncle Ho gets erased from the house. Every scrap of clothes, furniture, every hair in the bathroom, every half-eaten bit of food is gone. His bedroom has become like a cold, empty tomb. Grandma insists his old window be left open at all times, even when it's minus one outside. The only thing left by Uncle Ho is a tiny white pill I find amongst my socks and underwear.

School's getting a bit better; each day is passing quicker. I'm not as sad as before 'cos with Shils now gone, school is actually sometimes okay and not scary at all. Also with Uncle Ho gone I feel more safe at home. Though I wish I knew where Lai Ker was. So much has happened. I hope it won't be too long before we see each other 'cos he is my only real family left. But I know he will come back for me one day. I just know he will. Grandma isn't my real family. I guess Auntie Mei is my half family, 'cos I like her lots and she seems to care for me. But still she's not my true blue real family like Lai Ker. Like she weren't there the day the police came round and told us Mama had died, only Lai Ker. When I lay on the sofa crying, he sat with me and shook his leg and didn't say a word. After I stopped, he gave me ice cream - chocolate ice cream. Then he put the frozen lasagne in the microwave for our dinner. Before he gave it to me he cut all the burnt bits out, just like Mama would have done. That night while I was sleeping, or at least pretending to sleep, I saw him triple Sellotape the box with all my stuff nice and tight. He didn't cry once. But he did make lots of jokes and that helped me. He is my real family, no-one else, just him.

I quite like swimming now and can do breaststroke, which is a swimming move that sounds dirty but it's not at all. In fact, I'm quite good at breaststroke and our PE teacher asked me if I wanted to join the swimming club. Milly and Preema are in swimming club. They still hang out with us lots but I don't mind as much 'cos Milly has started dating the Cliff Richard lookalike and says she's "completely and utterly in love with him". She's still annoying but lends me lots of her DS games. She literally has all of them. Preema has a boyfriend too, but I think I fell asleep halfway though her story about her and Tony Porter. Jay is still my bestest friend in the whole world, but he's joined orchestra on Friday so we only hang out from Monday to Thursday. To celebrate him getting a solo piece in the West Hill summer concert, Jay's gonna treat me to Mr Chan's chips, not JUST the chips but also the fish as well!

"Yeah my dad is well proud that I got the solo piece. He said if I work hard maybe I can be a musician like him."

"Yeah, that would be cool. I can't wait to see you playing in a massive concert hall. It's cool that you don't mind playing in public no more."

"Well, you were my first proper audience."

I smile lots.

The shop is well busy today. There's a huge gang of kids - many of them have dyed hair and piercings. They're only a bit older than Jay and me. Each time Mr Chan turns to fry the fish, they reach over the counter to nick his chips. They're laughing and listening to loud music. The tallest guy with long purple hair lights a ciggie right in front of the sign that says *NO SMOKING*. The smoke fills the room and the air starts to smell like burnt fish. Mr Chan doesn't say a word; he rubs the sweat from his forehead with an old manky cloth around his neck. I've never seen him without the cloth round his neck. He starts to wrap the orders super fast without looking up once.

"HEY BOY, HAVE SOME RESPECT."

In the corner of the shop sits an old Indian man with a walking stick. I didn't notice him before; it was as if he was hiding behind the massive pot plant or something. He gets up and shakes his walking stick at the tall purple haired guy.

"HEY BOY, I'M TALKING TO YOU. I SAID HAVE SOME RESPECT. CAN YOU NOT READ OR ARE YOU BLIND?"

"What's YOUR problem old man?"

"YOU WANT TO KNOW MY PROBLEM? YOU WANT TO KNOW MY PROBLEM?"

I can see the old man's knees shaking but he walks closer to the purple haired guy and points his stick at the guy's face.

"MY PROBLEM IS YOUNG PEOPLE LIKE YOU. YOU NEED TO HAVE SOME RESPECT. IF YOU WERE IN MY SCHOOL WHEN I WAS A HEADMASTER IN INDIA, I WOULD HIT YOU SO HARD WITH THE STICK THAT YOU WOULD KNOW WHAT RESPECT IS."

"Well I'm not in India, I'm in London and I can do what the hell I want."

Jay walks up to the old man and I follow him. We're not going to let this bully get away. Jay folds his arms and looks up at the guy. He's like half the size of the guy.

"Yeah, listen to the man, you should have some respect."

"Or WHAT?"

Jay keeps quiet and just stares. He doesn't move, he just silently stares. They stand there locked in eye contact for a good ten seconds. Suddenly, Jay changes his stance as if he is about to use some kung fu moves to kick the guy's ass. He's doing the exact formation that Bruce Lee did in *Enter The Dragon*. Jay doesn't take his eyes off the guy once. The guy looks at me then he looks at Jay then back at me again. He puts his hands through his long, purple hair.

"You're not worth it."

The tall guy throws a twenty-pound note at Mr Chan.

"Keep the change."

One of his friends knocks the walking stick out of the old man's hand before they head off to whatever hole they came from. I pick up the walking stick and give it to the Indian man. He shakes his head while clucking his tongue.

"What is the world coming to? These young people have no respect. I wish your boyfriend used his kung fu to teach them a lesson."

I don't have the heart to tell him that Jay isn't my boyfriend and he definitely doesn't know kung fu. The old man tucks his shirt into his trousers, turns to Mr Chan and tuts lots.

"These children have no respect, you MUST tell them off. If they cause trouble you must call the police. They need to understand what respect is. When I was in India, I never dared speak back to my elders. If I did, my father would give me a big slap. I blame the parents. These children, they don't know any better because the parents don't teach them what is right or wrong. So you MUST tell them off okay?"

Mr Chan shakes his head and sighs.

"Yes, I tell them off then the next day my window is smashed. What can I do? I'm just trying to make a living."

A tiny Chinese girl in a worn out pink dress peeks out from behind the curtains in the back. She can't be more than six.

"Uncle, I've finished the homework Ma gave me."

"That's good, you can watch TV now before your mother comes to pick you up."

"But I'm hungry. Can I have some chips?"

"No, your Ma will give you proper food later. She is just working late at the restaurant. Just be a good girl and wait."

I see the pretty little girl nod and join her brother in front of the tiny TV. There's only a thin worn out sheet that separates us from their little world. Mr Chan sighs and puts some more chips in the fryer. Then he looks at us and puts on a sad smile.

"So, what would you like today?"

I've come home from school and I'm super sleepy after stuffing myself with chips. Jay and me shared a massive portion of fish. Mr Chan gave us the biggest one he had and also threw in some free mushy peas.

WAIT A SECOND!

Grandma is waving goodbye to a man from the RSPCA. The truck nearly knocks me over as it reverses out of our drive. I rush to the box the tortoise lives in. He's gone!

"You not looking after tortoise. He sleeping too much. So, I get better home."

"But Grandma, I need the tortoise for school work. Mrs Wilkins will kill me if she finds out the tortoise is gone."

"I call teacher, she understand situation. NO PROBLEMS. NOW TIME FOR HOMEWORK."

Grandma gives me her ice woman stare.

My tortoise has followed the same fate as Meow Meow. I go to my bedroom and scream into my pillow. I'm so tired. Tired of Grandma, tired of meanness, tired of rude boys, tired of families, tired of missing Lai Ker. I fall asleep and dream about tortoises and guys with purple hair and swimming in the pool that goes dark blue when you pee in it.

Chapter 37
Let Dem Eat Cake

I wake with a jerk to a loud knocking at the door. The clock says seven-thirty-two; I must have fallen asleep for at least two hours. The knocking continues. We never get visitors after six. Grandma doesn't like people butting into "Family Time". I hear the tapping of Grandma's new clogs across the hallway, the opening of the heavy oak door and a man's voice. I drift back to sleep, too tired to care.

The Visit
"It is so good to see you again, Mrs Wu."

Mr Haywood was making a rare house call. Headmasters only made house calls when a student had done something atrocious. This was the second house call he had made to Mrs Wu. The first was after Lai Xing Wu's scandalous business with the TF4 cards. Mrs Wu had filled Mr Haywood with lemon cake and organic Earl Grey, and graciously thanked him for looking out for her grandson. Mr Haywood assured Mrs Wu he would take Lai Xing under his wing and she was "not to worry about his future". He saw something special in Lai Xing Wu. With the right guidance, Lai Xing was the sort of young man who could reach far.

Headmasters and professors were among the only people Mrs Wu truly respected. Mr Haywood had a PhD from Cambridge and had written several academic books including a 400-page bestseller called *Spare the Rod, Spoil the Child*. It was a non-fiction book arguing the merits of corporal punishment returning to the school system. Mrs Wu had Mr Haywood's book on her shelf, it had been read and referred to many times. Nevertheless, Mrs Wu had never told Mr Haywood she was a great admirer of his work.

When Lai Xing got into trouble with the law, Mr Haywood was the first person Mrs Wu rang. She knew he was the only one who would understand the gravity of the situation. Dealing with unruly children was his speciality. The aged headmaster was someone who Mrs Wu respected and trusted. Most importantly, he was a gentleman who would be discreet. Mr Haywood persuaded Mrs Wu that the best solution for her grandson would be to spend a period of time with himself. Consequently, unbeknown to his younger sister, Lai Xing moved in with Mr Haywood as soon as he was discharged from hospital. Lai Xing was given a second chance after he had strayed from the path that led to good education, strong morals and a respectable job.

Three months previously, Lai Xing had started work at a Chinese restaurant called Green Dragon. He had acquired the job via his best friend Jimmy Tang. The work was difficult and the tips were appalling. However, what drew Lai Xing and Jimmy Tang to the greasy, dilapidated restaurant was the friends they made. There was a deep sense of acceptance and camaraderie they had never experienced before. They learnt how to play poker and were allowed to swear and speak their minds.

The friends were recruited to join an organisation called the Chinese Alliance Group (CAG). It was an organisation that believed in defending the rights of Chinese people in society. The founders of the CAG started off with the intention of being a voice for Chinese people. Through their hard work, a number of Chinese people had found justice. Previous examples were city workers that had faced unfair dismissal, restaurant owners facing discrimination and Chinese journalists who were silenced. Nevertheless, as the years passed, the direction of the group had changed and evolved. Their repeated efforts to be heard in society had not borne the fruit that they desired. Many petitions had been signed along with countless calls for new laws to support equal opportunities. All their hours of fundraising and organisation had seemingly come to nothing. The CAG slowly evolved into an organisation that believed in getting the Chinese community heard through any means possible.

With his passion for getting British Chinese people heard, Lai Xing was someone the CAG believed would one day have a crucial role in their organisation. They wanted Lai Xing to commit to their group by going to regular meetings and showing his allegiance by fulfilling all the assignments they gave him. Putting graffiti on his classmate's father's restaurant was only the start of their long term plans to assimilate Lai Xing into the group's direction. If he had not been caught with the graffiti spray, Lai Xing's next assignment would have been something a little more daring, followed by something a little bit more criminal, followed by something a little more sinister. If Mr Haywood had not stepped in and given Lai Ker a home in his spare room after his "graffiti incident", the young Chinese boy may have ended up taking quite a different path.

Mr Haywood was someone whom Lai Xing trusted, a father figure that had cared for him when no-one else did. He gave Lai Xing the best present a man can give a young lad. He gave him time. Over many chess games and cups of tea, a trusted friendship had been built with Mr Haywood. This close friendship with an upper class English man, an outsider, a *gweilo*, was something the CAG saw as a threat to Lai Xing's growth and identity. When Lai Xing moved in with Mr Haywood after his arrest, he was abandoned first by the CAG, and later by his best friend Jimmy Tang.

Mr Haywood sat awkwardly in the living room of Mrs Wu.

"I get chocolate cake, then we talk."

"Thank you Mrs Wu, you really are too kind. I still have fond memories of the exquisite lemon cake you gave me on my previous visit."

"That lemon cake from Harold & Sons, quite cheap price, £8.99. This cake made special from neighbour French chef. He use work in five star hotel you know. So little more money, £16.99. But you see if good."

"Thank you. You are too kind."

Mr Haywood lifted a large spoonful of chocolate cake into his mouth and dabbed his lips with a neatly pressed handkerchief from his pocket.

"Thank you for agreeing to meet with me, Mrs Wu. It is always such a pleasure to meet families that have such special interest in their children or in your case grandchildren."

"I do best I can. Not easy with these modern children."

"Well, Lai Xing has turned out to be a fine young man. He is quite exceptional in his mathematical abilities and I hear his rugby skills are good too. Nothing makes me prouder than to have a student who is talented both mentally and physically. "

"When he break law, I so mad, I don't know what to do. I don't want him stay and be bad influence on my granddaughter. I scared he come back make her break law too. Next you know, they have guns and drugs in room. But then you say can try live with you, so I think maybe see how he is with you. You look after hundreds boys over years. So trust you but hard as I never trust anyone."

"Mrs Wu, as you know, I like to take a keen interest in the future of Hampstead boys. Lai Xing has been a pleasure to have around. I live by myself, so it had been quite lonely and he is a lively chap."

"Yes, he loud mouth boy."

"Well, Mrs Wu it is completely your decision, but perhaps he is ready to see his sister again. He wouldn't admit it, but

I can tell by the way he talks about her, he misses her very much."

"Yes, maybe I let him see her soon. But she going through bad things herself, maybe wait a while first."

"Of course, as I said, it is completely your decision."

"I think about it."

"Yes, that would be good."

"I see when a good time."

"Yes indeed. Anyway, you must be wondering why I wanted to visit. Well, I wanted to give you the wonderful news in person. I am terribly excited to let you know that Cambridge has shown great interest in your grandson."

All the hairs on Mrs Wu's skin quivered in excitement at the sound of the word: Cambridge.

"Mrs Wu, they are very serious about offering Lai Xing a scholarship to study Mathematics when he finishes his A levels. This is an excellent opportunity for your grandson."

"Yes, Cambridge good school. I pleased he can go."

"Mrs Wu, you must be very proud of your grandson. Yes, he's had his troubles. But overall, he is a fine young man, you have done a good job."

"I guess he okay."

"In fact, brains seem to run in your family. I do remember your clever son. What was his name again? Oh yes, Ho. He was one of our best students. As I recall, he was a quiet boy, not like Lai Xing at all. But he was definitely a very smart boy. My son Richard was in the same class as him, they weren't close friends - more like acquaintances. Richard used to complain that Ho always beat him by a few marks in every subject."

Mr Haywood laughed at the fond memory while Mrs Wu shifted in her seat as if she had a painful itch on her rear.

"How is Ho these days?"

"He fine. How is your son?"

"My son. He… "

"He live nearby?"

"No."

"He live far away?"

"Not exactly."

"Where he live? He move overseas? He go America?"

Mr Haywood turned red under Mrs Wu's quick fire questions.

"My son... my son, he sadly passed away."

Mrs Wu's machine gun questioning style was given a rest and she slurped loudly on her tea.

"I sorry to hear about son."

"Thank you. It has been such a long time - more than twenty years. But it's never easy saying it out loud."

"How he die?"

Mr Haywood took a long sigh and looked at his feet. In Hampstead he walked up and down the corridor like an army general. In his presence, children would stand upright and straighten their shirts or run their fingers through their uncombed hair. In Mrs Wu's presence, he felt like a lost boy.

"Mrs Wu, sometimes things happen that only God can explain. You see my son was a very, very happy child. He was a good boy."

"I sure he good boy with good father like you. He lucky to have good father, not many so lucky."

"Well, I tried my best. I guess as parents you always want what is best, but sometimes you don't know how. You see my son was always a sensitive boy."

"Sensitive boy?"

"Yes, what a sensitive boy he was! I remember when he drowned his pet frog by mistake he cried for two weeks - only ceasing when my wife bought him a hamster. After a couple of years, the hamster died. He was inconsolable for a month until my wife got him a puppy. She was good like that."

Mrs Wu sat in silence; it was not an awkward silence. It was an appropriate one.

"She was good at giving him something new to nullify the pain of losing something he cared about."

Mr Haywood picked up his tea, the teacup started to shake against the saucer.

"When my wife died from cancer, I had nothing to give him to take the place of his mother. She was not like his frog or his hamster or his dog. Nothing could ever replace her. He didn't want to talk about it. At sixteen, he was at an awkward age - neither a man nor a boy. I have never been good at talking about my feelings myself. I suppose he got that from me."

Grandma quickly filled Mr Haywood's teacup with more tea. She believed a guest's empty teacup showed disrespect.

"Your son sad. When people sad they stop talking. They become silent, but silence good for heal pain."

"That's exactly what I thought too. I believed if I gave him his time of silence, it would heal him. Over time, it did. He started to go out with his friends and became more social. I mean he was sociable, but he still studied hard."

"He work hard, sound like good boy."

Mr Haywood absentmindedly sipped the hot tea. He jerked his head back when the hot liquid burnt his tongue.

"He was a good boy and really terribly smart too. Much smarter than me, but I never told him that. I thought if I told him he wouldn't have anything to aim for."

"Yes, I feel same. No push children get so, so lazy."

"Yes indeed. He did end up working very hard. He got straight As for his A levels and attended Oxford. When he was awarded a First Class degree I was so proud of him. I told him his mother would be proud of him too. He started to cry, I teared up too. It was an emotional day for the both of us."

"Good he go to Oxford, very good school."

"Yes, it was the proudest day of my life."

"Of course lots to be proud for."

"Yes, I was so very proud. In fact, I planned a small celebration at my home. All his friends and his girlfriend Sandra were there. But it was very strange because he didn't turn up. We waited for a very long time but he failed to arrive. The alarm bells started ringing when it was eleven o'clock at night and he had still not arrived. That was very unlike him, he was always on time, just like me. I sat in my lounge waiting - just waiting and waiting for days. They were the most painful days of my life. The not knowing was killing me."

Mr Haywood paused and his voice went hoarse.

"It was a week before I got the news. Two policemen came to my house. It was a Sunday morning. As soon as I saw their faces, I knew what they were going to say. They didn't have to say one word. I knew it already. My son was dead."

Mr Haywood's teacup continued to tremble. Mrs Wu gently took it from him and put it on the side table.

"They said it was a tragic accident, he had drowned off the coast of Coverack in Cornwall. His alcohol level was off the chart. They said he must have slipped in his drunken state and drowned. But I knew in my heart it wasn't an accident. My son was one of the best swimmers that Hampstead ever produced. Coverack was my wife's hometown."

Mrs Wu and Mr Haywood sat in silence to the ticking of the grandfather clock in the living room. Mr Haywood's half-empty teacup remained on the table. They sat in the stillness of their sadness.

Mrs Wu was the first to speak.

Her words came out slowly; her voice was choking as each syllable left her mouth.

"My son… my son…

… he very sick.

… he sick for many years.

… he like your son.

… he die too."

Mrs Wu's shoulders started to shake as she cried into her hands. Mr Haywood gently put his hand on her right shoulder. There were tears in his eyes.

230

Chapter 38
Crappy Birthday

Mr Haywood keeps giving Grandma these mid-week visits for really strange reasons. Like he wanted to see Grandma's gardener about growing the perfect rose bush. After talking for two minutes about squishing green flies and weeds, he spent two hours drinking tea with Grandma. Then yesterday, Mr Haywood came to receive cooking tips from our Chinese chef. The chef sniggered when Mr Haywood asked him how many tablespoons of ketchup were needed in sweet and sour pork. With a smirk, the chef told Mr Haywood sweet and sour pork was a cheap dish made up by Chinese takeaways for white people.

"Ketchup with chips, ketchup with sandwich, ketchup with fish, ketchup with chicken. Ketchup, ketchup, ketchup. What wrong with soy sauce? You know, if I cook this dish, my family in China disown me."

Grandma saved Mr Haywood from the angry chef and offered him coffee cake with walnut frosting. "This one made by expensive bakery, £5.99 a piece. I so shocked at price."

Mr Haywood's visits are becoming more and more regular. Sometimes he arrives really early in the morning - like before the birds have even got up. Grandma hands him a basket of steaming food and they have breakfast in the park. On Sunday afternoons, Grandma and Mr Haywood sit in the garden and read the newspapers together. Grandma starts with *The Straits Times* followed by *The Times* and finished with *The Sun*. Mr Haywood starts with *The Times* followed by *The Straits Times* and doesn't touch *The Sun*. They eat well expensive cake and drink loads and loads of tea. Grandma likes to boss Mr Haywood around. She tells him his trousers are too creased or he eats too fast or he needs to speak louder. When she bosses him around, Mr Haywood doesn't say anything, he just smiles. Sometimes they sit in complete silence or chat in low voices until the sun goes down.

Grandma's got Mr Haywood and I've got Jay. But Grandma and me don't have each other, in many ways we never did. We'll never be like those Grandma and grandkids in the fairy tales. The stories where cuddly Grandmas make pies for their grandkids and they laugh together and put flour on each others' noses. Grandma doesn't even shout at me any more. It's weird, like we both live in the same house, but it's like we're both not there. I think she's still mad at me 'cos of what happened with Uncle Ho. But I don't care 'cos I'm still mad at her for everything. Uncle Ho is safe in hospital isn't he? So why can't she let it go?

Today is the 30th of May.

It's Mama's birthday and it's horrible 'cos she's not here. I'm sad today but I'm also really mad that 'cos of Grandma, Lai Ker isn't here. She said, "He alive, that all you need know." When I ask her more she puts her hand in the air like those traffic wardens directing traffic when the traffic lights are busted.

When we were little, Mama would get her own cake for her birthday. It was always a frozen strawberry cheesecake from Iceland and we would wait all day for it to melt. I would put the candles on, Lai Ker would light them and Mama would blow them out. She'd always give us the cake first and we'd stuff our faces until we were full. After we were old enough to understand that Mama shouldn't get her own birthday cake,

232

Lai Ker and me pulled our pocket money together to surprise her with the fresh vanilla cheesecake from the bakery. Mama cried. But she said it was 'cos she was so happy not 'cos she didn't like the flavour.

Mr Haywood's got Grandma to buy a large, white kitchen table. I think he told her that she needs to be modern or something. It looks like a shiny ice skating rink with Grandma sitting on one end and me on the other. I'm too upset about Mama's birthday to look at Grandma when I sit down for breakfast. She ignores me as usual. Auntie Mei is STILL in Croatia with her crazy film. But I think she's having lots of fun. She is staying in a posh hotel and gets to order room service whenever she wants. Also, she's been drinking a lot of this drink called Rank-Jar. I wish she'd come back soon, the house feels all big and creepy and quiet when it's just Grandma and me. If a mouse were to creep across the table, we'd hear its little feet ice skating on the polished surface. I think of a little mouse with tiny white ice skates and it makes me smile. But then I remember that I want Grandma to know that I'm still mad with her so I quickly put on my serious face.

The usual stack of newspapers is lying in the middle of the table. My favourite pop star Justin Bird is smiling from the front cover in a diamante suit. The title reads, "Shock Love Child of Teenage Star", the newspaper is calling to me like a siren from a lighthouse. From the corner of my eye, I can see Grandma sitting super still. She's leaning against the kitchen counter and is not moving a millimetre. I KNOW she is waiting to see if I fall into her trap. I'm not gonna touch the newspapers; I'm not gonna mention Mama's birthday. I'm gonna eat my breakfast and go to school without saying a word. I crunch really hard onto my chocolate hoops, making as much noise as possible. If she opens her mouth and breaks the silence, it will annoy the heck out of her.

Chomp, chomp, chomp.
Silence

Crunch, crunch, crunch.

Silence

Chomp, crunch, crunch, chomp, slurp.

Silence

I glance briefly at Grandma. A little flicker of her being annoyed would be enough to make my day, but she is staring at the wall behind me. I give a loud burp.

Silence

What is she staring at?

I give the wall a quick once over, there's nothing weird. Grandma continues to stare at the wall, her eyes are blank and she is barely blinking; drool and Chinese porridge are dripping down from the right-hand side of her mouth.

"Grandma?"

Silence

"Grandma?"

Silence

I get out of my chair and zoom towards her. I pass Grandma's silver spoon, it's lying on the floor in a small pool of porridge.

"Grandma? Are you okay?"

She softly murmurs when I put my hand on her shoulder, but her eyes can't focus on me, they look to the floor and then to the wall again. Her body is flopping against the side of the chair like a fish losing its balance. A wave of panic churns through my body and I run to the phone in the hallway. The walls are starting to move like I'm on a rollercoaster.

I dial 999.

It rings once and I slam the phone back down. Grandma would be annoyed if I sent her to an NHS hospital. I claw at the stack of papers next to the phone, desperate to find the phone number of a doctor, a friend, a neighbour, anyone who could help me. On a crumpled piece of paper I see the name Mrs Lee, Grandma's mahjong friend. With shaking hands I dial the number. It rings three times and a lady with a Chinese accent picks up the phone.

"Hah-low?"

I slam the phone down again. Grandma would HATE for her friends to know she's ill. Once they knew she was weak, they would take over her monopoly on organising mahjong parties and charity events. I cry out in anger. Who can I call that Grandma would not tell me off for? I run back into the kitchen and shake Grandma; she still has the blank look on her face.

"WHO SHALL I CALL? WHO?"

She frowns a bit but doesn't reply. I run back into the hallway and open the drawer next to the phone. On a yellow post-it note in Grandma's scratchy handwriting is *MR HAYWOOD* and his telephone number. It's eight-thirty; Mr Haywood may have left home already. I ring his number. Please, please, please, please pick up. Please, please…

"Good morning. Mr Haywood speaking."

"Hello. Mr Haywood. It's Xing Li."

"Good morning Xing Li. How are you?"

"Look, Mr Haywood, my grandma is very sick. I didn't know who to call."

"What is wrong with her?"

"She can't move and she is drooling everywhere. I don't know what to do. I don't know who to call. I just don't know what to do."

I hear him breathe in as if someone has winded him.

"I will be there in ten minutes. Call 999 and tell them to come immediately."

He puts the phone down before I can explain Grandma's allergy to public health care. I listen to Mr Haywood. If Grandma gets super mad about being sent to an NHS hospital, Mr Haywood will get the blame. I pick up the phone and dial 999.

Chapter 39
A Stroke of Mad Luck

Grandma sits in the middle of wires, beeping monitors and a strong smell of cleaning fluid. Her back is hunched over and she sways from side to side like a wounded animal. A young nurse mops up her drool and tries to prop her up, but she topples to the side. She looks all fragile and broken and scared. The doctor says she's had a stroke; five minutes of oxygen was cut off from her brain.

Five minutes, that's all it was.

I watch the nurse carefully unbutton Grandma's silk shirt and fold it neatly into the cabinet next to the bed. I know I should look away, but everything seems to be in slow motion including my reactions. Grandma is naked from the waist up; her wrinkled skin is speckled with loads and loads of sun spots. I don't know what to do, she's really sick. I'm really confused 'cos a few hours ago I really, really hated her and now she's sick. But then underneath the shell of sickness, she's still Grandma. When the nurse starts to tug at the legs of Grandma's trousers, I find my jelly legs wobbling me out of the room, along the corridor and into the cold night air. Auntie Mei is probably on the evening flight from Croatia by now.

She will have to deal with Grandma, I just can't.

I sit down on a damp bench near the entrance of the hospital. For ages I watch emergency patients being wheeled in on stretchers, some gasping into oxygen masks. Their relatives' faces are full of fear. Sometimes husbands wheel their big pregnant wives into the hospital with a mixture of hope and stress. It's all very crowded and cold and dark and busy like on TV, but without the screaming and blood.

"Hey lil sis, you want to freeze to death or what?"

LAI KER!

I jump up from my seat and give him a huge hug that almost topples him over.

"Easy, watch the hair, watch the hair."

He grins at me and gives my hair a playful tug.

"Who gave you this bowl haircut?"

I'm smiling so hard my face hurts.

"Your fat girlfriend."

"Is that Kate Moss or Gisele?"

"You wish!"

AH-HEM

Mr Haywood clears his throat. How did he find Lai Ker?

"Good evening Xing Li, where is your grandmother? How is she?"

"She's in room 3B in the red wing."

Lai Ker suddenly looks all stressed.

"Is the old bird okay?"

I think of the beeping wires and the terrified half-naked Grandma swaying from side to side. I don't want to look at Lai Ker, it's too awkward. I look at Mr Haywood.

"Think you'd better go and see for yourself. I'm gonna wait here."

"But young lady, won't you be cold out here?"

"Nope I'm okay, I'll wait for my auntie. I'll be okay."

"Are you sure lil sis? Don't want to have to make ice cubes out of your frozen butt."

"Nah, I'll wait for Auntie Mei."

Lai Ker and Mr Haywood start to walk super fast into the

hospital. The wind is cutting into my skin, but I don't want to go into the hospital and have a nurse or doctor tell me off for not seeing Grandma. I don't want to see Grandma. I'm not sure if Lai Ker should either after what she did to him.

Auntie Mei arrives with her Louis Vuitton luggage and an enormous, white fur coat that is asking for red paint to be thrown on it. Her usually perfect face has mascara stains and she almost runs past me.

"Auntie Mei."

"Xing."

She engulfs me with a hug; the fur is soft and real.

"Xing, are you okay? I'm so sorry you had to go through this all by yourself."

"I'm okay."

"Where is she? What did the doctors say?"

"She's in Room 3B, the red wing."

"No private room?"

"No private room."

"Okay, let's go then."

I don't want to go, but Auntie Mei looks so pale and upset. She grabs my hand, pulls me into the hospital and I just follow her. We have to ask two hospital orderlies and one nurse before we find the correct room. It's a real maze.

Grandma's sleeping with a tube up her nose; her heart is beating at a steady rate. Mr Haywood is holding her hand. When he sees us, he lets go of her hand and goes beetroot.

"Miss Wu, I am so glad you have arrived. My name is Earnest Haywood. It's good to finally meet you."

"Thank you for coming Mr Haywood."

Lai Ker goes up to Auntie Mei and gives her a hug. She's happy to see him, but she doesn't look surprised; it's weird 'cos she acts as if she knew he was coming. Auntie Mei edges to the side of the bed and tears up when she bends over to peer at Grandma's peaceful face. Their noses are almost touching. It's been many years since Auntie Mei's been allowed to stand so close to Grandma. Mr Haywood reaches his arm out as if he wants to comfort Auntie Mei and then lets it hang loosely at his side instead.

"Miss Wu, the doctors had a quick word with me. I'm sorry you were not around."

"What did they say?"

"They said… they said your mother has had a stroke. The next forty-eight hours will be crucial to see how quickly her brain repairs itself. She is in no condition for them to do any further tests, but they are monitoring the situation closely."

Auntie Mei nods and holds Grandma's hand.

"My mother is strong. She will get through this, she always does."

"Yes, your mother is a strong woman. If anyone can get back from this she can. My cousin had a stroke many years ago. In the beginning, he was just like your mother. But two years on after therapy he became just fine. Well, he still walks with a stick, but he is fine."

"How old was your cousin - when he had the stroke?"

"About forty-two."

"My mother is seventy-two."

"Yes, she is elderly. But she is strong."

Mama once said that being strong was a blessing and a curse.

"When you are strong, people expect so much out of you. They rely on you to be the friend who they can turn to or the colleague who will stand up to the boss at work. You are the person who will have the right word, the one who will give them the strength to carry on. But when your heart is collapsing inside who can you turn to?"

Lai Ker's snoring by the window in the hospital.

I can't believe he's back and give him a pinch just to make sure. He tries to give me a punch, but I duck down just in time.

"Looks like you've been practising your ducking since I went away."

"Yeah, that's all I've been doing."

"Bet you have."

"What took you so long to return? I'm still bloody mad at you that you didn't contact me earlier."

"Yeah, I wanted to but I couldn't."

"'Cos of Grandma? I'm so mad at her."

"It was 'cos of Grandma, but don't be mad. She was trying to do what she thought best. I'm too nacked to tell the whole story. But the bottom line is it all worked out fine."

"Well, I'm still mad at her. Stupid old bag."

Lai Ker gives me a disgusted look as if I have just been sick on his shoes.

"Well, you shouldn't be. Grandma had a serious stroke and you should give a toss."

"I know she's sick but that don't change nothing. She's still a terrible person inside."

"Yeah, I know she was for most of the time. But she's okay, she's family."

"You're family. She's just blood."

"Then she's blood, you're so bloody stubborn."

"Look, A LOT happened when you were gone. So don't judge me for being pissed off at Grandma. I can hate her if I want and to me she's blood not family."

Lai Ker looks really angry and starts getting loud. Before he went away he never, ever got angry with me.

"FINE. But remember without her blood, you wouldn't be here. Without her blood, Mama wouldn't be here, without her blood, Auntie Mei wouldn't be here. SHE'S BLOOD."

"Don't shout at me, you're the one that buggered off 'cos of your stupid chinks have mouths. You're the one that left me behind. Mama would be so upset if she knew that you left me behind. Mama hated Grandma or have you forgotten how she shut Mama out?"

"Look, if Mama were here right now she would be next to Grandma in the hospital bed and you know it. Why can't you see it? Why are you so bloody thick?"

"Yeah, I'm so thick. I'm thick for ever thinking you were right about *CHM*. I'm thick for ever believing a word you said."

I lift up my trouser leg to show him my scar.

C H I N K

He keeps very quiet. I'm crying by now. I'm upset that after not seeing Lai Ker for so long we're shouting at each other. I'm sad about that the most. I feel betrayed like Lai Ker has joined the dark side and left me behind. He's meant to have my back. When Mama died he promised. I run and run out of the hospital and get a taxi home. But I don't know if it's my home any more.

Mama would be next to Grandma in the hospital bed.

Chapter 40
Sorry Seems to Be the Furthest Word

Lai Ker comes into my room and sits on the bed. It's about 1am and I was just dreaming that I was swimming with Auntie Mei and the sun was really hot.

"I've got a present for you."

He throws a massive box of Toblerone my way. It's my favourite.

"It took a lot, but I didn't take one bite out of it."

"That's a lot of will power for you."

"Yeah I know, didn't want a repeat of your twelfth birthday. My half-eaten chocolate Toblerone pressie was probably the *worst* thing to happen on your birthday."

"Yeah, it was the *worst* thing that happened."

We both give each other a sad smile that only we could understand.

"Look Xing, it's okay if you don't want to see Grandma. From what Auntie Mei told me a lot went down when I was away. So, I'm not gonna make you. Look I'm… I'm sorry that I didn't contact you and all. It's just Mr Haywood and Grandma thought it was best."

"What, they kept you away from me?"

"No, it weren't like that. It was more they tried to protect you."

"Protect me from what?"

Lai Ker looks down at his feet; they're still super hairy and yucky as usual.

"From me… "

"Why?"

"'Cos I was bloody messed up. I messed up."

"How?"

"I was a cocky bugger. Thought me and Jimmy Tang could change the world. But we couldn't, it takes more than beating the crap out of white boys and spray painting *CHM* everywhere to rule the world. Anyway, I'm okay now."

Lai Ker gives me a very soft pat on my leg near the scar.

"Are you like… like… okay?"

I think of Shils and what she did. After what happened, I was sure I didn't ever want to have *CHM*, but some days I'm not so sure. Like Jay says I'm brave 'cos I told on Shils to Mr Lewis and 'cos of that she got expelled and that is all I should think about, the good not the bad. All of a sudden, I realise that for the first time in weeks I'm awake at 1am. But I'm not awake 'cos of a nightmare. I'm not awake 'cos I'm scared or sad any more. I'm awake 'cos Lai Ker woke me up. I nod my head at Lai Ker.

"I'm okay."

"You sure? Like does anyone at West Hill need roughing up?"

"Thought you're anti-violence now."

"Easy, I may be a changed man, but if you mess with my family I ain't holding back. So does West Hill need a 'special' lesson in R-E-S-P-E-C-T from the Laister or not?"

I think of Jay and Milly and Preema and how they all called when they heard Grandma was sick. I think of the Cliff Richard lookalike and how two days ago in music class he asked Jay if he wanted to jam with him some time. I think about how I eat lunch in the canteen instead of the library every day and how I got an A for my history presentation where I had to stand up in front of everyone and give a long speech.

"It's alright. West Hill is alright."

"You sure?"

"I'm sure."

It's been five days since Grandma was admitted and the doctors are shocked at her rapid rate of recovery, but it's still hit and miss 'cos she's so old. Lai Ker says Grandma's speech is still limited to "Yes" and "No" as well as various random words such as "To", "Hard" and "Jam". The right-hand side of her body is paralysed and she has a droop on her face that makes her look like a melted wax figure. Lai Ker says she pushes away any hospital food she doesn't like - which is most of the food on offer. Auntie Mei's started to bring in Chinese food in a stack of tiffin tins. She says it takes her a while to work out what Grandma wants. Lai Ker says it's like they're playing charades but on the losing team.

Auntie Mei's lost her appetite since Grandma's been sick. Her face looks worn and pale and she has dark bags under her eyes that she tries to cover up with expensive concealer. For the first time in her life, she actually looks her age. She keeps trying to get me to visit the hospital and has a damaged look on her face when I say I'm too busy. Most of my evenings are spent with Jay's family. They sometimes do their mini concerts for me, which is really cool. Jay says if I want to talk, cry or swear, then he has my back. But if I choose not to talk, that's cool too.

I choose not to talk.

Auntie Mei's trying to get me to go again.

"Xing, I'm going to the hospital today so I will be back around seven. What time do you want to visit?"

"I'm sorry Auntie Mei, I can't today."

"Why?"

Yesterday I had dinner with Jay's family, the night before I had watched a film with Jay and the night before that I had Geography coursework. I can't think of an excuse today.

"I think... I think I have an English essay that is due in

tomorrow."

"You think or you know?"

"I think."

"What is the essay on?"

"I can't remember."

"Please can you check it is due in tomorrow? Grandma hasn't seen you since she was admitted. It has been FIVE days. Well, bring your diary here and let's have a look."

The guilt starts to travel up through my body and I bring my school diary. The English essay is due next week. Auntie Mei nods and has the beginnings of a smile.

"Excellent, you can visit Grandma then? I'll see you at 5pm sharp."

Chapter 41
Cat on a Wok Tin Roof

Jay says he has a "MAJOR" surprise for me. He says it will cheer me up for sure. I need all the cheering up I can get 'cos I really don't want to see Grandma. Sometimes Jay prays for Grandma and that God will heal her just as he instantly healed his mum from cancer. As I watch him screw his eyes up and pray for Grandma, I feel well bad 'cos I don't know if I want Grandma to be okay again.

"Xing, you'll love the surprise, I can't wait."

Jay's dreadlocks have been tied into a loose bun on top of his head. They look like a nest waiting for a sparrow to come and lay its eggs in. He pushes me into his garden.

"You're gonna love the surprise. At least I think you will."

I haven't seen him this excited since he found a rare digitally re-mastered calypso version of Handle's "Messiah". There were only eighty copies of the album.

Jay taps his leg as he opens the shed door. That's Mo's Art's fifth symphony he's tapping. There's a stench coming from the shed - a bit like urine and wood mixed together. Old woks and cooking utensils are scattered amongst cobwebs and empty plant pots. I hold my nose and duck under two cobwebs. Out of the shadows steps a furry black and white animal.

"MEOW MEOW!"

Meow Meow blinks and starts meowing and meowing and meowing. From the "I'm hungry meow" to the "Please pat me meow" and back to the "I'm hungry meow". I scoop her into my arms and her soft, furry body is purring on auto speed. Jay's smiling as if he's just won a backstage pass for the Royal Phil-ham-bionic Orchestra.

"That cat was well hard to find. It was like searching for Father Christmas and finding him in Barbados."

Jay pats Meow Meow's head and a wad of her moulting fur sticks to his sweaty hands.

"My dad and me had to visit like five cat shelters. They kept moving her 'cos no-one wanted to put her down."

Meow Meow's fur looks matted and messy, but she still has the round belly.

"When we finally found her, they were well happy to get rid of Meow Meow. They tried to fob off a scary looking ginger tom as well. After he hissed at me, my dad politely said nah."

"Thank you! Thank you! Thank you!"

"WAIT, there's more. When we brought Meow Meow home, we realised that she was kind of lonely, so we got her a friend."

Jay drags a HUGE cardboard box over and opens up the top. I hear a chomping sound and I KNOW who it is. The African spur-thighed tortoise is chomping a massive hole into the corner of the box. Jay and I carry the tortoise out, he's a bit lighter than normal but he's still as heavy as a toddler. Meow Meow's meows start to get louder and she sniffs the tortoise before playfully whacking its head with her paw. His long head goes back into its shell and she looks at me all confused. I start to laugh! Jay and me feed her a saucer of milk and she purrs and laps it up super fast with her rough tongue. The tortoise pokes his head out and sniffs the air before making his way s-l-o-w-l-y to the milk. His purple tongue darts up and down like a fat lizard. We watch them in silence like two proud parents.

"You know Xing, everything's gonna be okay. Whatever happens, you've got Meow Meow, you've got the tortoise and... you've, you've got me."

Jay's starting to tap again, but I don't recognise the song, the rhythm is really quick. Jay slowly puts his hand over mine. It's so light I can barely feel it but I know it's there. The grip of his hand starts off loose then becomes firmer. I hold his hand back and my heart starts to beat a little quicker.

"Xing you'll be okay. I'll make sure of that."

I nod and Jay slowly leans towards me. I can feel his soft dreadlocks brushing against my face. My heart's beating super fast now. I close my eyes and everything goes all quiet like we're both in a dark tunnel, just me and him. He kisses me with his light, velvety lips. It feels all warm and nice and amazing.

I want it to last forever.

When I finally open my eyes, my lips are tingly and nice. But I'm too shy to look at Jay, so I smile a silly smile and hold his hand and look at the tortoise.

He sticks his tongue out and I could swear I saw him wink.

Chapter 42
Forgive and Regrets

Grandma is sleeping when I arrive. Her veiny lids are tightly closed and she has a frown on her face. Mr Haywood leaps up and offers to get me a drink. I ask for a Coke and he gives me a squeeze on my shoulder as he walks out. The curtains have been drawn around Grandma's bed and a low watt energy saver bedside lamp is switched on. It feels dark and eerie. I sit on the edge of the bed next to Auntie Mei. I give a big sigh and try not to look at Grandma. I watch the second hand as it ticks around the clock.

Tick

Tick

Tick

Tick

Maybe if I stare hard enough I'll be able to make time go faster like the Japanese guy in Lai Ker's comic. Auntie Mei looks at me and shakes her head. Then she waves at me to go into the corridor for a chat.

"Xing, I need to talk to you about something."

"What about?"

"I want to know when exactly are you going to stop?"

"Stop what?"

"When are you going to stop being angry at Grandma?"

"I'm not angry at Grandma."

"Then, why don't you ever want to visit her?"

"It's not that I don't want to visit her, it's just that I have better things to do."

"Better things than visit your sick grandmother?"

I keep quiet.

Auntie Mei would never understand what's going on. How can I explain to her that I don't want to see Grandma 'cos I'm so MAD at her? I'm mad at Grandma for not saying a kind word to me when Mama died; I'm mad at her for blaming me about what happened with Uncle Ho; I'm mad at her for cutting Mama out of the family 'cos of Papa; most of all I'm mad at her for not caring about what happened with Shils. She's my grandma. She's meant to love me and look after me and make me feel safe. She's meant to encourage me and hug me when I am sad.

But she doesn't.

Auntie Mei grabs hold of my hand. I try to push it away, but she grips even harder. I can feel her diamond ring softly pressing against my skin.

"I know that you're angry at Grandma."

I don't reply, a lump has grown in my throat and I'm desperate to swallow it down. Auntie Mei carries on holding my hand.

"You're angry at Grandma. I'm not saying you're wrong to be angry. But what you need to know is that she does love you."

"She never showed me that she cared for me."

Auntie Mei shakes her head really slowly.

"Xing Li, Grandma is always thinking of you, she just finds it difficult to show it in an obvious way. She does care for you."

"Like when?"

"Like the incident with Shils."

"What do you mean?"

"Do you know that after you were hurt by Shils, Grandma immediately called the school?"

"No."

"Well she did. She demanded they give her the Teddinghams' number and also the numbers of all the girls involved. Your grandmother can bulldoze people down to get her way. When she had all their numbers, she called all three of her lawyers to ask their advice. It resulted in a meeting with the Teddinghams."

"But she made a sick deal with them. She was too scared to stick up for me, so she let it go."

"That's where you're wrong. Grandma always had you in her heart. You see if we had pressed charges towards Shils and a case was made it would have dragged on for months. You would have to recollect the incident over and over again. It would be a horribly traumatic experience for you. Not to mention once the press got wind of the story. So, your grandmother did what she did best. She fought for her family, but she fought in her own way."

"How did she fight?"

"Grandma made a watertight deal with the Teddinghams. They tried to negotiate but you know Grandma's stance on negotiations."

"No negotiations."

"Exactly. Grandma made them sign a document that would force Shils out of the country so you would never see her again."

"How did Grandma get them to sign such a document?"

"She managed to get witness statements from all the girls involved. Through bribes, blackmail, anything she needed to do. Then she threatened to blacken the Teddingham names and ruin Shils' future. Mr Teddingham had been planning Shils' future since she was a baby. He was already going though a messy divorce with Shils' mother after he left her for his Chinese mistress. Something like this would ruin his reputation forever. So, he agreed to send Shils away. You don't have to worry about seeing that girl's face in this country ever again."

251

Shils is never ever coming to get me. NEVER EVER again!

"How about all the other bad things that Grandma did, like getting rid of Meow Meow and cutting out Mama and hitting me with the feather duster?"

I'm hoping Auntie Mei can explain all those things too. But she sadly shakes her head.

"Your grandmother isn't perfect, I know, and I have no excuses for the all the mistakes she has made. What you have to understand is Grandma was not always the woman she is now."

"What do you mean?"

"Xing Li, you have to understand your grandmother's life was not always easy."

"You mean she had it bad during the war? Grandpa told me."

"Yes, that was part of her pain. But there were other circumstances too… "

"Like what?"

Auntie Mei lets go of my hand and looks to her feet.

"It started when I was about seven or eight… I found her crying in her room. She pushed me out with a ferociousness that I had never seen before and slammed the door shut. Pa and her had started to argue a lot. Real shouting matches with smashed furniture behind closed doors."

I think of the kind gentleman who brought me scones and listened to my problems.

"Dinner times were tense and quiet; to make it worse your grandfather would crack jokes to break the silence. There was a bitterness in her that grew and grew. Uncle Ho's illness did not help. Pa refused to visit him. He said his mental son was a terrible embarrassment to the Wu name. Sometimes I think he didn't love Uncle Ho at all."

Auntie Mei starts to shift uncomfortably from side to side.

"I… I found some letters when going through her old things."

252

"Letters?"

Auntie Mei's voice is starting to tremble.

"The hospital needed proof of identification. I knew she kept all her important things under her bed in a chest. I've never opened the chest. Never felt the need to until now I suppose."

"Did you find what you were looking for?"

"Yes, I opened the chest and true enough her birth certificate was there with lots of jewellery and stacks and stacks of letters. I should have been satisfied with getting what the hospital wanted. But I'm human, how could I not have taken a little peek at the letters?"

"Who were the letters to? What did they say?"

"The letters were to a man called George Tan who lived in Singapore. She had written to him every week for over forty years."

The tremble in Auntie Mei's voice is starting to grow really big and she leans against the wall.

"You know Xing Li, my first reaction was anger. I was furious that Grandma would have a secret lover while making your grandfather out to be the villain. She always told me that Grandpa had mistresses and a secret temper. He did stay out a lot, sometimes overnight. But as I read the letters, I realised Mr Tan was not her lover. He was more of a friend, her only real friend. He was the one person she could tell everything to. I should have been satisfied after reading a few letters, but I couldn't stop. There were so many things about her I didn't know. I wanted to know who my mother was."

Tears start to drip down Auntie Mei's pointed cheekbones. She quickly wipes them away and continues.

"Your grandma was desperately sad. She was sad about her marriage, she was sad that your mother was not in her life, she was sad she didn't understand her modern British children, she was sad she had left Singapore. She was sad because she was losing herself in this big country. You need to read the letters to understand who Grandma really is."

The tears are at full flow and Auntie Mei doesn't try to hide them. She opens her pink handbag, takes out a key and puts in gently in my hand.

Chapter 43
Three Blue Letters

Mr George Tan
93 Sennett Road, Singapore 8789
Republic of Singapore

31 January 1968

Dear George

Today very cold. I wrap up in long coat, scarf, gloves, thermal underwear, boots. I miss Singapore and hot sunshine. I can't wait 'till we go back to Singapore when husband finish studies. He very angry these days, don't know what to do. His temper never so good. One moment smiling, laughing, next moment angry, shouting. Since baby boy arrive he worse. I sometimes relief he go out so much. But then feel lonely when just me and children. Feel lonely in this country I do not understand. Feel sad when people look at me strange and make funny noises like Ching Chong, Ching Chong and ask me go back China.

I not from China, I from Singapore but they don't know difference.

Today I walked to supermarket to get milk for son. It tiring having a baby, I don't know how I cope. Think maybe I will not have any more children. Three enough trouble, especially my boy. He's hungry all the time, must be cold weather.

When I go supermarket, it is hot because of heater so I take off my coat and scarf. I put it on the floor for moment because it is so hot. Then woman tell me off. I think she from Liverpool or Scotland, but I cannot tell her accent. She said, "In England we don't leave our coats on the floor, we are not like YOU villagers in Japan."

I am so shocked, my mouth is wide open and then I leave the shop in hurry. I leave so quickly, I make terrible mistake and leave baby behind. I am halfway down road and realise baby left behind. I give a big scream and people look at me like I mad. I run back to the shop. I terrified something happen to son – my lovely baby. When I get to the shop, baby gone. I start crying until manager of shop say baby ok. He sleeping in staff room. My heart bounces with joy and I am the happiest I ever been. Happiest I been since I gone to London. I don't bother even when manager tell me I terrible mother leave my baby.

Sometimes I think about life. What life be if I stayed Singapore? What I be if not got married so quick? But what can I do? My father said I too old to be single. Needed to get married before I got too old. I know stupid thoughts. But still think sometimes of what would have happened if I did not get married. If I did not move to country that is not my home.

I have to go baby crying. Hungry again. Write soon ok?

Yours
Rose

Mrs Rose Wu
68 Queens Drive
NW8 0HZ
UK

7 May 1985

Dear Rose

I hope you are wrapping up warm. I heard on the news that it has been the coldest of winters for many years. In Singapore, the weather is still as hot as ever, we are going through a heat wave and at times I think my fan is going to explode from being used all day.

Today, I met the new batch of soldiers that I will be in charge of. There is always an excitement in the air - a bit like the first day of school. I really think this lot of young men will be a good team not like the lousy team I had last time. Modern life has made men lazy! I look at them and I feel a great sense of responsibility. Some of them look so young as if they were still in secondary school.

My mother has been wanting me to marry a girl of her choosing. She has been hassling me day and night. She cannot understand how someone nearing forty could not be in need of a wife. But I am happy being by myself. Perhaps, being by myself for so long has made me selfish.

My mother forgets that I was the only child for fifteen years before my sister arrived. Sometimes, I wish I were a young boy again without a care in the world. Remember when we used to search for frogs in Kallang river near our houses? Those were happy times weren't they? I often remember those childhood days before the war - when everyone called you Rose because you became red so easily. How about the days we spent with Ah Boon, Mei-Fang and Raja? How mischievous we were! Do you recall when we sneaked into the back garden of old Mr Wen and stole his apples? Ah Boon split his pants on the fence as we tried to escape from that horrible dog! How about when we stole some peanuts from the Kacang Puteh man - how we laughed when he chased us with his old trolley spilling over with nuts. I almost wet my pants from all the laughter. Life was a lot simpler then. To be young!

I was extremely sad when I read your letter about Ho. Please do not keep saying you are a bad mother. He is getting the help he needs and will be better in no time. Teenagers are more resilient than you think. I am sure he is getting the best treatment and with your support he will bounce back soon. You must never lose hope. Remember when my sister suffered from postnatal depression? She was so bad, we wondered if she would ever get better. But here she is, nine years on with my two beautiful nieces. Promise me you will never lose hope?

As for what you wrote about your husband, well, I was not surprised he once again washed his hands over the matter. We would expect nothing less from the fair-weather father who has lost his way. All I can say is the less contact you have with him, the better. He needs to learn that being a father is more than just providing a roof over a child's head. As mentioned before, if he ever touches you again, you must go straight to the police. You are always welcome to stay with my sister or myself if things get too tough. Here I go again, speaking rubbish of your husband and I'm sorry if I have overstepped the mark as usual. But I worry for you, my dear friend.

I really do wish you nothing but hope and happiness. I will be praying for Ho and thinking of you.

Yours
George

Mr George Tan
93 Sennett Road, Singapore 8789
Republic of Singapore

21 February 1986

Dear George

Today is the saddest day of life. Please don't judge me. I never sleep all night, woke up 11pm, 3:30am, 5:05am, 7:30am. Thinking up and down about day. Thinking why decision had to be made. But know have to do it.

I went to clinic by taxi. Was a sunny day which is odd, but cannot enjoy. My heart is in pain, cannot enjoy it. When arrive, nurse gave me robe. I wait for hour then they put me to sleep. When I wake up, I take taxi home. Happen so quick. Husband don't even know I slip out.

Now I sit at home in bed. Daughters think I got cold. They have no idea my heart broken. Keep thinking did I make good decision? But what choice I have? Ho need me to support. I all he have, how can support when have look after baby? What if baby be like Ho? I know I do right choice. Yet, still feel so sad. Why feel sad if right choice? Maybe because I love too much. When you love it only cause pain. Love baby who gone too much. One day everyone I love will go to join baby. Then pain worse and worse. Don't know if can take pain. If feel large heartbreak today when never met baby - what more for children I met? Will not survive any more heartbreak. Cannot survive unless be strong. Please pray I stronger and stronger every day. So I can be hard like rock and not hurt ever again. How I forget what I have done? Please tell me. How I forget my pain? How I can smile again?

Yours
Rose

Chapter 44
Wu and Peace

I feel so lonely here. Who I can talk to?
Who can understand? They not Singaporean.
When you ask them "How are you?" they say,
"Fine Thank You." So I tell them I am fine
too, but I'm not. I don't know who I am
any more or why I here. I see my children
becoming more English every day. Every
day they less Chinese, I feel they become
further and further away. It breaks my
heart but don't know how to stop it.

I've been reading Grandma's letters all night. Each piece of
paper opens a door into her past, her dreams, her pain. She
was super confused just like me.

When Grandma was little, she lived in a very large household
with two brothers, one sister, four step-brothers and two
step-sisters. Apart from her youngest step-sister in Sydney,
Grandma has outlived all her siblings. It was really sad,
'cos my great grandma died giving birth to Grandma. Then
my great grandpa married his mistress who was a "Hungry
Ghost Festival singer". Basically, she specialised in karaoke
sessions for the dead.

Grandma was a quiet child and when she grew up she weren't a looker, but the one thing Grandma had was tons of brains. By the age of five she was writing short stories and reciting classical Chinese poems. She respected her father a lot and got his attention by getting good grades in school. Whenever she showed him her report card of straight As, he would give her a short nod to show her he was well pleased. She wrote to George:

The two-second nod was all I lived for.

Grandma married Grandpa 'cos her father said so. He said she was getting way too old at twenty-five. Also, Grandpa had rich parents but he didn't do very well in school. His parents thought if he married Grandma the kids would be brainy. Both of them didn't choose to get married, they did it 'cos in those days you had to listen to everything your parents said.

What is this thing called love? Making the most of bad marriage is all I have.

When Mama was five and Uncle Ho was in Grandma's belly, Grandpa wanted to further his studies in the UK. They packed their belongings and moved to a foreign country with tea, toast and terrible tube lines.

In one of her letters she says: **With Chinese, they offer you to come for dinner after first meeting. With English takes many years before you get past "How is the weather?" conversations. They only can speak long when drunk.**

The only person Grandma could pour her heart out to was her old childhood neighbour George Tan. His parents were quite rich 'cos they owned a huge furniture factory. I guess in some ways, George was to Grandma a bit like Jay is to me. Grandma shared everything with him. She told him she needed to be louder and stronger, if not, she would be bullied. Like Lai Ker she had *CHM*. Grandma wrote a ton about the fights she had over the years.

264

Today I go green grocer and he try give me bad cut of meat. He say "YOU people won't know the difference when you mix all your food together for your chop suey." I so mad, what he mean "YOU people?" Does he mean meat only nice when cook burnt on BBQ? I have never shouted in public in my life. But today I shout back at him. I am shocked at myself. I shocked I can scream so loud. I feel bit sorry it so loud, so paiseh. But then also don't know what else to do...

Grandma learnt to shout lots. She yelled at queue jumping teenagers who told her to "go back to China" and delivery men who spoke to her in slow motion as if she were a child. She screeched at taxi drivers who told her that her Chinese ingredients were too smelly for their cars and librarians who showed her the kids' section. Grandma's fights turned into wars. She could not conquer Uncle Ho's illness, but she could mow down the doctors that treated him. She was unable to save her marriage, but she could force Grandpa to another country. She couldn't force her daughters to keep their culture but she would make sure we didn't make the same mistake.

The longer Grandma stayed in London, the angrier she became. Every day was a battle for her and her mouth grew bigger with each fight. While Grandpa got in good with the Brits by getting drunk a lot and learning to speak the Queen's English, Grandma wrote long letters to George Tan about the British sickie culture.

Asia has work hard culture I miss so much. When you call in sick you better be in hospital have your leg amputee after terrible car crash. People call in sick here a lot. Mondays popular so are days after bank holiday and rare, sunny days in winter. They always give the excuse of "flu", this an illness that cover any symptom. THAT make me so mad when I see lazy neighbour sunbathing not go work. If husband let me, I definitely work but I not allowed.

Grandma left Singapore as a dainty quiet girl but had changed into a loud-mouthed lion. The gritty London air changed Grandma just like it had changed Lai Ker and just like it had changed me.

After reading her letters, I get why Grandma got into fights a lot; why she had to have *CHM* 'cos if she didn't shout, people would squish her down. In a weird way, I also understand why Grandma tells me off lots, 'cos even though it's warped, it means she wants what is best for me. Like I know she cares now 'cos she let us stay with her and she stuck up for me with Shils. Also, she chose me to come with her to visit George Tan in Singapore 'cos in a strange way she wanted to share me with him. It's like she needed me there or something. But then, I don't want to be exactly like Grandma. I don't want to be angry and sad and annoyed and fighting with people all the time. I want to be happy and grateful and peaceful and strong. I want to have a mouth so I can speak up when things are not right. Like when I stood up to Grandma for Auntie Mei and told my classmates how to say my name and wrote to Mr Lewis about Shils.

I'm a *Chinese person with a mouth*, but I'm a Chinese person with a heart too.

Chapter 45
I Love You Forever and a Week

Grandma is lying flat on her back like a stiff life-size porcelain doll. Her eyes are closed and her breathing is so quiet I have to put my fingers under her nostrils just to check. I touch her chin gently. She looks all peaceful and for the first time in months, I don't hate her any more. I notice she's got the same round chin as Mama and me. It was what Mama called the "Wu half moon chin".

She stirs and her eyes flicker as she moves from her dreams to the real world. She doesn't seem to know it's me at first and frowns a massive frown. There's a spark in her eyes and she looks really surprised to see me. Her mouth opens as if she wants to speak and ends up coughing instead. I give her a glass of water and she flaps her arm that works to ask me to come closer.

"I… I… I… I… "

Her voice is tiny and weak like a little bird chirping for its mama.

"What do you want to say Grandma?"

"To I you, to I you."

The words in her mind have been jumbled up like a jigsaw puzzle. The doctor says the words might return; they might not. Grandma urgently points at me and then back to her chest.

"Is it your chest Grandma? Is it painful?"

"N… N… No."

"Are you feeling unwell?"

"N… N… No."

Grandma starts to wiggle her hand as if trying to draw a shape in the air. It looks like she's trying to draw a circle or a crescent or maybe a heart. I'm not sure and I can see the sorrow in her eyes. She's been carrying all this broken sadness for so long and now I finally know why.

"I'm sorry Grandma, I don't know what you are trying to say. Is it to do with your body?"

"N… N… No."

She keeps pointing at her chest and then she uses my hand to pat her heart.

"You ME. YOU ME."

"Is it about you and me?"

"Y… YES."

Her last Yes sounds firmer than all the previous Yesses. It's loud and strong and reminds me of the person inside her decaying body.

She's still here, it's not too late.

I lean down and whisper into her ear.

"I know Grandma. I know about everything - about Shils, about Grandpa, about you. I'm sorry for being mad at you."

"NO."

"I'm sorry Grandma… "

"NO."

Grandma grabs my arm, and pulls my hand towards her chest. She doesn't let go even when I try to pull away.

"NO YOU. M… M… ME… ME SOR."

She puts my hand on her heart and grips me tightly around my wrist, refusing to let go.

"ME SOR… ME SOR… "

Her eyes fill with tears.

"ME SOR… ME SOR… "

I try to let go but she continues to hold my hand over her

heart. Letting go is not an option, not until I understand her secret pain. Not until I understand her love for me and her love for Mama. I hold Grandma's tiny hand. Her grip is warm and firm. I sit with her until she closes her eyes. I sit with her until it's dark. I sit with her until the silence is no longer awkward.

Acknowledgements

The One Up There: Daddy God, you mended me, loved me and made me smile again.

The Dowdeswell Ghetto Clan: Papa, Loong Ker and Chung Ker whose jokes, stories and love mean everything to me. We share laughter, shouting, crying and secret memories dear to my heart. I am happiest when I am near to all of you.

My Literary Soulmate: Wf Graca who is always there for wise words, long, late night letters and shopping trips.

The Super Agent: Lorella Belli, you have been so amazing! Your belief in me, quick-thinking, entrepreneurialism and sound advice has meant the world.

The Risk Takers at Legend Press: Lauren, you really "got" my book from day one! Your encouragement, positivity and hard work have been bananalicious. Lucy, for always finding new angles, answering my long emails and trying out fun ideas. Tom, you gave my book a home and for that I am forever grateful.

The PHS Survivors: Louise and Trina, friends forever and a week. Trolls, secrets, boys and "getting" me even after all these years.

My Super Creative "Fam": Karen, JJ, JL, Zu & Migs for all your prayers, support and great snacks!

A "Lala": Stella, you have been more than a friend. You are a "therapist", and buddy for long walks and long lunches.

The Roast Beef Gang: DIY Dad and Nasi Goreng Mum. Your food and care speaks volumes.

The Adopted Ones: big sis Marie and younger bro Luke Lukus for your kindness, Mandarin translations and hospitality whenever I visit.

The Writer Whisperer: Jean, my old English Language A level teacher at night school. You told me "Some people can write, some people can't. You can." Your words gave me confidence and keep me smiling to this day.

All the Pioneers: my fellow British born Chinese and Singaporean writers who have amazing stories but still struggle to get published. Keep going; keep believing and never give up!

Banana Writers
- Where Asian writers get unpeeled -

Dear readers

Thank you so much for buying my book and supporting my journey as an author.

I hope you will support other new East Asian and South East Asian writers at:

www.bananawriters.com

There aren't enough books being published by East Asian and South East Asian writers. With readers from over twenty countries, Banana Writers is a voice for new and talented writers.

Join me in the battle to help new writers get "unpeeled".

Yours bananaly

PP Wong
Editor-in-Chief Banana Writers

Come and visit us at
www.legendpress.co.uk

Follow us
@legend_press